Hooked By You

Kate Sweden

Wild Magnolias Press

For the readers who live for slow-burn spark and
sharp-edged banter,
who know connection is the sexiest kind of risk,
and who believe the wild has a way of calling us home.
This one's for you.

Contents

Chapter 1

Patagonia or Bust

EMME

THE KNOCK CAME BEFORE I'd even made it to my second cup of coffee.

Not polite. Not casual. One of those sharp, militarized raps that said, *open this fucking door or I will, and you won't like how I do it.*

I opened the door to our office suite—early, quiet, and blessedly empty except for me—and there she stood.

I blinked. Summer Wilder did not do mornings. At least, not at the office. She was a ten-o'clock arrival, calendar-blocked to the minute, blazer crisp, coffee waiting. I was the early riser. Not because I liked mornings—God no—but because I liked claiming this slice of stillness before the day went feral. It was an unspoken arrangement between sisters: I opened, she closed. I got peace, she got control. It worked.

Until today. Summer Wilder. COO of Wilder Horizons. Eldest sister by seven years. Already dressed like a minimalist power icon—tailored black trousers, crisp white blouse tucked just so, delicate gold hoops catching the light, AirPods still in, manila folder in hand like it contained either a hostile takeover or a kingdom blueprint.

"Don't say no," she said by way of greeting.

I raised an eyebrow and backed up to let her in, the scent of burnt espresso and copy paper clinging in the air. My hair was still damp from the world's fastest blowout, a few polished waves pinned back with gold clips. Lip gloss, heels, tailored pink blazer—the full Vendor Relations Barbie starter pack. That's me—smile painted on, charm set to high. Charm's expensive currency, and some days the cost showed in my jaw, sore from grinning at ghosts, while my phone lit up with numbers I didn't want to call.

My shoes were off under my desk only because I'd swapped into fuzzy slippers for these sacred pre-nine a.m. hours, when no one was around to judge me for preserving my arches.

Summer marched straight to the kitchenette and glared at the coffee machine. She jabbed a button, twisted the wrong dial, and stared down the chrome beast like it had personally betrayed her. The machine sputtered, hissed, and blinked a red light. She kept jabbing buttons.

"Is this thing still broken?"

"No. You're just banned," I said, watching as she smacked the side like it was a vending machine. With a sigh, I slid in, shooed her aside, and coaxed the machine into purring within seconds. I handed over the mug—black with just a splash of cream, Summer's idea of indulgence. She took a long sip, grimaced anyway, and muttered about the death of decent caffeine.

I flopped onto the sofa, legs tucked under me, and flipped open the folder she handed me. Heavy cardstock pages. Stiff. Smelled like ink and recycled ambition. "You're in a mood. And early. Who are we conquering today?"

Summer turned with her mug, took one sip, and wrinkled her nose like it personally offended her. "You."

"I'm already conquered. HR has the paperwork to prove it."

"You're going to Patagonia."

I laughed. Then realized she wasn't laughing.

"Wait. Seriously?"

She nodded and leaned one hip against the kitchenette counter, all business now. She squared the folder's edges on the counter before she spoke. "We've got two scouting reports, three unaffiliated client pings, and a whisper from that freaky travel concierge Rayann blackmailed into sending us next year's high-wealth trends list. Patagonia's on it."

If anyone can sway a freak, it's my sister Rayann—Sales Director and goddess who could sweet-talk a cactus into producing vodka.

"Logistics aren't the problem," I said quietly. "Vendors are already courting me—someone pitched glacier-side wine tastings yesterday. I love the hustle. Access, though, is the real issue. Patagonia doesn't bend for outsiders. If Summit strikes first, they'll lock down the gates before we even book a flight."

If Summit landed Patagonia before us, they'd scoop our highest-paying clients, corner the luxury market, and brand Wilder as second-best. We didn't survive on second place.

"Trends list or not, Summit Expeditions is already circling," Summer added. "They've been sniffing at Patagonia for months. We move first, or we move out of the way. And don't waste your charm on him," Summer said flatly. "Rumor is, the last scout Summit sent came back after forty-eight hours—said he barely spoke a word. Just get the deal. "

I stared at her. "You want me to fly to the literal bottom of the planet—"

"Top of our opportunity funnel."

"—to freeze my ass off in the name of luxury?"

She gave me a pointed look. "Our clients want what's remote, curated, and impossible to replicate. Patagonia checks every box."

"Penguins and frostbite. Very aspirational."

"Don't forget status-driven suffering. That's trending hard. Think *cryotherapy meets altitude sickness.*"

I swore under my breath and shoved a throw pillow over my face. "I hate it here." And for half a second, I almost meant it.

"No you don't," she said mildly. "You love it. The negotiations. The thrill. The adrenaline hit of getting somewhere first."

She wasn't wrong. I pulled the pillow away and studied the top sheet again. Elevation stats. Micro-climate notes. Vendor portfolio. Then—

A lodge photo.

Jesus.

The place looked like a painting. Or a conspiracy theory. All stone and timber, perched on the edge of a cliff like it dared the mountain to move. Balconies jutted toward the horizon, glass walls swallowing every inch of view. A sweep of alpine forest spilled below it, roofs dusted white, smoke curling from a chimney like someone had staged the world's most decadent winter postcard. Even the driveway looked dramatic—cut into the rock face, winding up like it only allowed the worthy.

Dad had a map on his study wall once—faded paper, corners curling—where a red pin marked this very stretch of Patagonia. He used to say it was the one place that slipped through his fingers. Looking at the lodge now, I felt the pin prick me back. I remembered standing on a stool in his study, tracing the edges of that map while he swore one day he'd plant a flag there. It had been years since a place—not a person, not a paycheck—hit me like that.

"You're sending me *here*?" I asked quietly.

Summer nodded. "It's called *Refugio Cielo*. The owner's an ex-architect. French. Rugged. Off-grid for seven years."

"Why do they always have to be French?"

"Because you respond well to accents and sexual hostility."

"Fuck off."

She grinned. "He runs everything himself. No social media. No press. No confirmed affiliation. But he's booked out six months in advance with clients who sign NDAs just to get on the waiting list."

The corner bore a logo—mountain peak, crossed tools, survival wrapped in luxury. The paper cut into my palm, like it sensed the name it guarded: Luc Moreau.

Oh great. A name like a wine I couldn't afford—French, ex-architect, vanished from the design world a few years back. No interviews. No comeback. Just silence—and a lodge balanced on a cliff like defiance.

Summer was still talking. "You'll evaluate the property, secure a preliminary contract, and gather local vendor options for expansion. If he plays nice, we keep him solo. If not, we launch our own high-altitude outpost. Either way—"

"Wilder wins."

She toasted me with her mug. "That's the spirit."

I got up and walked to the window. Sunlight flashed on the glass, humidity clinging to my blazer, jasmine warm and thick in the air. Outside, a car horn bleated twice, lazy traffic edging past the square, petty noises that felt obscene against the silence I was already craving. Even the storm's aftertaste lingered on my tongue, metallic and damp. I pressed my fingers to the pane and imagined Patagonia instead: wind sharp enough to flay the skin awake, air so thin it scraped your lungs clean, silence so profound it roared. Miles of wilderness that gave no fucks about polished logos or curated guest experiences.

My skin prickled.

Not from cold.

From *curiosity*.

I flipped into hunter mode so fast it scared me.

Wilder Horizons wasn't just a company; it was our father's legacy. He'd started with nothing but charm, grit, and a refusal to settle for ordinary, building luxury adventure travel experiences in places most people couldn't even find on a map. After he died, the six of us inherited more than his contracts and client list—we inherited the mandate to keep it alive. Summer, the oldest, took COO, weaponizing calendars and color codes to keep the whole machine running. Juliette, next in line, stepped up as CEO, steering global strategy and turning his dream into an empire. And me? I was the one who knocked on impossible doors and made people open them. Which was exhilarating, sure—until you looked up and realized you were always chasing, never arriving.

"Flights?" I asked, already calculating layovers and luggage weight.

"You've got a little bit of time. Still a few deals to close and a PR mess to untangle first."

"Perfect. My favorite kind of vacation prep."

"Add it to your to-do list."

I turned back to the folder. There was a small note clipped inside in Summer's handwriting: *Don't try to charm him. Survive it, if you can.*

I smiled.

Too late.

I was already plotting how to melt the frost right off Mr. Luc Moreau.

Even if I had to do it in three layers of thermal underwear.

Chapter 2

The Edge of the Map

EMME

THE FIRST TIME I saw Patagonia in person, it was through a smudged oval window and a thin, mean layer of cloud that refused to move. For the last twenty minutes of the descent, the pilot said something soothing in Spanish and then casually mentioned crosswinds, and half the plane made the sign of the cross. I pressed my forehead to the plastic and watched a continent made of knives appear: jagged mountains punched out of the earth, rivers the color of melted steel, and long bruised stretches of steppe that didn't care if anyone ever loved them.

Beautiful. Brutal. Probably no Wi-Fi.

A hand tapped my shoulder from the aisle. A girl of maybe twelve offered a peppermint with solemn ceremony, which I accepted like it was a sacrament. We were in this together—me, the peppermint girl, the pilot, and the wind that had apparently decided today would be sport.

The wheels kissed the runway, skidded a whisper, and then grabbed hold. Everyone clapped the way only people who have just survived a minor spiritual crisis can clap. I applauded too, quietly, mostly because my heart had decided to return to my chest from wherever it had vaulted during the last turn.

Welcome to El Calafate. Winter. Gray light. Two jet bridges total and a terminal that looked more alpine outpost than airport. My phone pinged three times in a brave little burst before the signal gave up:

BRYNN: Send penguin pics or I riot

RAYANN: Do NOT fall in love with a mountain man. We barely survived your pilot era.

SUMMER: Flight? Customs? Keep receipts. Also check in with Juliette re NDA language for landholder contracts.

I typed back with half-numb fingers. Landed. Not dead. Will seduce a glacier on your behalf.

The doors opened. The wind hit hard enough to make me rethink every packing decision I'd ever made. I tucked my scarf tighter and followed the small exodus to customs, my answers ready to go—tourism, short visit, vendor meetings. No need to overshare with border patrol.

By the time the subtle hum of fluorescent lighting delivered me to baggage claim, the turnstile had already coughed up duffels, hard-shells, boxes wrapped in mystical layers of plastic. My suitcase did not appear.

I waited through hope, bargaining, denial, and rage, and we all know what comes after rage. In this case, acceptance looked like a punishingly cheerful airline officer behind a plywood kiosk with a sign that said EQUIPAJE DEMORADO. Delayed luggage. A concept so universal it needed no translation.

"Color?" he asked.

"Gold with black corners. A decal that says Wilder Horizons in block letters." He looked bored despite my internal crisis. "And a pink bow on the handle."

"Ah." He typed with the concentration of a surgeon. "Tampa. No llegó. Maybe mañana."

It didn't arrive. Maybe tomorrow. My ass.

I stared at him, then at the window with its view of a parking lot that had surrendered to ice. "I have meetings in the mountains. I can't do mañana."

He shrugged in an elegant, sympathetic circle. "The bag has its own adventure, señorita."

He handed me a form and a pen attached to the counter with string. I filled it out while recalculating my available options. I had my ride-or-die leather boots in my carry-on—chunky-heeled, city-girl tough, mountain-trip ready—and one emergency dress rolled into a packing cube: soft gray knit, warm enough for Andean wind, fitted enough to mean business, and still unapologetically feminine. Add in travel-sized toiletries, minimal makeup, and one backup pair of underwear, and I was basically thriving.

The rest—thermal base layers, merciful socks, and my weatherproof jacket that made competence look chic—was somewhere over the Caribbean, living its best life without me.

"Any chance it's on the next flight?" I asked.

"Any chance," he said, which was not an answer.

I stepped away with my claim number, my carry-on, and my dignity filed under "to be continued." The automatic doors breathed open. Cold slammed into the cavity behind my ribs. Imagine the world's cleanest knife driving itself right through your coat and into your very good intentions. I pulled my knit cap lower and walked out into it.

The sign where a driver should have been held a blank rectangle of fog, as if someone had exhaled on it and never wiped it clean. Two men in parkas held placards for other names—European, some American, one Japanese tour—and still no Wilder. I checked the email thread with the transfer company.

Confirmed: El Calafate

Airport pickup. Señorita Emme Wilder. 12:20 PM arrival.

Driver: "Martín." White 4x4.

No Martín in sight. No white 4x4 either. Just a row of vehicles with frosted windshields and a scruffy mutt making his morning rounds like head of airport security.

"¿Emme?" a voice said near my elbow.

I turned. A man of indeterminate age, leathered by weather and possibly by a lifetime of scolding clouds, peered at me from beneath a wool cap. A scar cut through one eyebrow, which would have been threatening if his other eyebrow hadn't lifted with pure hospitality. Behind him, a sheepdog waited in the passenger seat of an aging pickup, its gray-and-white coat and mismatched eyes giving it the patience of a diplomat.

"Sí," I said, relieved that my vowels decided to cooperate. "Wilder."

He nodded once. "Cielo." He pointed toward the parking lot, then at me, then toward the parking lot again, an efficient charade that made the point—Refugio Cielo. Let's go.

"Martín?" I asked.

Another nod. "Sí."

His truck was less "white 4x4" and more "art project": a pickup from a decade that had not fully embraced airbags, its bed protected by dented steel and prayer. The dog was already in the passenger seat but, with one look from Martín, hopped gracefully into the back like it was protocol. I climbed in, careful of the bolt that had decided to live its life freely instead of holding the handle down.

What the fuck kind of bullshit did you send me into here, Summer?

Martín turned the key. The truck coughed, complained, and finally gave in. The heater howled to life, and the wipers looked as tired as I felt.

The road out of El Calafate stretched flat and endless, fences blurring under a sky that couldn't quite commit to blue. Then it gave up on being civilized—pavement turned to gravel, gravel to dirt, and dirt to pure optimism. Sheep scattered politely.

I tried my phone. A brave bar of signal appeared, then ran for its life. I recorded a voice memo out of habit, which might upload before the end of days. "Note to Summer: consider adding 'satellite thing' to the standard scouting kit. Note to self: buy better hat. Note to Dad—" I stopped. I didn't like speaking to ghosts out loud, even my favorite ones. "Fine. Note to Dad: you would have loved this road. It's more suggestion than plan."

Martín drove the way men who've always driven in weather drive—with the belief that if you just keep the nose of the truck pointed at the horizon, the rest will work itself out. He didn't speak unless speaking needed to happen, which I found oddly restful. The dog—Gitana, he offered when I asked—sat behind us, occasionally resting her chin on the console between the seats, accepting my absentminded scratches like a queen accepting tribute. Sentinel. Sheep whisperer. Emotional support cloud.

"You know Cielo?" I asked when the truck did something that might have been sliding and might have been dancing.

"Todos conocen," he said after considering. *Everyone knows it.*

"Luc?" I added, soft, as if the name might spook something.

He shrugged without moving his shoulders. "El francés."

The Frenchman. Apparently out here, that was introduction enough.

"Friendly?" I ventured.

Martín considered that too, which did not immediately inspire confidence. "Callado," he said finally.

Quiet.

"Married?" I don't know why I asked. Maybe I do.

Another shrug, another small head tilt that said maybe he was, maybe he is, maybe he doesn't tell truck drivers his secrets. Fair.

We climbed. The landscape changed in small, deliberate steps—scrub turning to wind-battered forest that refused to quit. A flash of dark water cut through the trees. Lago Viedma. Blue-black, sharp, cold enough to teach respect.

"The road?" I asked as our path narrowed into a goat trail that had probably been consulted but not obeyed when someone painted it on a map.

Martín made a noise that wasn't a word. The truck lowered its center of gravity out of respect and we crawled.

Twenty more minutes. The sky darkened, brightened, darkened again in a very efficient cycle that suggested weather here didn't arrive; it ambushed. A snow squall swept through fast, dusting the windshield before disappearing like it had changed its mind. Somewhere ahead, a condor made very clear to a smaller bird that this was not a shared airspace.

And then we crested the last bend, the one where the world had been holding its breath, and there it was: Refugio Cielo.

It didn't look built so much as grown, pulled from the rock by someone who understood both defiance and mercy. Stone base sunk into the mountain, timber rising in clean planes and angles that caught the light like contoured cheekbones on a red carpet. Glass faced the valley in long, generous spans. Balconies reached for air. Smoke lifted from a chimney with the kind of restraint that implied control over all the elements. It was fucking stunning.

Something moved behind one of the long windows—just a shift of shadow, the suggestion of a figure. The feeling wasn't being watched so much as being measured by the land itself. The same sensation I'd had looking at the photo in Summer's folder, multiplied by cold and altitude and the sudden knowledge that when I breathed I could feel every edge of my lungs.

Martín pulled into a small clearing that barely qualified as a parking area. Gitana jumped out first, clearly running the operation. My door stuck, then gave way all at once, and the cold hit every cell like it had a job to do.

"Gracias, Martín," I said, payment already counted out in my wallet. He shook his head once, palm raised in refusal. "Luc," he said, tipping his chin toward the lodge as if the word itself were coordinates. "Él paga." *He pays*.

I nodded, tucked the money away, and hauled my carry-on by the handle. The absence of my suitcase hit like another gust. I looked down at my ankle boots—great for a light snow, questionable for glaciers—and the coat I used to call warm. It wasn't. I pulled my gloves higher, wrapped my scarf tighter, and started toward the steps cut into the rock.

The door was solid wood, heavy enough to suggest it kept out more than weather. The handle was worn smooth, the kind shaped by years of use. I stepped into the covered entry and waited, breath fogging the air. No bell. No voices. I was about to knock when the handle clicked and the door eased open.

The first thing I felt was heat—woodstove, radiant floors, that instant relief after hours of wind. Then I saw him—broad shoulders, dark sweater, built like someone who trusted stone more than people. He filled the doorway without crowding it. Taller than I expected, taller than I usually allow. The sweater fit his frame too well to be an accident, too practical to be intentional. Dark hair, shorter than in the few feral images a search algorithm had coughed up—roughly trimmed, like he'd taken a blade to it out of practicality, not neglect. Stubble that had decided to be a beard by the weekend. Eyes—impossible to name at first. Gray? Blue? Winter before the storm.

Of course he looked like that. Because the universe never misses a chance to test my professionalism in low-oxygen conditions.

"Bonjour," he said in a voice that came from the same place as the stone—deep, rough-edged, accented enough to make me forget every vowel I knew. Then, after making very sure he'd read my face correctly, "Buenas tardes." And finally, as if English were a tool he only sharpened when necessary, "Good afternoon."

"Bonjour," I echoed, light and easy, the way tourists say it to sound worldly. His gaze flickered—just a split second, like he'd caught an accent where there shouldn't have been one. "Emme Wilder." I offered a hand and my smile—the one for men who don't realize they're already signing the contract.

He looked at my hand, as if he planned to make sure it didn't do anything dishonest, then took it. Warm. Not crushing. Absolutely in control of how this would go without needing to say it out loud.

"Luc Moreau," he said, and somehow it landed like more than a name—like a promise or a warning or both.

"Thank you for the rescue," I said, nodding toward the truck now idling its way back down the hill. "Your driver found me."

"My neighbor," he corrected, as if the word driver created a job where there was only a favor. "You are late."

"So was the plane. We made it a group effort," I said lightly. "Also, my suitcase is currently on a beach vacation without me. I hope it posts pictures."

The corner of his mouth entertained the idea of amusement and, very generously, agreed. "Come in," he said, stepping back.

The lobby—if that's what passed for one—was sleek, restrained, the kind of space that whispered money instead of shouting it. Slate floors warmed my bones through the soles of my boots. The ceiling lifted into beams that made a cathedral of the space without the guilt. A long wall of glass looked over the valley and the lake beyond, winter unfolding in silver and smoke. The air smelled like cedar and the ghost of coffee.

The main room centered around a stone fireplace big enough to roast a bear—if one were into that sort of thing. Not the compact woodstove I'd felt when I first stepped inside, but its sleeker, grander cousin meant for guests to admire. "You heat the place with wood?" I asked, because apparently practical questions would keep me from staring at his mouth.

"And sun," he said, his eyes flicking toward the view where dark panels blended into the roof line. Pride didn't move his voice; accuracy did. "In summer. In winter, the wind likes to take what it can."

"Sounds like the wind doesn't share well."

He gave the faintest shrug. "It's Patagonia. The wind negotiates with no one."

At a low table, a ceramic teapot waited on a trivet, steam curling. Luc poured without asking, handed me a cup, and then one for himself. Mint. Maybe something cut from a garden that had made private arrangements with the frost.

"You came alone," he said, as if confirming a datum he'd already entered into a ledger.

"I did."

He took that in. "Your Spanish is... enough?"

"For survival," I said. "For charm, I need more."

"Charm?" he repeated, tasting the word the way an engineer tastes a weld—testing it for integrity.

I sipped the tea and let the warmth move through me. "Persuasion, then," I corrected. "My job."

"Vendor relations," he said, as if he had a copy of my folder, with the corners squared and the ink still smelling expensive.

"Among other sins."

He didn't smile exactly. "Your father founded Wilder Horizons."

The tea went briefly to the wrong place. I recovered, set the cup down carefully. "He did," I said. "Patagonia was one of the places he wanted to see."

Luc nodded without looking away from the lake. "Sometimes the place decides."

We stood like that for a time that wasn't uncomfortable. The quiet stretched, filled only by the faint pop of the fire. "I believe you have a room for me," I said finally, business reasserting itself like muscle memory.

He looked at me then, really looked, as if he could see both the heels in my carry-on and the absence of my suitcase. "I have one ready for you," he said. "The others are... occupied."

A private lodge with NDAs and off-season guests. Interesting. "Corporate retreat?" I guessed.

"Not corporate." He let the words stop there in a way that made the border visible. I admired a man who could articulate a line by saying nothing.

"I'll take whatever you have." I smiled again—the brave kind, because it was my last one and I intended to get mileage out of it.

Jet lag, lost luggage, and the audacity of showing up alone in Patagonia—yeah, brave was the only kind I had left.

"And could I trouble you for the Wi-Fi password? I should let my team know I made it."

"You will not," he said, and for a second I thought I'd misheard. Then he gestured toward a small slate placard near a shelf of books. In perfect lettering:

NO SERVICE.
NO EXCEPTIONS.
TALK TO EACH OTHER.
TALK TO THE WILDLIFE.
CALLS AVAILABLE IN EMERGENCIES ONLY.

Someone had carved it with the satisfaction of a man who'd personally declared war on Wi-Fi and won.

I laughed, because the alternative was a minor meltdown. "I'll write the email now and send it when I'm in town," I said with what I hoped passed for grace.

"No town today," he said simply. "The pass will close. Snow."

"Tonight?"

He lifted a shoulder a fraction. "Now." As if summoned by the word, the gray deepened, the air thickened, and flakes began to show themselves against the window, slow at first, then with conviction. He nodded toward the hallway. "Your room is ready."

Chapter 3

The First Rule of Cielo

EMME

W^{E WALKED A HALLWAY} lined with black-and-white photographs—glaciers, climbers, scientists, dreamers. A woman laughing into the wind. A man standing in water cold enough to sting just looking at it. The kind of faces that believed curiosity was worth frostbite. My footsteps sounded loud against all that quiet.

He opened a door and let me step in first. The room was simple and perfect—the kind of perfection that costs a fortune to look effortless. Pale wood. White walls. The air carried a faint cedar warmth, clean and sharp.

A bed built low and solid, layered in wool blankets that looked warm enough to make promises. A single chair faced a window that turned the valley into a live feed of weather and light. On a narrow bench: a folded sweater, a knit cap, and gloves—practical things, placed with care. Someone had thought ahead.

"I wasn't expecting—" I started, and stopped, because everything in the room was already saying it for me.

"You lost a bag," he said, and somehow the sentence wasn't unkind. "These are extras." A pause. "Clean."

I touched the sweater with two fingers, felt the softness and the weight. It was still warm, like someone had only just folded it. "Thank you," I said. The words stayed upright.

"Leave your laundry by the door in the morning," he added, pragmatic as stone. "I'll send someone."

"Someone who isn't you." I smiled so he could choose whether it was teasing. He decided silence was the correct response.

"Dinner at eight," he said instead. "We eat together. Whoever is here. If you don't come, we keep your plate for breakfast."

"Communal," I said. I didn't hate it. I wanted to—because shared tables make control harder—but some small, homesick part of me born of sisters and noise liked the idea of a place where everyone belonged.

His gaze dropped to my boots. "You'll need different shoes," he said, and before I could launch my speech about competence, added, "For the snow. Downstairs, left. Take what you need."

"You have a boot room," I said, delighted despite myself.

"I have a boot religion," he corrected. "And you're a pilgrim who's walked into the mountain in church shoes."

I laughed—real, unguarded—and it startled both of us. His mouth acknowledged the sound, brief as sunlight between clouds. "I'll see you at eight," he said, stepping back.

"Luc," I heard myself say. He paused in the doorway. "Thank you. For the sweater. For... this." I gestured toward the window and everything beyond it—the lake, the gray, the land watching from its own distance.

He nodded, equal parts greeting and promise. "It was always here," he said. "Someone just had to say it could matter."

The door closed with a quiet click.

Silence filled the room, but it wasn't empty. It had weight and texture, the kind you could run your hand through to feel the weave.

I went to the window and pressed my palm to the glass, the way I had in Maris Key when Florida heat made even decisions sweat. Here, the cold bit back. Wind whispered along the eaves like it knew secrets. Snow feathered, gathered, slid. I could still hear the wind. I could almost hear my father's voice too, buried somewhere under the floorboards where old promises go to keep warm. *If you can still hear traffic, Emme, you haven't gone far enough.*

I hadn't heard traffic for hours. Felt like days.

I unzipped my carry-on and gave the contents a hard look. It wasn't much, but it would have to hold the line. My toiletry kit had survived, thank God—bare bones but functional. The portable steamer had made it, which felt like divine mercy. My boots. The dress. Make-up. Two silk camisoles that had seemed impulsive in Paris now felt like foresight. A black cashmere scarf. And my battered Tampa Rays cap, tucked into the corner like it always was—the only constant in years of terminals and time zones.

I stared at it all and decided that optimism, while not a plan, could still qualify as strategy.

The sweater Luc left for me waited on the bench—heather gray, thick enough to stand on its own, soft enough to disarm me. I pulled it on over my camisole. The sleeves fell to my knuckles, and warmth arrived where diplomacy had failed. It was the kind of practical kindness that shouldn't feel personal—and somehow did anyway.

The mirror reflected someone who looked less Barbie and more woman capable of negotiating with glaciers. Not bad. My hair—long, black, slightly wilder than I preferred—had rebelled against the flight and the wind. My face was wind-flushed, eyes sharper than they had any right to be after twenty hours of travel. Trim. Functional. Healthy enough to look like I belonged in weather that didn't care about opinions. I straightened my shoulders, adjusted the cap sleeves, and decided I'd pass—for now.

I headed downstairs. The boot room delivered on its myth. Racks of footwear organized by size with military affection. The room smelled like leather, wool, and melted snow. Shelves of gaiters, wool socks, hats knitted by someone with opinions. A note on the wall read:

RETURN WHAT YOU BORROW. LEAVE IT BETTER.

Below it, in smaller handwriting: *or i will find you —*
L.

I had yet to meet another staff member, so I assumed
L was both manager and enforcer. I chose a pair that fit,
tested my footing on a rubber mat like I was about to
take the stage.

Back upstairs, the snow had gotten serious. It didn't
fall so much as assemble itself from the air, like the
mountain had decided weather was a group project. The
light went navy, then charcoal. Somewhere deeper in the
lodge, a door closed. Voices—low, plural—moved past,
then faded.

At 7:58 PM, because I refuse to arrive late to any table,
I followed the scent of cumin and woodsmoke to a room
near the lodge's heart. A long table. Six places set. A bowl
of something thick and red at the center, steam rising like
a blessing. Cumin and smoke curled into the air, warm
and immediate. Two women in their sixties sat together,
faces shaped by decades of sun and laughter. A man with
the bearing of a guide—calm, steady, windproof. Another guest, young and self-conscious in expensive fleece,
proving that performance fabric can't repel insecurity.

"Buenas noches," I offered.

"Buenas," the women chorused, eyes bright. "You're the American." They said it in Spanish; I nodded, which was easier than confession.

Luc arrived without sound, which seemed unfair for someone his size. He carried bread wrapped in a towel, still warm, and set it down with a restraint I could drink. Steam curled up as he loosened the towel. He poured wine like a man who respects the grape but doesn't worship it. When he took his seat at the end of the table, he didn't preside so much as anchor.

We passed bowls. The stew—*guiso*, he called it—was thick with lamb and lentils and a slow heat that worked its way from tongue to chest.

The women introduced themselves as Teresa and Mariela, retired teachers from Mendoza who hiked slowly and gossiped fast. They'd come south to "see if our knees still function and if red wine works at altitude," Teresa said, raising her glass like a toast to gravity itself.

The guide was Rafa, hired to consult on a new trail that refused to stay where maps told it to. He had the kind of calm shoulders that came from decades of rescuing tourists who'd misjudged daylight.

The fleece man—Elliot, from London—confessed he worked "in finance," in the tone of someone apologizing for an illness. When pressed, he said he managed "client portfolios," which told us nothing and everything at once.

"*Y tú?*" Mariela asked me. "You are here for hiking or...?" She gestured with her spoon, circling in the air until it landed squarely on *business.*

"Work," I admitted. "Vendor negotiations."

Teresa nodded sagely. "Ah. So you tell people what to do."

"Only the ones who pay for the privilege."

That earned a round of laughter and a refill of wine. Rafa said something about tourists who think contracts can outwit the weather. I said something about clients who think the internet can fix logistics. Teresa decided we should all start a consulting firm immediately.

Luc didn't say much—he didn't have to. He listened, a steady presence at the far end of the table, hands resting loosely around his glass. Every so often, his gaze would flick toward whoever spoke, and they'd straighten a little, like plants finding light. Even the chatter softened, drawn toward him without effort.

When my bowl was empty and my bones remembered heat, I hesitated, weighing timing against curiosity. "Would it be rude," I asked, glancing toward Luc, "if I asked a few questions about the lodge?"

Teresa grinned. "She can't help herself," she said, delighted.

Luc's eyes met mine across the table. "You may ask," he said simply.

"How many rooms?" I asked.

"Twelve," Luc said. "Never more than twenty-four guests. I like silence. And walls that survive winter."

"Guides on staff?"

"Two," he said, nodding toward the calm man. "The rest local. Seasonal. People who'd be here even if I wasn't."

"NDA for every guest?"

"Yes."

"Emergency comms?"

"Satellite. In the office." The unsaid *not for your email* hovered politely between us.

"Do you work with outfitters in El Chaltén," I asked, "or exclusively independent vendors?"

His attention sharpened; I'd stopped skimming the surface. "Independent," he said. "El Chaltén in summer is a city. Cielo is not a city."

"Your capacity in high season?"

"Full."

"Waitlist?"

He gestured toward the sideboard where a black note-book lay open with the reverence usually reserved for scripture and schedules. "Always."

I wanted it—the book, the partnership, the certainty that comes from being first in and last out. I wanted to say Wilder Horizons and hear him say yes like it was a promise.

Instead, I reached for another slice of bread and let the moment pass. You don't take a mountain by rushing it. You pick your line, test your hold, breathe.

After dinner, no one seemed in a hurry to leave. The teachers were the first to sigh contentedly, declaring they'd had "too much wine and not enough sense to climb stairs." Rafa promised to check the trail conditions in the morning and told Elliot not to wander off looking for Wi-Fi. Elliot laughed weakly, which only made Rafa repeat it.

Luc began clearing plates with that same deliberate economy he applied to conversation—methodical, silent, exact.

I stood to help. Old habits. He looked genuinely startled, like he hadn't imagined the woman with the glossy hair and the corporate smile knew what to do with a stack of dishes.

"I can manage," he said.

"I can help," I countered, already reaching.

He gestured for me to sit, not impatiently—more like a man unused to being assisted. "Guests don't clear tables," he said.

Later, in the hall, as guests drifted to rooms and snow pressed its weight against the windows, he stopped beside me at a pane of glass pretending to be a wall. "Tomorrow, you see the property," he said.

"Good."

"Early," he added, a word that sounded like a test.

"I do early," I said, thinking of those quiet pre-nine hours in Maris Key when the world still believed I was gentle. "And Luc—"

He paused.

"I know why you built it this way," I said, nodding toward the dining room, the firelight, the proof of care in every corner. "People come here to remember they exist."

His gaze lingered on my face with the kind of attention that feels like standing under weather. "Yes," he said simply. "And you? Why are you here, Miss Wilder?"

The way he said my name—with that accent, low and deliberate—did things to my body I hadn't budgeted for.

Classic, Emme. Falling for the stereotype in real time.

"Because my family builds bridges to places that don't want them," I said, before I could stop the honesty. "And I wanted to see if this one would hold."

He looked at the snow, then back at me. "We'll see."

He said goodnight. I said it back. We both stayed a moment too long, then pretended we hadn't.

In my room, the mountain pressed its body against the glass, and the silence rearranged itself into something living. I could still feel the table's grain under my palms, taste mint and smoke and salt. The sweater smelled faintly of cedar and smoke, and something warm I didn't have a word for. The wool warmed fast against my skin.

I took off my earrings, lined them like punctuation on the nightstand, and slid under the blankets that had held a hundred temporary lives. Before turning out the light, I tried my phone one more time. The screen glowed, stubborn and useless. I opened the notes app and typed a message that would send when it could.

Landed. Lost the suitcase. Found a mountain. Met a man who speaks in complete sentences and means them. Contracts later. Trust me.

I set the phone face down and learned the shape of the quiet. Then—

I slept.

In my dream, a map I knew well shifted under my hand. The red pin in Patagonia glowed warm against my palm. When I lifted it, the color bled—slow, certain—drawing a line I didn't recognize yet. It headed toward glass, and smoke, and a man whose name tasted like winter.

Morning would come early. I had work to do. The mountain would have its say, and I'd be ready to listen.

Chapter 4

Control,
Interrupted

LUC

THE LODGE WAKES BEFORE the guests do. Timber schools you that way. You learn to hear weight in the walls and wind in the joints. Before coffee, before heat, before names, there is the quiet check: doors latched, ash shaken down, pilot light steady, pressure in the lines. The mountain gives you mornings like this if you've earned them. I don't waste them.

At five, the kitchen is mine. The light over the prep table is a small sun. The floor keeps last night's warmth. I set water to a slow boil and grind coffee to the notch the grinder knows by heart. Seventeen clicks. Not sixteen. Not eighteen. The difference is bitterness. People pretend they don't taste it. They do.

Bread first. Dough overnight, shaped now, steam in the oven by habit and by superstition. I align the mugs handle-left. Six. We have six in-house. I plate the butter, taste the guiso I finished at midnight, adjust heat with cumin and salt. The wind pushes at the glass, then thinks better of it. Good. Stay out there.

Rafa will be here before six. We review the day then. There's a line of weather anchored over the pass. It will slide or it won't. If it slides, I send guests to the low loop. If it holds, no one leaves the balcony. People think snow is soft. Snow is a decision.

I'm mid-inventory on the shelf above the sink when something shifts that isn't weight or wind. A scent—citrus and something faintly floral—threads the air like a wrong note. It's not mine and not the lodge's. It's warm skin and a shower I didn't turn on.

I don't turn. I watch a reflection gather in the oven door: dark hair pulled back; knit sweater I folded last night; the kind of focus people mistake for gentleness until it lands on them. She moves lightly and straightens what is already straight.

"Good morning," Emme Wilder says to the room that belongs to me.

She's barefoot. Socks, not bare feet. Fine. The slate holds heat well but not kindness.

"This room is staff only," I say without raising my voice.

"I'm staff-adjacent today," she says, carrying a row of mugs to the counter like she's done it a thousand times. 'You were out,' she adds. 'I'm preventing a caffeine em ergency.'"

She reaches for the grinder.

"Arrête," I say. *Stop.*

She does. Instantly. Turns. Waiting.

It's a small thing, how the world stays where you leave it. The grinder at seventeen. The knives edge-in. The sugar jar sealed tight so it doesn't clump and attract damp. You keep enough of those small things steady and the big things feel possible.

"You'll change the setting by bumping it," I tell her. "You won't hear it. You'll taste it."

Her mouth curves. Not a smile so much as a bracket around one. "Seventeen clicks. Not sixteen. Not eighteen," she says, soft, and sets her hands back at her sides. She was watching. Of course she was.

She doesn't leave, though. She threads herself into the room's edges. She opens the drawer with the linen. She chooses the good cloths, not the stained ones. She is tidy and exact but she touches things that are mine.

"Guests don't work in this room," I say, pouring water off the boil into the filter in a slow, steady circle.

"I'm not a guest," she says, voice even. "I'm an investment. And I hate sitting still."

The grounds bloom. I wait the seconds they need. The oven hiss changes pitch. I pull the bread, listen to the crust sing, crack it with my thumbs. The smell is clean and generous. Her eyes close. It's involuntary. There's a small sound in her throat she didn't know she made.

"Assieds-toi ," I tell her. *Sit.*

Her brow lifts, like she maybe understood the word. "I can set the table," she says.

"I didn't ask."

She looks at me a fraction too long, then chooses a stool and sits, ankles crossed, hands on her knees. She obeys well. She resents it slightly. Both are true.

I pour her a cup and set it down on the wood. No saucer. This isn't Paris. She wraps her fingers around the heat like she hasn't been warm in years. The sweater fits her enough. The room fits her less. Good. Some edges should stay sharp.

"I was going to make a pot for the others," she says. "Teresa looked like the kind of woman who pretends tea is enough and then drinks coffee as if it's a secret."

"I make the first pot," I say. "Rafa takes the second. Guests pour their own after that."

"Ritual," she says.

"System," I correct.

"Same church, different liturgy."

A corner of me almost laughs. I don't. I slice bread, slide butter across the grain with the back of the knife, lay the knife down edge-in.

"You sleep?" I ask, because I watched the light under her door go dark before mine did. Because it matters if she can climb the stairs without catching the rail by the fourth landing.

"Enough," she says. "The mountain talks in its sleep."

"It says the same thing awake."

She studies me over the rim of the mug. People think silence is empty. It isn't. It's crowded. You learn to stack your thoughts in it or they fall on you.

She stands again. She can't help it. She opens a cupboard and finds the chipped enamel pitcher no one uses and fills it at the sink. She takes it to the dining room, humming under her breath. Two notes, no melody. She sets the pitcher in the center of the table and steps back to see the room the way guests will.

In the reflection of the window I watch her move three chairs by a finger's width each. It changes the sight line from the head of the table. She probably doesn't know that is what she changed. She probably does.

"You're in the way," I say. Enough to carry. Not loud.

She turns. There is color in her cheeks. "I can be in a different way," she says. "Tell me where."

"In the dining room, staff cross on the kitchen side, guests on the glass side. You'll get under people's elbows if you move on the glass."

She nods once. She moves where I told her. It should be the end of it.

It isn't.

She brings the small clay cups out of the drawer guests never open and lines them along the sideboard. She finds the basket I forget to fill with blankets and fills it. She lights the candles on the mantle I don't light on storm days. The room warms in a way I didn't authorize.

The back door opens at last, cold folding itself into the warmth like an insult. Rafa's boots sound out the count I know by heart. Two step, pause, heel down. He shakes the snow from his jacket on the mat and lifts a hand.

"Generator is sulking," he says. "I'll run it before breakfast."

"Run it after," I say. "It will start cleaner once the line warms."

He grunts agreement, then notices Emme, the mantle, the candles. He hides his smile badly.

"Señorita Emme," he says. "You found work."

"Work found me," she says, and passes him half a slice of bread with butter done right. Rafa is a simple man about simple things. He blesses her with a nod that makes my jaw tighten against nothing.

Teresa and Mariela drift in soon after, parka-slow and already gossiping. The Brit—Elvis, or Elliot, something with an E—appears last, bright fleece and nervous apology. The storm has come down a shade and presses the glass with both hands. The room has the shape I give it every morning, and also a softness it didn't have ten minutes ago. People sit easier. I don't.

I set the pot on the table and reach past Emme for the stack of plates. She has set them out with the side plates under the dinner plates. That's not how it goes here. This isn't a hotel. You don't stack weight for the table to carry; you stack it for the hands that will.

"Plates separate," I say low, so it is between us. "It keeps the table from feeling formal. People talk more if they don't perform first."

"I want them to rest," she says.

"I want them to listen," I say.

Our eyes hold for a count. She steps back. I separate the plates.

The conversation moves around us. Names, knees, weather. Elvis-Elliot tries a joke about the Wi-Fi and is punished by silence. Good. Learn fast.

I pass bread. Guiso steams into the air like a promise kept. Teresa sighs her half of Mendoza into her bowl. Mariela asks Rafa about the trail like she is buying real estate. He tells her nothing and she thanks him.

Emme pours water for Teresa without asking. She drops a wedge of lemon in it. We don't put lemon in the water at breakfast because the sour lives in the coffee and the stew this early and the tongue gets confused. It's a small thing. It is my thing.

"That's not—" I begin.

Her head tilts. "Your ritual," she says, and lifts the lemon out with a spoon. She doesn't drip. She learned fast by watching.

I don't correct her again because she already corrected herself and because the room is watching from behind their spoons. The trick with control is never to show it to the audience. Control is backstage work. If it makes the stage, you've failed.

When the bowls are half-empty, the wind punches the south windows hard enough to lift conversation off the table. People turn, look where the weather wants them to look. Elvis-Elliot laughs at his own fear. Teresa does not. She reaches for Mariela's hand under the table like they've done it for fifty years.

Emme stands. This is where most people tell stories or make noise. She doesn't. She leaves, fast, and returns with blankets. One for Teresa's knees. One for Mariela's shoulders. She doesn't touch their heads because she understands dignity. She moves to the Brit and folds a blanket over the back of his chair like it always lived there.

La pièce respire de nouveau. Putain d'elle. The room breathes again. Damn her.

"You're in the way," I say. The words are quiet and still somehow hit the table like metal.

Her eyes lift to mine. She doesn't flinch. She doesn't smile like a shield either. "Then show me where you stand and where I can stand without crowding you."

It takes a second for the words to land in the space my temper usually keeps empty. She didn't apologize. She offered a map.

I point to the kitchen side, the arc from sideboard to end of table. I show her the line where staff cross and where they stop. I hate that she makes me name the things I know by bone. I do it anyway.

After, we eat. Conversation returns in small increments. The candles she lit do nothing for light and somehow help anyway. I let them stay. It costs me nothing except the habit of blowing them out when no one is looking.

Rafa takes the second pot. I wash the first. The rhythm returns, not the same and not broken. Emme clears nothing. She stands where I marked the floor for her and does not cross the line. I respect that more than I want to.

The pass will close. I call Martín and tell him to send word to the families down-valley that the supply run won't clear the pass until tomorrow. He says something about old snow and new snow not liking each other. He's right.

By the time the bowls are stacked and the table wiped, only the small sounds of winter remain. The women drift toward the hearth. Elvis-Elliot remembers an email he can't send and sulks. Rafa pulls his hat down and goes to wrestle the generator into reason.

I dry my hands and find Emme still at the edge of the kitchen, where I left her.

"You touched too much," I say. "Next time, ask."

Her chin lifts a fraction. "If I'd asked, you would have said no."

"Yes," I say.

"Next time," she says, "try thank you."

It's not insolence. It's a door she leaves open because she must not believe in locked ones.

"Tour in twenty minutes," I tell her. "Boots. Hat. No city shoes."

"I already found your boot religion," she says, and turns away before I can answer.

When she's gone the room feels too orderly. I move the enamel pitcher back to the shelf where it belongs and I blow out the candles, then light one again and leave it. It annoys me and it stays. That's the kind of compromise people call growth. I call it a truce I didn't negotiate.

Rafa reappears in the doorway with a hand against the jamb and a brow raised at me that says what he always says without words: you don't like being seen.

"Generator?" I ask.

"Obedient," he says. His mouth twitches. "The señorita helps like a guide. Not like a guest."

"I noticed."

"She listens when you draw the map."

"We'll see," I say.

He leaves. I put the knife edge-in. I check the grinder. Seventeen clicks. My hands are clean and still not steady. The scent she brought into the kitchen clings to the air, citrus and something I don't have a word for because I haven't needed it.

The mountain presses its shoulder to the windows. I press back.

Twenty minutes. Boots. Hat. No city shoes.

I tell myself I am taking a client to see the property. I tell myself the line will hold where I drew it.

Outside, the wind shifts and the powder skates off the eaves. Inside, on the mantle, one candle burns when it shouldn't. I let it. Only for now.

Chapter 5

Bossy, But Not

EMME

I MET LUC AGAIN exactly nineteen minutes later. He was already waiting, of course—dark jacket zipped to the throat, wool hat pulled low, gloves hooked through one hand. The kind of clothes that didn't shout *guide* or *owner*, just *prepared*. Even bundled, he looked carved from the same slate and quiet as the mountain itself—solid, self-contained, mildly disappointed the rest of us insisted on breathing in it.

Outside, the wind practiced its vowels. Inside, the world smelled like cedar and coffee, warm and honest.

It wasn't the coffee or the view making my pulse misbehave.

It was him—too calm, too contained, too... something.

Dangerous, if I let it be.

And I refused to be the woman who caught feelings over efficient outerwear.

"Ready?" he asked.

"I was born ready," I said, and immediately regretted the tourist bravado. He looked at me the way people look at weather forecasts they already know are wrong.

Before stepping out, I layered up—Luc's gray sweater over one of my camisoles, then pulled on the same black pants I'd worn the day before. They'd survived a flight, what would count as a snowstorm by Florida-girl standards, and an existential crisis, so they could survive this. In the boot room I'd found a basket labeled *base layers — borrow and return* and claimed a pair of thermal leggings that looked one wash past glory. Add the loaner parka folded near the door, the hat and gloves he'd left for me, and I was more or less Patagonia-ready. Mismatched but warm—progress, at least, until I saw my suitcase again.

We stepped into air that redefined cold. It didn't sting—it settled. Slow, thorough, everywhere at once. I'd worked in enough winter markets to know how to layer, but Patagonia had its own rulebook.

The path from the lodge curved downward, snow-packed and narrow, each step a quiet reminder that the elements here didn't negotiate. My breath came out in controlled clouds, the sound small against the hush.

Luc handed me trekking poles without ceremony. No lecture, no warning label—just trust wrapped in practicality. His gloves brushed mine as he passed them over, warm from use.

Summer owed me for this.

I'd handled altitude in the Andes, frost in Iceland, even a blizzard that trapped me in a Lapland hostel with three drunk Finns and a heater older than sin.

And okay, maybe one of them was cute, and maybe he kept me a little warmer than the others—but even that didn't compare to this brand of cold. Air so pure it burned, landscape so unreal you almost forgave the burn for what it showed you. Patagonia didn't posture; it simply existed at a level most climates couldn't afford.

Still didn't matter.

Not here.

"Keep your weight behind the step," he said.

"I've been walking for years," I told him.

"Not here," he said, which was somehow not condescending—just fact.

I tried not to like the way he said it. Bossy, but not. A heat curled low in my stomach anyway, traitor that it was.

We moved along the ridge in silence. His version of tour guiding was apparently to exist near a view and let it do the talking. Below us, the lake caught the wind and changed color by the second—steel, pewter, silver. No filter could do it justice. I wanted to take a photo but it felt rude—like photographing a prayer. I lowered my phone without thinking.

When we reached a lookout framed by black rock, he stopped. "The lodge faces north," he said. "For light. For heat. For the way storms come from the south—you can see them before they decide."

I turned toward the valley. Clouds drifted low and heavy, stitched by light. "You designed it," I said, already knowing the answer.

He nodded once.

"It feels alive."

He looked down at his gloves, maybe to hide the way his mouth almost softened. "It should. Everything else up here is."

I could've asked more—about blueprints and builders, about how he found this spot—but his shoulders had that precise set I was beginning to recognize:

the weight of a door closing quietly. The line of his spine sharpened, a quiet no.

So I talked instead, because silence with him felt like trying to read between languages. "You know, most lodges sell the illusion of wilderness. Yours actually lets it win."

He glanced at me. "And what does your company sell?"

"Access," I said. "Luxury, safety, curated danger. We give people adventure with a warranty."

"That's not adventure," he said.

"I know," I admitted. "It's marketing. But it keeps the lights on."

He adjusted one of the poles I wasn't using right. His gloved hand brushed mine, light, businesslike. The touch traveled through fabric anyway. "And you think this place needs your marketing."

"I think the right people should find it," I said. "The kind who treat quiet like a resource, not a reward."

For the first time, his mouth tilted toward something that might have been amusement. "You talk in proposals even on mountains."

"Hazard of the job," I said. "Also maybe genetics."

We kept walking. Snow crackled beneath our boots; the cold had a sound all its own. He paused sometimes to point—a stand of lenga trees twisted by wind, the blue spine of a glacier far off, paw prints pressed deep into the snow where a fox or maybe a puma had passed hours before. Proof that something out here lived by different rules—and survived them. A flash of rust moved through the brush ahead—a fox, lean and unhurried, its tail a streak of flame against the gray. I startled anyway, a tiny betrayal of nerves. Luc's hand closed around my elbow, steady but brief, like gravity remembering its manners.

"Zorro colorado," he said. "They own the place."

"Noted," I said, pretending I hadn't jumped.

When we looped back toward the lodge, I caught sight of the stone foundation, the clean geometry of it against the slope. "You built it yourself?"

"With help," he said. "Locals. Friends. My father." There was a pause that felt like it should have included another name. He kept walking, so I didn't chase it. I just matched his pace and let the silence settle.

Back at the door, he brushed snow from his gloves—efficient, steady, wrist flexing under the leather. The kind of movement you notice even when you pretend not to. "You walk well," he said.

"High praise."

"It's rare," he said. "Most people fight the ground."

"I negotiate," I said.

That earned half a sound—almost a laugh, mostly a sigh. He stepped ahead to clear the last drift from the threshold, boots leaving sharp prints across the stone. When he opened the door, a wave of heat rolled out, sharp as sunlight through whiskey. He held it a beat longer than necessary before motioning me inside. Warmth hit my face, rich and immediate.

I unzipped my parka, fingers stiff, trying to look like someone who'd done this a thousand times instead of someone who'd nearly face-planted on Patagonia's welcome mat.

My chin lifted on instinct—*fake it, Florida girl.*

"I'll draft the proposal this afternoon," I said, voice steadier than my hands.

He nodded. "Lunch runs one to two."

"Communal again?"

"Not exactly," he said. "Buffet. People come and go. There's food, coffee, wine. Enough to make silence optional."

I started up the stairs and heard him add, almost to himself, "You move through rooms the way weather does."

When I looked back, he was already gone.

Weather changes things without asking permission.

Figures I'd show up in work clothes to reason with a mountain.

By the time I reached the landing, my legs had stopped pretending to be warm. The quiet was so complete it felt curated, like Luc had personally interviewed every sound before letting it stay. Even my footsteps felt padded, as if the floor wanted secrecy. The hallway lights glowed low and gold. Someone had tucked a small vase of dried flowers on the windowsill—simple, wild, deliberate. Everything in this place had purpose, which was both impressive and deeply unnerving for a woman who built her career on controlling chaos. Nothing here seemed accidental—not even the air.

My room waited the way it had last night—warm, spare, too honest to flatter. But there, just inside the door, sat my suitcase. Upright. Untouched. A tag still dangling like proof of a miracle. Rafa must've brought it in while we were out—quiet, efficient, making sure I'd find it.

"Well," I said out loud, "look who found her way home."

She looked rougher than I remembered—scuffed at the corners, one zipper bent like it had survived a bar fight with baggage handling—but she was here. And inside was everything I'd thought I could live without for twenty-four hours.

I knelt, unlatched the case, and was hit with the familiar scent of travel: soap, leather, something faintly floral from a bottle that had somehow not exploded. Relief had a smell, and it was mine.

I pulled out my thermal base layers, the blazer that had no business in this hemisphere, my notebooks, and the small packet of hotel coffee I'd forgotten to remove. The color and order of my things steadied me. Luc might thrive on stillness, but I worked better when surrounded by evidence of motion. My hands moved automatically—fold, smooth, stack.

I traded the day's layers for comfort—black leggings, a soft sweater, and my favorite fuzzy slippers, the ones I wear under my desk at the office before my sisters get in. The floorboards creaked in approval. Patagonia might've been trying to kill me outdoors, but inside, it made surrender feel civilized.

I pulled my hair into a loose knot, settled at the small desk by the window, and opened my laptop. The screen blinked to life, cursor waiting—impatient, arrogant, like it knew how easily I'd let work talk me out of sleep.

A soft knock pulled my attention toward the door. Three taps, even and unhurried.

Luc. It had to be.

I hesitated a second before opening it. He stood there holding a mug, steam curling into the hall light, and a covered plate. No coat now—just a dark flannel and that same impossible calm. The steam curled between us before either of us spoke.

"I thought you might need this," he said. "You mentioned work."

I blinked. "You deliver room service now?"

"Only when it seems necessary."

The coffee smelled exactly right—strong, smooth, a hint of cinnamon. The way I'd taken it that morning.

"You remembered what I put in it," I said before I could stop myself.

He shrugged, a movement more habit than humility. "It's a small lodge."

I took the mug and dish, careful not to brush his fingers. "Thank you."

He nodded once, already turning away, as if that were all the conversation required.

When the door clicked shut, I stood there longer than necessary, the cup warming my hands. The cursor still blinked on the screen behind me, patient now, waiting for me to decide which one of us was the distraction.

Proposal: Wilder Horizons x Refugio Cielo – Initial Assessment

Normally, this part came easily. I'd evaluate, quantify, categorize: target demographics, accessibility ratings, marketable experiences. Luxury adventure was, after all, a product—comfort disguised as courage. But nothing about Cielo fit that model. It wasn't built for clients who wanted curated wilderness; it was for people who needed to remember they were small.

I typed: *"Refugio Cielo operates on scarcity—the kind that feels sacred rather than inconvenient."*

Then paused. Deleted. Rewrote.

"Cielo's appeal lies in its restraint. Twelve rooms, twenty-four guests, and silence treated as a resource."

That felt closer.

I kept writing, fingers warming as the words found their rhythm.

"Guests aren't pampered here; they're trusted. The experience is designed to remind them they belong to something that doesn't need them."

Which is probably why it worked on me.

I stopped again. That one might be too honest for marketing copy. But it was true.

Luc's version of hospitality was a paradox—impeccable care delivered through distance. No small talk. No artifice. He served warmth like it was a controlled substance: carefully measured, never spilled. And somehow that made it feel rare.

I tried to translate that into bullet points.

Key Differentiators: Silence, privacy, isolation, authenticity, ecological integrity.

Risks: Accessibility, limited capacity, temperament of owner.

I smiled at that last one. Temperament of owner could fill its own appendix.

He wasn't difficult exactly. Just precise. Every gesture had intent: the way he placed things, the way he moved through a room without disturbing the air. Most men that disciplined hid arrogance behind efficiency. Luc hid history.

I thought of how he'd said *locals, friends, my father*—and how the sentence had ended there, clean but not complete.

There was loss in this place. Not loud, not tragic, just absorbed into the walls the way light sank into the wood.

I added another note to the file: *Partnership proposal must protect the integrity of the environment and the autonomy of the host.*

"Autonomy of the host."

God, that sounded clinical.

But it was what he wanted—to keep the world from touching what he'd built. Which meant my usual approach wouldn't work.

Wilder Horizons specialized in creating bridges. Luc Moreau had built a fortress.

I stared at the cursor, blinking like judgment.

Maybe the proposal shouldn't be about expansion at all. Maybe it should be about protection. Licensing. A strategic partnership that offered Wilder Horizons exclusivity without interference. A model that let Luc keep his silence while still profiting from it.

I leaned back in the chair, sipped my coffee, and watched steam curl against the windowpane. Outside, the mountain looked half erased by low clouds, like a secret withdrawing its permission.

Somewhere below, I could hear faint conversation from the dining area—cutlery, laughter, the clink of glass. Lunch had started. I pictured the buffet he'd mentioned: soup, bread, maybe that same guiso reheated until it achieved legend. The thought of sitting across from him again so soon made something in my stomach shift. Not nerves—just a charge under my skin, like I'd stepped too close to a live wire. Warmth prickled low in my pulse.

I added a final note under "Considerations": *Partnership may depend on earning trust of owner—slowly. Approach with respect, not persuasion.*

Then, because I couldn't help myself, I muttered, "And maybe bring a parka to the next negotiation."

The cursor blinked back at me, unamused. I closed the laptop halfway, like shutting a mouth, and glanced toward my suitcase. Half my wardrobe looked ridiculous now—tailored dresses, silk blouses, heels. Winter pieces or not, none of them belonged here. None of them belonged with him. Still, I found comfort in folding the pieces, smoothing out creases, making order out of travel wrinkles. It was a small ritual that said, *I'm still me.*

When I reached the bottom of the case, a small envelope slid free. A note from Summer, written before I left: *Don't charm him. Survive it, if you can.*

I laughed softly. "Too late."

Chapter 6

Blueprints for One

LUC

THE GENERATOR CHANGED PITCH. Not trouble, just the kind of wind-gust correction you only hear when you live with a machine long enough to call it by its first name. I set my mug on the table and waited for it to settle. It did. Obedient again.

I cleaned the edges of the blueprint with the side of my hand until the paper lay flat, square to the grain of the table. Order gave the mind a hallway. You could walk down it without bumping your shoulders.

Footsteps overhead crossed once, twice, then stopped. A chair protested softly. Typing resumed. She was still working. Time and hunger, both ignored. I told myself that wasn't my business.

The clock on the stone pillar said 16:40. Juliana would be checking the smoker for me—local woman, steady hands, here three days a week. Sometimes kitchen, sometimes cleaning, sometimes the run into town when the valley forgot something. Early dinner prep. I gathered the drawings, slid them into their sleeve, and put the pencils back in their exact place in the drawer. I turned off the lamp and stood a moment in the blue of the window, letting the mountain reduce everything to scale.

On the way to the kitchen, I heard Rafa singing something off-key when I pushed the door. He cut the note in half and grinned like he'd been caught stealing the moon. "Jefe." *Boss.* He lifted the lid on a stockpot with theatrical reverence. "The soup says good evening."

Steam rose, clean and herbal. "¿Qué es?" *What is it?"*

"Caldo verde with charred leek. Juliana got the good sausage from town."

Juliana snorted without looking up from her knife. "I got the normal sausage. He's dramatic."

"Normal sausage," Rafa repeated sadly, "that dreams of being better."

He slipped me a spoon. I tasted. Salt right. Heat gentle. Body enough to convince a person they were not alone. "Bueno." *Good.*

Rafa's eyes flicked past me toward the main room. "Our guests? The teachers already took cake. The Brit never stops eating. And the fancy woman"—his mouth tilted—"the one who works like she is the boss of winter? She did not come for lunch. I saved a plate."

My jaw answered him before I did. "She has a name."

"Sí. Emme." He watched me too openly. "You want me to take her food?"

"No." Too sharp. I eased it. "I'll take it."

Juliana didn't pause the knife. She never did. But the humor in her voice was a small knife of its own. "Of course you will."

I ignored her and covered the plate. The kitchen lights threw an honest heat. I poured a fresh coffee before I could stop myself, trying to remember what she'd put in hers that morning—and why I cared. Beyond the window, the sky was moving toward ink. Snow took its first breath.

I carried the plate and mug out to the main room, crossed the hall, and climbed the back stairs that didn't creak when you stepped on their inside edges. At her door I stopped, braced the plate and mug in one hand, lifted the other—and didn't knock.

On the other side of the wood there was movement and then stillness, the kind that sounded like a thought landing. She'd asked this morning if she could use the fiber line at the desk by the window. I'd said yes. She had thanked me like I'd given her a light in a storm.

I knocked once, not hard, not tentative. She opened after a pause—slippers, sweater sleeves pushed to her elbows, hair pulled up. The sweater fit like it had been made to prove softness could have structure. For a second my breath caught, shallow and stupid. I shifted the plate in my hand to give it something to do. The heat from the mug curled up between us, carrying cinnamon and something else that didn't belong in a hallway.

A gust hit the window behind her, a quick crack of wind against glass, sharp enough to jolt the breath I'd just steadied. I pulled in air, steady again. Or close enough.

Ressaisis-toi, mec. Pull yourself together, man.

She smiled, light and professional. "You deliver room service now?"

"Only when it seems necessary."

Her fingers brushed the mug. "Thank you." Her fingers tightened on the mug for a fraction of a second, as if the warmth steadied more than just her hands.

I nodded once, said something that probably wasn't a sentence, and left before the air could turn into something else.

On the way back down the stairs I told myself this was hospitality. Nothing more.

By 6:00 PM, the guests had fallen into their routines. The teachers took the corner by the fire, arguing gently about chess rules they both knew perfectly. The Brit stationed himself near the window, sketching the glacier between sips of hot tea. It was the kind of noise I preferred—contained, familiar, nothing sharp around the edges.

Rafa brought out the picada—local cheeses, thin slices of chorizo, olives, a few pastries still warm from the oven. Juliana followed with bread and that look that always asked if I'd eaten, which I hadn't. She caught my eye and lifted her chin in a question I didn't answer.

A few minutes later, Emme came down carrying her empty plate. That alone earned Juliana's raised brows. Guests rarely returned dishes themselves. She set it on the counter with quiet efficiency, asked for another coffee, and took a small pastry while she waited.

She joined Teresa and Mariela by the fire for a few minutes, polite conversation, quick laughter—easy, practiced warmth that didn't sound forced. Then she excused herself, promising to be back down before dinner, coffee in hand and the firelight still moving in her hair.

Super. Maintenant, je la suivais. Putain de génie. Now I was tracking her. Fucking brilliant.

I went back to the table and unrolled the drawing again, even though I knew I wouldn't work. I wanted to make sense of something. A wall, a doorway—anything that stayed where I put it.

The lamp hummed. The pencil waited. I redrew the same line three times, erased it twice, and still didn't like the angle. I shifted the ruler, changed the scale, checked a measurement I already knew by heart. Nothing was wrong, but nothing was right either.

An hour passed like that—small corrections pretending to be progress. Graphite smudged the side of my hand. The air cooled, the fire sank, and still I couldn't leave it alone. I kept tracing the same section, convinced that if I just held the line steady enough, the rest of the world would fall back into order.

Then, footsteps on the stairs. Not the hurried kind that meant a question. The measured, end-of-day kind. I didn't have to look to know who it was. The air changed when she entered a room, not louder, just recalibrated somehow.

She crossed the threshold and paused. Most first-timers paused there. The room offered a choice: fire or window. Warmth or the dark that made you honest.

She went to the window first and looked at the night like she had a conversation unfinished with it. Then she turned and came toward the table.

I was rolling the last of the blueprints when she stopped beside me.

"May I?" she asked, nodding toward the drawings.

I hesitated, thumb still on the edge of the paper. "They're not finished."

"That's the best part." She leaned closer, careful not to touch the table, eyes scanning the plans as if she were learning a language. Something in my chest kicked—small, unruly—and I sat a little straighter, as if posture alone could shove the feeling back where it belonged. No questions yet—just quiet understanding. Most people pretended to be interested; she actually looked.

"You design everything yourself?"

"Everything I can afford to get wrong." The words came out before I could edit them. I cleared my throat. "This one's for next season. A few structural improvements. Small things."

"They don't look small."

"They're not meant to."

I heard myself explaining angles, load points, the way the corridor light would change at different times of day.

My voice steadied once I had something technical to hold onto. I showed her where I wanted to turn a storage room into an extra guest room—something less formal. More personal, maybe. She listened—really listened—a silence that filled the room instead of emptying it.

I started to roll the drawings again, more to stop talking than to finish, when movement near the doorway caught my eye. Juliana stood there wiping her hands on a towel, expression somewhere between exasperation and affection.

"Go on," she mouthed. "I've got it." She crossed to the long table, laying out plates and folded linen like she'd been waiting for this moment. Two glasses appeared beside us—red wine, good enough to make a point. Juliana didn't look at me, but the pause before she set them down was pointed in a way that made heat crawl up the back of my neck.

"Gracias," Emme said softly.

Juliana smiled, one of those knowing smiles that didn't need translation, and went back to her work.

The smell of roasted vegetables drifted from the kitchen. The teachers were already choosing their seats. The Brit poured water like it was a ritual. The clock on the pillar said 19:55. Dinner.

I capped the pencil, slid the drawings into their case, and straightened. "You should sit."

"You should too."

Teresa, who had been polishing the same glass for three minutes, went very still in the way of a woman who wants to witness something and also not influence it. Rafa saw it and became interested in a salt jar he had filled an hour ago.

"Thank you again for the plate earlier," she said, as if we were moving along a list and didn't want to lose our place. "It was delicious."

"You don't need to thank me."

She tilted her head. "You think I only thank people when I need to?"

I opened my mouth and closed it again. "No."

"I thank people because I see them." She hesitated. "And because it's nice."

Rafa dropped a spoon in the kitchen like the percussion line to a joke he wasn't going to say out loud.

I turned to speak to one of the teachers. I didn't get that far. "How is the work?"

"Complicated," she said.

That wasn't what I expected. "Complicated how?"

"More than I thought it would be." She looked toward the rafters as if the answer might be there. "You. This place. It's not what I expected."

"You mean it's worse."

"No." Her mouth softened. "Better. Just different. Wilder Horizons works with luxury, but this—" she gestured around her "—this is alive. It breathes. That's... unusual. I want to get it right."

Her gaze dipped for half a second, a shadow passing through before the professional calm returned. She reached out, resting a hand on mine as if it were the most natural thing in the world—light, brief, sure.

My body didn't get the memo. Every muscle went still, like the table had grounded current through my skin. Her hand was warm, steady, human. Nothing dramatic, but it felt like it left a mark. My pulse stumbled, stupid and loud in the quiet—loud enough I was sure she'd hear it if she stayed a second longer.

She didn't seem to notice. Her eyes flicked back to the spot where the plans had been a moment earlier.

I told myself to breathe. *Putain, ressaisis-toi.*

I didn't know what to do with that. Praise wrapped in sincerity always landed like a mistake. I'd spent years making sure the work spoke for itself so I didn't have to.

"Most people don't care about getting it right," I said finally.

"Then they shouldn't be in charge of showing it to the world."

We didn't speak for a minute. "Your lodge." Emme's voice found me again. "It's... precise."

I glanced at the timber above us. "It had to be," I said.

"The way the corridors angle. The way the rooms sit into the hill instead of on it. The window heights." Her gaze swept the space, cataloguing it. "You designed it to make people look out, not in."

"Most people look at themselves wherever they go," I said.

"And you wanted to interrupt that."

"I wanted to make it difficult."

She looked back at me. "For them."

"For me."

She considered the arrangement of words, like it was a floor plan with good traffic flow. "How long did it take to build?"

"The parts you can't see took the longest."

"That's always true." She swiveled her body to face me. "In my line of work, the parts you can't see are called favors, patience, and backup plans."

"And in mine they're called footings and wind loads."
I paused. "And patience."

"The thing we both pretend we have." She smiled,
quick and knowing.

"Speak for yourself."

"Do you need anything for your work? A printer.
More outlets."

She shook her head. "I need a conversation with a
glacier that answers back. Failing that, I need your rates
and availability for Q3, Q4, and probably next year."

"I'm booked."

Her mouth didn't move but the air around it did.
"Completely."

"Yes."

"And yet you're thinking about turning a storage
room into a private guest space."

I let out breath I hadn't planned. "You are not restful."

"I'm not here to be."

Wind tested the window and found it solid. She took
the last bite of bread and set the plate aside with the kind
of neatness that made a person trust her to land a plane.

"Walk with me after dinner," she said.

The words surprised both of us. I saw it. She saw that
I saw it. She recovered first.

J'avais survécu à la journée. Visiblement, ça ne suffisait pas. I'd survived the day. Apparently that didn't cut it.

The invitation sounded simple. The look that followed wasn't.

"Not far. I want the kind of night air that clears out the tabs in my brain."

I told Juliana we would be five minutes. Juliana pretended to worry that five would become thirty and gave us each a scarf she had knitted out of some unkillable wool. Outside, the cold was an animal that waited politely at the door and then put its paw on your chest. We stepped onto the path that ran the length of the south wall, the one we kept scraped so guests could see the stars without breaking their necks.

Snow spoke underfoot in the good way. The edge of her sleeve skimmed my arm, a warm line in the cold that shouldn't have mattered but did. Air found the back of my throat as she pulled the scarf higher and breathed out once, seeing what her breath would do.

"Did you build this walk to be exactly this long on purpose?" she asked after a few steps. "Long enough to think. Short enough not to leave?"

Something in her expression loosened—the kind of shift you only catch if you're paying attention—then she reset it with a small breath.

"I built it to keep people from wandering into the dark."

"You don't like when people do that."

"They get lost."

"Sometimes that's the point."

"Are you trying to get lost?"

"No." She laughed, tweaking her scarf. "Not tonight."

We stopped at the turn where the path decided it had gone far enough. The lodge threw a warm shape against the snow. In its windows, our reflections were taller than we were and kinder, as reflections are.

"You don't like that I skipped lunch," she said. "Why?"

"I don't like people making the place carry them when they could carry themselves."

"I'm not asking it to carry me."

"I know." I tried again. "I don't like to watch energy go out and not come back."

"That's... very scientist of you."

"It's very builder."

When we turned back, she walked a fraction closer to my shoulder. By the time we reached the door, the windows had fogged again from the heat inside. "Thank you," she said again, and this time it landed in a place that made sense. "For the path."

"I didn't build it for you."

"I know." The small smile again, the one that shifted my whole center. "But it still works."

She didn't look away right away. For a beat too long, she just... stayed. Present. Open. Something in her posture wavered—subtle, unreadable—and it held me there with her. She moved toward the stairs. At the first step she paused, considering. She looked like a woman standing in a doorway, not sure which side she belonged on. Then she went up, quiet on the inside edge where the wood didn't complain.

I stood in the main room long enough to hear her cross the ceiling above and stop. Her floorboard rhythm found mine. The generator settled to the low contented hum it used when the temperature held steady. Juliana pretended to scrub a perfectly clean counter. Rafa asked if we needed more salt.

I went back to the table and unrolled the drawing one last time. The note in the margin had not moved. It didn't need to. I added two measurements and a question mark, then put the pencil down and let my hand stay open.

You build for one and call it safety. Then someone comes along who knows how to live in the space you made and does not ask your permission to fit.

I rolled the drawings, capped the pencil, and left the table exactly as I'd found it.

Order restored.

Nothing else needed fixing.

That's what I told myself.

Which was a lie I could almost believe if I didn't still feel the warmth of her hand ghosting across my skin.

Chapter 7

Weather Permitting

EMME

THE WIND WOULDN'T QUIT. The beams above me groaned like old ships—solid, tired, built to hold their ground long after people gave up trying. It clawed at the eaves, rattled the shutters, shoved a draft through the seam of the window like it was trying to find a way inside. I stared at the dark ceiling and counted each groan of timber until the numbers blurred.

Sleep wasn't coming.

I shoved back the blankets and found my socks with my toes, then slid into my pink fuzzy slippers to calm my nerves. The floorboards were cold through the wool. I wrapped my cardigan tighter and told myself a cup of tea would help.

Downstairs, the lodge was a cathedral of wood and hush. The walls held the day's heat in uneven pockets—warm near the hearth, cooler by the windows where frost feathered the glass. The fire in the great room had burned low, amber coals pulsing behind the grate. The room smelled of charred oak and wool, the faint musk of boots drying by the door, all of it threaded with the metallic bite of storm air sneaking through the seams. Every few seconds the wind surged, pressing snow against the tall windows until the glass shivered.

And then I saw him.

Luc sat in the far chair, one elbow on his knee, a line of light carving his profile. A radio murmured beside him, all static and low Spanish vowels—something about *el paso cerrado* and *vientos fuertes*. Shadows from the fire moved along the stone hearth, climbing and falling like they couldn't decide which way the night leaned.

The storm had closed the pass.

We were officially sealed in.

He looked up, surprised but not startled. "You're awake."

"So are you," I said, keeping my voice soft so it wouldn't disturb the air between us.

"I don't sleep well when the wind sounds like this."

I filled the kettle without asking permission. The metal clicked against the sink, loud in the quiet. "Tea?"

He hesitated, then nodded once.

When the water boiled, I poured it over two bags of chamomile and carried the mugs toward the fire. He watched me the whole way—eyes shadowed, unreadable, but something in his shoulders eased when I set one mug beside him.

"Gracias," he murmured.

"De nada," I answered, even though my accent probably made him wince.

The radio crackled again. I caught a few English words—"gale force," "roads impassable." He turned the dial lower until the voice became another layer of weather.

For a while we didn't speak. We just sat, two strangers sharing borrowed warmth, listening to the weatherman report the same bad news in both languages. The lodge held its breath around us—the old timbers settling, the roof flexing under the wind, every part of it reminding me I was in a place built by a man who understood how to make wood stand its ground.

When I finally looked over, he was studying the fire. The light cut along his jaw, the faintest stubble catching gold. He looked different without the daylight—less carved, more human.

He must have felt me watching, because his mouth tilted. "Do you always wander at midnight?"

"Only when the wind keeps me up." I sipped my tea. "You?"

"Only when the wind keeps the mountain up."

I smiled into the steam. "That sounds like an architect's answer."

A short breath of amusement. "Old habits."

He leaned forward to adjust the log with the iron poker. Sparks lifted, tiny constellations that vanished before they could mean anything.

"Do you always babysit the weather?" I asked.

"It's better than being surprised by it."

"You don't like surprises."

He looked at me then, properly looked, and it felt like standing too close to the fire. "Do you?"

"Depends who's bringing them."

The corner of his mouth twitched—almost a smile, almost not.

The radio faded into a faint waltz of static and wind. I cradled the mug between my palms and watched the snow blow sideways across the window. It was hypnotic, that much whiteness moving without destination.

After a while he spoke again. "The pass will close completely by morning. Two, maybe three days before they clear it."

"You sound disappointed," I said.

He shrugged. "Guests expect schedules. I prefer to keep them."

I tilted my head. "Control issues?"

He huffed something that might've been a laugh. "Maintenance."

"Mm. I'm familiar."

He glanced at me, one brow raised.

"I work in vendor relations," I said. "Keeping people happy while they're trapped together is practically a degree."

That earned an actual smile, faint but real. It flickered and was gone.

He studied me again, slower this time. "You came here in the middle of winter. Why?"

I laughed quietly, more at myself than him. "My bossy sister thought it would be good timing—quieter, fewer distractions. Realistically, it's the best window to secure contracts before high season hits."

"Bossy sister?"

"Summer. She's the COO. She calls it leadership, but we all know what it is."

He looked amused. "There are others?"

"Five. I'm number five, which means I spent my childhood yelling over everyone just to get an opinion on pizza toppings. I got good at being heard."

"Clearly."

His tone wasn't teasing, exactly. More...observing.

"She thinks sending me south in the middle of Patagonia's winter is character-building."

"Has it built character?"

"Ask me when I see daylight again."

He laughed softly, low and unexpected. It loosened something in the air. The firelight caught the edge of his jaw, carving warmth where there hadn't been any. I found myself smiling into my mug just to keep my hands busy.

"What about you?" I asked. "Any siblings?"

He shifted, elbows on knees, gaze still on the flames. "A sister," he said after a pause. "Still in Paris."

"Older or younger?"

"Older."

"And she thinks you're crazy for living here."

His eyes lifted to mine, the flicker of surprise brief but visible. "She does, but she understands."

There was more behind it—a door half open—but I didn't push. The silence after felt companionable, the kind that didn't need more attention.

The fire cracked. I shifted, resting my chin on my knees. "Curiosity gets people killed out here," he said suddenly.

"Then it's in good company."

That drew another look from him—half admiration, half warning.

"You don't scare easily."

"I'm the fifth of six girls. I stopped being scared around age seven."

He smiled again, this one slower, as if it snuck up on him.

For a while we just listened. Wind. Fire. Static. His hand drifted to the radio dial, thumb brushing the metal. The rhythm of it felt personal, almost intimate—the way he needed noise the way some people need prayer.

I followed his gaze to the structure around us—the thick beams, the joinery so precise it felt reverent. "You built all this," I said.

He nodded once. "Every beam."

"From the plans you drew in Paris?"

His jaw flexed. "Those plans were for someone else. This place was for me."

"So the rumors are true—you walked away from the city to build a refuge."

He didn't answer. The fire popped; his silence filled the room faster than the heat did.

"Was it supposed to be temporary?" I asked gently.

He stared into the flames. "Everything is."

I felt the weight of it land between us—a truth wrapped in regret. Whatever sent him here hadn't been a whim; it was an exile.

I wanted to ask more, but his shoulders had already straightened, the wall rebuilding itself stone by stone.

He rose, setting his untouched tea on the table. "Forecast says clear skies in two days."

"Good," I said. "I was starting to think I'd have to start a snowshoe division."

That earned a small sound—half chuckle, half sigh. "Until then, patience."

"Not my strong suit."

"Then you'll learn." He paused. "Good night, Miss Wilder."

He moved toward the stairs, shadows folding around him. For a heartbeat the firelight caught on his wrist—a leather bracelet, worn and dark. Then he was gone, the creak of the upper landing fading into the wind.

I sat a minute longer, letting the quiet stretch. The fire hissed softly, a reminder that warmth always costs something.

I finished my tea and set the mug beside his. The snow outside had swallowed the world whole.

Some men build walls. Some, whole mountains. He'd done both.

Chapter 8

Fault Line

LUC

THE FIRE HAD BURNED itself down to memory. From my room above the great hall, I could still smell it—smoke and cedar, faint and warm, clinging to the wool of my sweater. The beams creaked overhead, deep and familiar—a reminder that even solid things shift in the dark. Usually that steadied me. Tonight it felt like a question I didn't want to answer.

I tried to read. The book lay open across my knees, lines of text about proportion and light. I'd taught myself those theories by heart years ago, but repetition had always been comfort. Tonight the words drifted apart before they reached meaning. The rhythm that used to quiet my mind refused to catch.

Her voice kept sliding in instead—low, thoughtful, distracted. Too smooth for a woman who said the wind kept her up. Too dangerous for a man who suddenly didn't mind the noise. *Maybe we build what we need most.*

An offhand remark, tossed between talk of timber and insulation, but it wouldn't leave. I'd built this place to last against every kind of weather. I hadn't realized I'd built it to keep anyone out.

My brother once said nearly the same thing. *You build like you're afraid the walls might leave.*

He'd been grinning when he said it, charcoal dust across his knuckles, music spilling out of some old radio in the shop. We'd been sketching a roofline, arguing about the curve. He wanted it wild; I wanted it right. I can still hear the scrape of his pencil across the paper—careless, confident, alive.

After that, everything got quieter.

I snapped the book shut before the memories got louder. The air in the room felt thin, stretched. I crossed to the narrow window set into the interior wall—one of the lodge's quirks—overlooking the great hall below. From here I could see the last of the fire guttering in the hearth, light spilling upward to warm the beams and the rough-hewn railing of the gallery.

Movement caught the corner of my eye. Emme stepped from the hearth's glow, passing through the pools of gold that climbed the stairs to the guest wing. She'd slipped off her sweater but still held it close, hair loose and catching the firelight in glints of copper against black. She moved quietly, careful not to wake the house, and paused at her door as if listening to something I couldn't hear.

When she disappeared inside, the light seemed to pull in on itself. The hall went still again, leaving only the tick of cooling wood and the echo she'd left behind.

I should have gone back to the book, but the page had already given up on me.

Instead, I thought about the way she'd laughed tonight—quietly, like she didn't want to disturb the peace but couldn't help it. The way she watched a fire the same way architects watch a horizon: judging its lines, guessing what it might do next. The faint scent of citrus that trailed after her when she passed me earlier. My pulse misbehaved. So did the rest of me. And my dick. I sat back on the bed, told myself to think about the schedule for tomorrow, the repairs, the paperwork. None of it worked.

Christ. Five years up here, and one woman walks through a room and my body forgets how to behave. C'est quoi ce bordel? What the hell.

"Brilliant," I muttered into the dark. "La première fois que mes propres dessins me trahissent." *The first time my own designs betray me.*

For a second I almost let go of the argument. *Maybe I should.* It had been a long time. My hand drifted lower before I caught myself. *Merde, c'est pas bien. No. This wasn't right.*

The air cooled enough to steady me. I pulled the blanket higher, the soft wool warm against my skin. The room smelled of ash and cedar and the faint, impossible trace of her perfume carried up through the vents. Sleep, I told myself. Tomorrow there would be contracts to review, pipes to check, roofs to inspect. Ordinary. Safe things.

Outside, the wind turned again. I watched it lift the snow from the roof and scatter it into nothing. I'd survived five years of Patagonia's winters, but apparently not one American with opinions.

Sleep didn't come easily. Neither did forgetting the sound of her laugh.

The storm buried the night in white and woke the morning slow. I came up out of thin sleep to the hush I knew too well—the kind that turns footfalls into secrets and makes the world feel padded. The windows were a blank sheet. Fresh drifts leaned against the lower panes like a dog that had decided the door was furniture.

The clock blinked 7:12 AM. *C'est quoi cette merde. What is this shit?* I never oversleep.

Ressaisis-toi, Moreau. Le monde n'est pas censé tourner tout seul. Pull yourself together. The world isn't supposed to run by itself.

The boiler thumped once—faithful. Good. I shrugged into a sweater and went down the service stairs. The kitchen hall held a blue-gray light, the kind that comes before the fire has decided it wants to live. My phone buzzed on the counter—a missed call from Juliana, timestamped just after dawn, and a voicemail waiting.

I hit play. Her voice filled the quiet kitchen, brisk and unbothered: "The pass is closed. Rafa and I made it home last night before it shut down. We'll be back when they clear it. Until then, don't do anything stupid."

A beat. "Y cuídate, por favor." *Take care of yourself, please.*

"Noted," I said to the empty room. "Fais pas le con aujourd'hui." *Don't be an idiot today.*

Elvis-Elliot had left his boots like a breadcrumb trail to the hearth. The teachers' coats hung in a clump, thawing. Someone had stacked yesterday's mugs by the sink as if proximity to the dishwasher were the same as virtue.

I set the coffee to drip and laid kindling in the wood stove. The first catch is always a held breath. Then flame: a small, determined animal that decided to be bigger. Heat moved into the room the way music enters a church—reluctant and then everywhere.

I heard her before I saw her. A soft cough, those furry slippers quiet on wood, the whisper of a sweater sleeve against a doorframe.

"Good morning." Emme stood at the edge of the hall, hair braided over one shoulder, sleeves pushed to her elbows like she'd made a decision and time could keep up if it wanted. She looked warm, even with the storm pressing the glass.

"You're up early," I said.

"Couldn't sleep. The wind." She smiled, the quick kind that's more for herself than anyone else. "Also I promised Juliana I'd help if the roads closed."

Of course she had. I should have expected that and yet I didn't, not in the way that matters. Some guests fake helpful. Emme wore it like muscle memory.

"The kitchen's yours," I said, and meant it.

"Careful," she said, crossing to the counter, "I'll take that as a binding contract."

The coffee finished with a sigh. She poured two mugs, set one by my hand without asking how I took it. I watched her inventory the space the way a good manager does—mugs, plates, stove, the way the teachers clustered by the windows of the great room like penguins by a glacier. She moved through it all with purpose, sleeves still pushed, braid swinging like a metronome.

Elvis-Elliot appeared, cheeks pink from the cold he had not yet encountered. "Any chance of the snow stopping in time for my afternoon hike?" he asked no one and everyone.

"Small chance," I said.

"Micro," Emme said, and it was the correct word. He looked between us, recalibrated, then drifted toward the fire, narrating his resilience to it.

She looked at the teachers and said, "Hot breakfast in thirty. Sit. Warm up. No grading required." They sat, laughing, already halfway to obedience.

I'd built her wrong in my head. All professionalism, no pulse. Not this rhythm. Not this certainty.

Emme moved around my kitchen like she'd been briefed by the building itself. Gas on. Skillet. Eggs. The soft clatter of bowls syncing to the beat of her hands. I stood in the doorway and forgot to be irritated by the idea of anyone else handling my space.

"You do most of the cooking yourself?" she asked without looking up.

"Mostly," I said. "Or Juliana when she's here."

She made a small noise. "Control or enjoyment?"

"Yes."

She laughed, low. That voice again.

She cracked eggs with one neat tap, whisked them with a flick of her wrist that told me she'd done this a thousand times. She found the sourdough, sliced it, slid the bread onto the plancha and the eggs into heat. I set out chèvre and the last of the roast peppers. She kissed salt into her palm, scattered it from above like she trusted gravity to do its job.

"Move," she said, nudging me with her hip. "You're in my light."

I moved. Instinct, apparently.

"Putain de femme chiante," I murmured, soft enough to deny it later. *Damn bossy woman.*

She laughed without turning. "I know all the French ones," she said. "You'll have to get more creative."

The teachers started a quiet conversation about nothing urgent. Elvis-Elliot read a guidebook aloud to himself. I watched Emme run the lodge the way a good river runs a valley—confident, practical, shaping without shouting.

Juliana called. "Jefe? You okay?"

"We're fine," I said. "Stay with your mother. Don't try the pass."

"You promise you're not doing anything stupid?"

"On my honor."

"Emme?"

"She's boiling the water you forgot to boil."

Juliana laughed, said something in rapid-fire Spanish about saints and Americans, and hung up. A minute later, her text buzzed through—a single red heart.

La maman poule. Mother hen.

Emme slid plates across the counter: eggs with goat cheese and peppers, toast glossy with butter, a bowl of fruit that had somehow survived the night without turning to stone. Steam rose. Eyes widened. The lodge exhaled.

Elvis-Elliot chewed with theatrical appreciation. "Remarkable, really. I didn't expect—well—this level of...depth."

"Eggs," Emme said. "They're famously complicated."

He missed the tease entirely. The teachers didn't; they snickered into their plates.

I ate standing at the pass, the way I always do when the room is fuller than it looks. She nudged a second slice of toast toward me without comment. I didn't say thanks. She heard it anyway.

After breakfast, the rhythm set in. Emme loaded the dishwasher with the ruthless logic of someone who has trained plastic to obey. She set the teachers up at the long table with maps and pencils and a loose snow day schedule they invented on the fly: sketch the valley from memory, trace the flow of light, write two lines about the sound of snow. She talked to them like they were interesting and capable, which is the exact trick most people never learn. They adored her within ten minutes. Fifteen for the Brit, who took longer to melt.

I chopped wood by the side door, listening to the thunk of the axe bite the round, the release as the grain gave up its argument. Through the glass I watched Emme show Teresa how to coax the espresso machine into not behaving like a sulking cat.

The storm brightened in that way storms do when they're busy wrecking the rest of the world. Inside, the lodge grew warmer, the kind of heat that makes you forgive winter for existing. By midmorning, she disappeared into the pantry and came out with a tray of mugs and a jar of honey I'd forgotten I owned. "Tea rounds," she announced. "Hydration is not optional."

"You're not staff," I said, because someone had to say it.

"I'm everything," she said, as if it were a simple fact. "Contracts, vendors, chaos control. Pick a hat."

"Bossy," I said.

"Effective," she said.

Couldn't argue with that.

"What do you need?" she asked me quietly, when the others were busy sugaring their tea.

I almost said nothing. It's a religion up here. Instead: "If the power flickers, keep everyone entertained. I'll start the generator."

She nodded once. "Copy."

She helped me check pipes. Passed me wrenches without being told which ones I wanted. We argued about a draft under the west door like two people who were both right. She found the extra blankets in the cedar chest and stacked them by the hearth like we were expecting an invasion of cold and had decided not to be polite about it.

"Lunch?" she said at noon, and I realized time had become a rumor. We improvised: stew from last night stretched with beans and tomatoes, bread warmed on the hearth stones, a salad that pretended it was summer. The Brit told a story about a failed proposal on a glacier, terrible and funny in equal measure. Mariela fell in love with the light on the east wall for a full minute and didn't apologize.

Between ladles of stew, Emme asked me questions that were not actually questions. "You built the gallery window to listen without being seen." Not *did you—you did*. "You reinforced the roofline here because the wind shifts wrong in March." "You kept the old stone in the threshold because you wanted the building to remember what it was."

I made a face. "You collect confessions as a hobby?"

"Only the useful kind," she said. "And only when they'd rather be told."

"Putain," I muttered, and she smiled like she'd found the switch.

After we cleaned up, she taught the others a card game that required loud laughter. Elvis-Elliot lost twice and declared himself philosophical about it. When the conversation drifted to Patagonia in summer, Emme didn't sell; she painted. Trails like silver threads, ice that rang when it broke, guanacos with opinions. They booked next year in their heads without knowing they'd done it.

Putain, elle n'a même jamais vu la Patagonie en été, et elle la vend déjà mieux que moi. Damn, she's never even seen Patagonia in summer, and she's already selling it better than I do.

I kept trying to mind my work. I checked the generator twice, the weather report three times, the roofline from the east stair. Every return to the hall found her in a different orbit, always where she was most useful, never making it about herself. Watching her felt like checking a beam and finding it stronger than the math.

At some point she stole my scarf and looped it around Teresa's shoulders with a quiet, "You'll think better when your neck's warm." The woman blinked fast, once, then kept playing cards like gratitude was private.

"Why are you like this?" I asked when the table erupted over a disputed rule.

"Like what?" she said.

"Competent," I said, which was not the word I meant. The word I meant would have been too much for daylight.

She shook her head. "You hired me to be competent."

"I didn't hire you."

"You will," she said, smooth as a guarantee.

The storm eased toward afternoon, wind stepping down a rung. Outside, the eaves wore tinsel from spindrift. If peace had a temperature, we'd reached it.

I caught her watching the door the way people do when they've learned to keep part of their attention on exits. It wasn't fear. It was habit. I knew that, too.

"You can stop," I said, quiet.

"Stop what?" she asked.

"Running the whole world."

She looked at me like I'd said something intimate without meaning to. "Can you?"

"No," I said, because the truth is easier in winter.

She laughed—quietly, like she didn't want to disturb the peace but couldn't help it. My body remembered last night and made its opinion known. *Putain de merde.* Control is a tool; it is not a cure.

By late afternoon the teachers had set up a small gallery of their sketches on the mantle and were praising each other as if praise were a renewable resource. Elvis-Elliot conceded that stew could, in certain geographies, constitute cuisine. Emme collected mugs and compliments with equal ease and put both in the right place.

Juliana texted a photo of her mother beating her at cards and the single word **safe**. Rafa followed with **snowball war** and a victory emoji. The pass would open tomorrow, maybe. The world would tilt back to its usual angle. Or not. The lodge didn't care. It had weathered worse and would again.

As the light thinned, I stood at the edge of the gallery and watched Emme tuck a blanket around the back of a chair the way you tuck a child into bed—casual, certain she'd be believed when she said *there, that's better*. She glanced up, caught me watching, and didn't look away.

Later, as she passed me in the hall, she nodded toward the window. "That drift's going to make your morning interesting."

"Because of the curve in the ridge," I said.

"Because everything worth building is supposed to test you," she said.

I should have argued. Instead I said, "You always talk in proverbs?"

Her mouth curved. "Only when they fit."

"Putain," I said, almost smiling.

She went to her room. The hall sighed back into quiet. The storm took another step toward gone. Sleep would be another negotiation. But the lodge, at least, was warm. And something I'd kept locked behind precision had found the door and rattled it—politely, for now.

Chapter 9

Cold Hands, Warm Trouble

EMME

B Y MORNING, THE WORLD had rearranged itself into white and silence. The storm had blown itself out overnight, leaving behind a valley so bright it looked airbrushed. Snow stacked thick on every ledge and branch, the peaks cut against the sky like clean slate. The wind was gone. In its place—stillness, except for the soft scrape of a shovel somewhere near the outbuildings.

I paused by the hall window, close enough to feel the cold radiating through the glass without leaving a mark. Outside, the landscape had settled into a hush of white and quiet. Luc moved through the courtyard below, methodical and unhurried, carving paths from doorways to walkways. He didn't stomp or slam the shovel; he used it the way he used words—efficient, deliberate, precise. His jacket was open at the throat. His breath rose like smoke.

I told myself I was just timing him. Market research, right? Observational data for when Wilder Horizons inevitably needed to hire local crews.

Sure.

Behind me, footsteps approached fast. "He's been out there an hour," Elliot said, appearing in a fleece that looked one size too big and enthusiasm that fit none of us. "I should get a few shots before the light changes—post-storm recovery, staff in action, that kind of thing. The guests will love it."

Before I could respond, he cracked the window an inch and called down, "Luc! Mind if I film a little?"

Luc didn't even pause the shovel. "Not today," he said, voice carrying clean through the cold air. "Trails aren't stable yet."

Elliot sighed, shutting the window. "He's impossible."

"He's right," I said. "Half the courtyard's still under a snowdrift."

Juliana appeared behind us, tablet in hand. "If you need something to do, Teresa and Mariela are heading toward the meadow for bird counts. Luc already cleared that route—it's within the inner grounds and perfectly safe."

Elliot brightened immediately. "Perfect. I'll take the GoPro, make it educational."

Juliana smiled, which for her looked suspiciously like strategy. "Excellent choice."

When he hurried off, she turned back to me with a knowing little wink—unexpectedly gentle, almost motherly. It caught me off guard.

"I'm going to bring him coffee," I said, more to fill the silence than explain myself.

Juliana's brows lifted like she knew exactly who *him* was. "There are fresh thermoses in the kitchen. Take two."

So I did. The stainless steel was warm against my palms, the air already sharper near the door.

Outside, the world was clean and quiet again. I zipped my jacket, pulled on my gloves, and stepped into the courtyard. The snow squeaked under my boots, air biting at my nose.

"You're starting without me?" I called.

"You're still on coffee number one," he replied without looking up. "I needed progress."

"I see." I crossed the last few steps between us and held out one of the thermoses. "Fuel for the overachiever."

He paused mid-shovel, glanced at the thermos, then at me. Surprise flickered—quick, genuine—before he took it. "You didn't have to."

"I know," I said, matching his earlier tone. "But you looked like you'd earned it."

Something in his expression softened, the kind of shift you almost miss if you're not watching closely. He unscrewed the lid, tested a sip, and gave a small nod that felt heavier than words.

"Then let's double your progress," I said, reaching for the spare shovel leaning against the wall.

We worked in companionable silence for a while—him clearing long, efficient rows, me redistributing snow in what could generously be called enthusiasm. The sun caught on the edges of the drifts, scattering light everywhere. I'd been here what felt like long enough to stop gawking at the scenery, but today it demanded a second look. Everything sparkled. Even Luc.

He stopped to adjust his gloves. "We'll need to check the east trail after this. It drifts deeper."

"I heard," I said. "Because you built it that way."

He cut me a glance. "For wind protection."

"Mm-hmm. Nice cover story."

His brow lifted. "Cover for what?"

"For keeping people out."

That earned me the faintest quirk of his mouth. "You included."

"Temporarily."

He didn't answer, and the silence turned warm instead of cold.

The east trail started just past the storage shed, where the wind had piled snow waist-high in sculpted waves. Luc broke the surface with a shovel, then his boots, testing each step. I followed in his footprints, partly for safety, mostly because it was easier—and warmer.

When he bent to check the trail markers, I packed a snowball the size of a tangerine and threw it.

Direct hit.

It exploded across his shoulder, a satisfying burst of white. Luc froze. Slowly turned. His expression was pure disbelief.

"Did you—?" he started.

"Absolutely."

He blinked once, then scooped up snow with surgical precision. "Don't," I warned, laughing. "I'm unarmed."

"Poor strategy."

The next snowball landed squarely against my thigh. I yelped, retaliated, missed by three feet. He raised a brow. "Weak arm."

"You have no proof." Another throw—closer this time. He dodged, smooth as instinct. "Architects shouldn't move like that," I muttered.

"Design demands coordination."

"Show-off."

The next volley escalated fast. I ducked behind a drift, popped up to fire, shrieked when he advanced. He didn't run—he prowled. Calm, relentless. Every snowball he lobbed hit with unnerving accuracy.

"Okay, truce!" I gasped, laughing so hard my stomach hurt.

He stepped closer, eyes bright. "Now?"

"Now—" I started, but the ground betrayed me. My boot slipped on packed ice, and I went down with a startled noise that might have been a curse or a laugh.

Luc lunged to catch me. Momentum took over. He landed half on top of me, his gloved hands braced in the snow on either side of my shoulders. For a second, neither of us moved. Our breaths fogged the same air. His jacket brushed mine, and I could feel the heat of him even through layers. His eyes, that storm-dark gray-blue, fixed on mine.

"You missed," he said quietly.

"Pretty sure I didn't."

Something flickered between us—heat, awareness, restraint—and then he pushed up, offered a hand. I took it, letting him pull me upright. My heart was still running laps.

"Trail's clear enough," he said, voice rougher than before.

"Good," I managed. "Wouldn't want any accidents."

He didn't look at me when he answered. "Too late."

Back at the lodge, Juliana was waiting by the door, coat unbuttoned, eyes sharp as always.

"You're smiling," she told Luc.

He frowned. "I'm cold."

"Mm." She turned to me. "He's lying."

Luc muttered something in French that probably wasn't a compliment. Juliana smiled wider. "Whatever it is, keep doing it. We like when he stops scowling."

I laughed, shaking snow from my hat. Luc shot me a look that landed somewhere between warning and embarrassment, then escaped down the hall muttering about inventory.

By late afternoon, the adrenaline had burned off, replaced by the comfort of routine. The lodge hummed with activity—Luc and Rafa checking roofs, Teresa and Mariela reappearing from hibernation, the kitchen alive again. I settled upstairs in the small office nook by the window, laptop open, fingers thawed enough to type.

The contract draft glowed on-screen. I wanted it perfect—clean clauses, fair percentages, language that made sense even to someone reading it on a mountaintop after a day and a half of no Wi-Fi. Wilder Horizons didn't cut corners, and neither did I.

Still, my focus kept drifting—to the courtyard below, where Luc's jacket still hung on a railing, and the faint memory of his laugh when snow hit his face.

I shook it off, scrolled back to the clause on liability waivers, and decided I'd earned a break.

To: Wildlings

Subject: Dispatch from the End of the World

Still alive. Storm's over. The world looks like a snow globe someone forgot to shake again. I helped dig out the east trail this morning. Luc takes shoveling as a competitive sport. I threw a snowball. He retaliated with the precision of a sniper. 10/10 would not engage again without armor.

Also: local wildlife sightings include three foxes, six questionable hares, and one Frenchman pretending he's not flirting every time he says the word safety. *Photos attached for morale purposes.*

I attached a few shots—sunlight on the ridge, the path we'd carved, a candid of Luc adjusting his gloves, head turned just enough to catch the sharp line of his jaw. I hesitated, then hit send.

Replies came fast.

RAYANN:

Holy hell, Emme. If he looks that good in fleece, I'm afraid to ask what he looks like out of it. Are we sure Patagonia isn't a euphemism?

BRYNN:

Confirming: the man has bone structure that violates international law. Also—Jerrick is still in Maris Key. Legal's wrapped up. He's still smug. But enough about him—what's *this* situation, sis?

JULIETTE:

Focus, both of you. Emme, keep the updates professional. Also send higher-res photos for brand assets (purely for research).

ANNIE:

Did you see penguins yet??

SUMMER:

Contracts first. Distractions later.

RAYANN:

Translation: Summer wants the next selfie to include a signature line.

I snorted coffee through my nose laughing. The sound must've carried because a knock followed a second later.

Luc leaned on the doorframe, brow raised. "Everything all right?"

"Fine," I said, swiping tears of laughter. "Family email thread. Dangerous territory."

He nodded like he understood all too well. "Coffee?"

I held up my mug. "Already made some."

He didn't leave. His gaze flicked from the screen to me, pausing when he saw my reflection in the glass—loose braid, sleeves rolled, Tampa Rays cap on backward.

"What?" I asked.

"Baseball," he said. "You watch?"

"It's *my* religion." I turned in my chair, grinning. "You?"

"Fútbol," he admitted. "But my sister's husband is American. Obsessed with baseball. He makes me watch when I visit."

"Then you've suffered."

He leaned a shoulder against the doorframe. "You like suffering?"

"Depends who's pitching."

That earned the smallest laugh. "You work too much."

"Says the man who was out at dawn rebuilding the world."

"Someone has to." He hesitated, then added, "Don't work too hard. The generator still needs servicing."

"Yes, Daddy," I said, because he walked right into that one.

His head dropped, a quiet laugh breaking through. "Tomorrow—if the roads hold—we can go to town. You mentioned meetings."

I blinked. "You're volunteering as chauffeur?"

"Guide," he corrected. "The roads are narrow."

"Very noble of you."

He tilted his head, echoing my earlier tone. "For what?"

"For taking pity on me."

His mouth curved slowly, the way light stretches just before sunset. "Wouldn't be the first time."

"For the record," I said, "I allow this."

He nodded once. "Then we'll leave at nine."

After he left, I sat staring at the doorway, my heart doing its own snowball ricochet in my chest. The cursor blinked on the contract document. Somewhere outside, the last of the ice slid from a roof, landing with a soft thud. The sound pulled me back to work—but not completely.

I added one last line to my email thread.

PS: If anyone asks, I'm perfectly professional.

PPS: Stop laughing, Rayann.

That night, the temperature dropped again, freezing the melt into glitter. From my window, I watched Luc cross the courtyard with a lantern, checking each outbuilding before shutting them down for the night. His shadow moved across the snow—tall, steady, precise. For a man who built solitude like a wall, he carried light better than anyone I'd ever met.

Tomorrow we'd drive to town. Meet local partners. Discuss logistics.

That was the plan.

But plans in Patagonia had a way of bending toward weather—and people—you didn't see coming.

Chapter 10

Fieldwork

LUC

I TOLD HER THE roads would hold if we left before the frost returned. She didn't argue, which either meant she trusted me or didn't care that much about frost. We rolled out at gray light in the Defender, tires finding the packed strip between shoulder-high snowbanks. The mountains were a row of sleeping animals to our left. She watched them with a look I'd come to recognize: not wonder, exactly, but appraisal. Emme cataloged things, then decided how to love them.

"Town name?" she asked, tucking a pen behind her ear. "So I don't write 'that adorable stone place' on expense reports."

"San Piedra," I said. "Locals call the old quarter Las Piedras Viejas. You'll like it."

"I plan to," she said, and smiled at the windshield.

She rode with a laptop on her knees and folders in a canvas tote that had already learned Patagonia's grit. The smell of coffee lived in the cab, warm and determined. She'd brought two thermoses. One ended up on my side without comment. I didn't thank her out loud. I drank it.

The road dropped into the valley and the town appeared the way it always did, not suddenly but like a page you were already reading. Low buildings. Painted doors. A church tower that had been repaired three times and still leaned as if listening. Smoke threaded up from chimneys and was taken apart by wind.

"Everyone knows you," she said when three people waved before I'd found a space.

"It's a small map," I said. "Names repeat."

"Then let's add mine."

She had three meetings. That was the story she told the morning. I told the morning I was only driving her. Both of us lied a little.

The first stop, the vineyard, sat on the edge of town, short rows staked against weather that didn't promise kindness. Carmen met us at the gate, dark hair in a scarf, hands already purple at the edges from practice pours. We kissed cheeks. Emme followed the rhythm, light on her feet, then switched to Spanish that landed a beat behind perfect but arrived smiling.

"Gracias por vernos," she said. *Thank you for seeing us.* "Me encanta su enfoque... sostenible." She found the word, rolled it carefully, and pointed at the solar panels as if punctuation could be a gesture.

Carmen liked her immediately. Most people did. It wasn't an accident. I translated when idioms turned slippery. Mostly I watched. Emme asked about water use, composting, transport miles, the way supply actually moved through a valley that turned to glass in winter.

A small line appeared at the corner of her mouth—a focus line, not frustration. She cared about answers more than most who toured this place.

She listened to answers. She didn't promise what Wilder Horizons couldn't give. She didn't apologize for wanting standards. When her Spanish stuck on "terroir," she let her hands do the rest, fingers sketching the slope and soil like wind over the rows.

"You don't wait to be perfect," I said on the way back to the truck.

"Not a luxury I have," she said, then softer, "or want."

The second stop was the outfitter's shop. A bell rang when we pushed the door. The woodstove radiated a heat that smelled like old pine and long stories. Coils of rope hung in neat loops. Boots lined a bench, soles outward, the way I liked order to declare itself.

"Luc," said Matías, clapping my shoulder hard enough to mean it. He looked at Emme with a grin that had been earning him trouble for as long as I'd known him. "Pareces muy limpia para ser un caballo." *You look too clean for a horse.*

Her eyebrows did one elegant skate upward. Then she replied in Spanish that sounded like a postcard from Mexico City that had taken the train south and learned to swear on the way: "Dame quince minutos y una montaña. Luego hablamos de limpio." *Give me fifteen minutes and a mountain. Then we'll talk about clean.*

I didn't have to translate. Even Matías understood she'd just told him she could handle herself—and probably his horse, too. Her chin stayed lifted a beat longer than her smile—pride she didn't try to hide.

Matías laughed so loudly the bell over the door declared a second arrival. He poured steaming maté—the herbal drink they all lived on up here—handed her the shared gourd, and watched the way she tilted it. She did it wrong. He fixed it with the gentle impatience of an older brother, and she took the correction as if it were a new tool she'd been wanting. They talked routes, guides, emergency protocols. She took notes in English and dotted them with Spanish nouns when the English felt too far from the ground.

"You're not translating," she said to me at one point without looking up.

"You're not needing it," I said.

We wrapped up at the outfitters and headed back into the cold, driving across town toward her final stop of the day. The artisan cooperative lived in a former school-house. Sun came through tall windows and made the wool glow like a low fire. Women sat in a loose circle with looms balanced on their knees. There were ceramic bowls whose glazes looked like the lake at noon. A child slept under a table, hand closed around a wooden truck.

"This is beautiful," Emme said, and because beautiful is a word that can break from overuse, she didn't press it. She looked. She asked who wove which piece and whether it could scale without losing its hands. She bought a scarf the color of sky before snow and wrapped it once around her throat. It found her heat like it had been waiting.

I knew most of the artisans. They knew my habits, which doors I knocked on, which I designed and built.

We exchanged the arithmetic of winter: how much wood left, how many nights imagined. Emme fit into the circle without making herself smaller. When she stood, three of the women hugged her, and one kissed her forehead. She blinked. Then she laughed, surprised by her own softness. Her hand went to her sternum for a second, as if something had landed there before she could deflect it.

"San Piedra likes you," I said outside.

"San Piedra has taste," she answered, then shook her head as if a compliment might get stuck in her hair.

We walked the old quarter slowly, because there are places you don't hurry. The church steps were uneven, the stone slick where thousands of feet had polished it without meaning to make anything shine. The murals showed climbers with the kind of faces that marry patience to obsession. I told her how a flood had lifted the bridge and set it down three meters away, and the town had simply moved the footpath to meet it, because sometimes the earth decides and people can learn.

"What do the mountains keep?" she asked when we reached the ridge where wind had nailed prayer ribbons to the air.

"Secrets," I said.

"That's a cop-out answer."

"It is also true."

She stood in the gold of afternoon and let it put her in its pocket. The scarf moved once, small, in a gust. I felt the pull to tell her we should go, before the light became lie and frost turned the road into a story of mistakes. Instead I pointed at the restaurant across from the plaza.

"Lunch," I said. "Carmen's cousin. Good fire, better wine."

"Company card," she said instantly. "If you treat, it's a date. If I treat, it's business."

"So not a date."

"Not unless you're charging consulting fees."

"Expensive ones."

She laughed, then narrowed her eyes as if she'd over-shared and needed to gather herself. "I'm serious. It's work. Also, women picking up the check in front of men who know everyone sends a message."

"What message?"

"That I'm not looking for a shortcut," she said, and pushed the door.

La Parrilla de Isabel was one long room with a grill that turned meat into memory and a chalkboard wine list that changed when someone felt like writing. We took a table by the window. I ordered a Patagonian pinot noir—cool-climate, clean on the nose, the kind that respected the air here and didn't pick a fight with the smoke. She arched a brow when I asked for a bottle instead of a glass.

"You're very serious about wine," she said.

"I am very serious about things that ask to be taken seriously," I said. "And some that don't, but should be anyway."

She considered this. "Like what?"

"Knives," I said. "Lightning. People who say they are fine."

The bottle arrived. I tasted it, nodded, and poured. She brought the glass to her nose and tried to hide the way she wanted to get it right.

"What do you get?" I asked.

"Red fruit. Something... clean." She frowned a little. "Like someone opened a window."

I could have told her about acidity and structure. I let the window be enough.

We ate slowly. She refused the steak at first and then took a bite and closed her eyes in a punctuation that had nothing to do with language. I watched the room in the way you do when you know a place well enough to sense its changes. Somewhere behind us someone told a story that lifted and fell like a rope being coiled. A man in a cap tapped a rhythm on his glass without noticing.

She set down her fork and looked at me over the rim of her wineglass. "So how does a Frenchman end up at the end of the world?"

I smiled at that, because it was a fair question and a good one. "By mistake," I said. "And then by choice."

Her brows lifted, waiting. "That sounds like a story."

"Most stories start with someone else's idea of adventure," I said. "This one just ended with mine."

Something in my voice must've shifted—just enough to make her study me longer than politeness allowed.

"Tell me," she said when the second glass loosened the knots I kept tied behind my ribs. Not unkind. Not careless. As if the question had been resting on the table between us and she only just now put her hand on it.

I reached for words the way you reach for a railing in the dark. "It starts with someone I don't mention often."

The words scraped up slow, like they'd been buried too deep.

"My brother was younger. Reckless in a way that made reckless look like a plan. We mapped a motorcycle trip from Mexico south—then further, if the map didn't mind. He died before we left."

She didn't speak, just held my gaze like she knew the shape of the wound. Her fingers tightened once on the stem of her glass—quiet, precise—before she eased them again.

"I went anyway," I said. "There are places where the road feels like intention. Patagonia was one. I kept waiting for the feeling to pass."

"It didn't," she said.

"No."

"And the lodge?"

"He was an architect too. We dreamed of building something together. I thought if I designed a place with enough clean lines, the noise would stay out—people, sometimes, the world, often. It worked, for a while."

She touched the stem of her glass. "Until it stopped working."

I almost said, *Until you.* I didn't. Outside, the sun moved a degree and made the plaza look like a photograph taken one minute later.

"What was he like?" she asked, voice even, like we were speaking across a river and she didn't want to raise a wave.

"Larger than his weight could justify. He laughed in rooms I wasn't ready to enter. He taught me to ride too fast and apologize too late."

"And you loved him," she said, not a question.

"Yes."

She didn't stack condolences on top of that. She poured herself a little more wine, then placed the bottle nearer to me without comment. She'd already learned that I liked to control the pour—and she allowed me the fiction.

"Why Argentina?" she asked after the plates had been cleared and the knife marks on the wood between us looked like a map of a country neither of us owned.

"Because the space is honest," I said. "And the wind tells you what it wants."

"That's not a cop-out," she said.

"I'm learning."

"So am I."

We stayed longer than I meant to. She knew it. She let me pretend otherwise. At the register she produced the company card with a look that made arguments unnecessary. Carmen's cousin smirked at me as if to ask whether I was losing my touch. I smiled back and said nothing.

On the way out, a woman stopped us to ask if we wanted empanadas to take for later. Emme said yes in Spanish that put the weight on the wrong syllable and somehow made the word sweeter. We stepped outside. The wind had opinions. She pulled her scarf closer.

"Cold?" I asked.

"I'll live," she said, then shivered in a way that was half theater and half true. The smile that followed didn't match the cold.

We crossed to the truck and climbed in, the cab freezing enough to make her breath fog the air. I angled the heater vents her way without making a thing of it.

She pretended not to notice.

The road home had frozen in pieces. I knew where they would be and let the tires find the quiet parts. She sang under her breath to a song the radio barely caught. I didn't recognize it. I wanted to.

We reached Refugio Cielo under a sky the color of her scarf. I parked beside the main steps, the engine ticking as it cooled. For a moment neither of us moved.

"Gracias por hoy," she said finally. *Thank you for today.* Careful, not shy.

"De nada, Emme," I answered. Her name was different when I said it. Most names are, but some more than others.

She unbuckled, then turned toward the lodge lights. "Tomorrow," she said, "I'll follow up with Carmen and Matías. And print a draft for you. If you'd look it over, I'd appreciate it."

"I'll look," I said.

We walked inside together. The air was warmer, thinner, touched with woodsmoke. At the stairs she paused like a woman choosing a hallway in a house she hasn't finished exploring.

"And Luc," she said, steadying the words before they left her, "thank you for telling me about your brother."

I nodded. She disappeared down the corridor, her steps soft against the wood. The door at the end closed. The quiet folded back in, the way it always does when a presence leaves but doesn't quite go. The cold leaned once against the windows, then let the night seal itself.

I had planned to be back by noon. It was full dark. San Piedra had taken our day and returned it to us changed. That is one of the things towns are for.

Inside, I left the keys in the bowl and the scarf color in my head. In the quiet after a door closes, you can hear what a place thinks of you. The lodge said the same thing it always said: order restored. The lie of that sentence did not bother me as much as it had yesterday.

Chapter 11

Pipe Dreams

EMME

THE DRIVE BACK FROM town left my bones humming. Vendors confirmed, samples secured, three handshakes that translated to actual contracts if I didn't say one stupid thing in the recap email. Luc drove the Defender with one hand—palm flat on the wheel, wrist flexing with each turn, casual and certain, like the machine existed to obey him. Watching a man handle that much power with quiet control shouldn't have felt erotic, but my body disagreed. Every downshift sent a shiver somewhere it didn't belong.

Seriously, Emme. Get a grip. You need to get fucking laid.

We pulled into the drive. The sky had the color of stainless steel about to rain, and Refugio Cielo took it the way a cathedral takes a storm—shoulders squared, doors quiet, everything ready.

Inside: warm wood, the clean-thyme smell Juliana preferred, a bowl of clementines that hadn't been there this morning. The place felt... reset. Or maybe I did.

"You're back late," Juliana's voice floated from the pantry. She stood with a clipboard and a pen tucked behind her ear like a hairpin, surrounded by a small kingdom of neatly stacked flour, beans, and glass jars of something that looked like pickled swagger. Relief flickered across her face, quick as a match, before she sighed. "Coffee's fresh. The sink is not."

Luc set the keys on the counter and crouched beside the open cabinet. "I'll take a look."

Of course he would. The man couldn't walk past a problem without fixing it. He pulled a wrench from the drawer and pushed his sleeves up to his elbows. The shirt stretched across his back, and I forgot how to end sentences.

"I'll just... put these away," I managed, gesturing toward my bag.

Juliana's look said *coward* in three languages.

Upstairs, I set my laptop on the desk, hung my coat, and tried not to think about forearms or gear shifts. I just needed ten minutes. Maybe less. Long enough for dignity to reboot.

I padded back down to the kitchen for a quick coffee grab before I hunkered down to work—and stopped.

Luc was flat on his back beneath the sink, one arm buried in the pipes, shirt riding up just enough to make composure a team sport. He cursed something low and dangerous in French. *Putain de tuyau stupide... je vais t'arracher le cœur.* The sound curled through the air like heat. My pulse stuttered. "Damn," I murmured, mostly to myself, "I didn't know pipes had hearts."

Luc didn't hear me—or if he did, he ignored it. Juliana's pen stopped mid-note, eyes flicking up just long enough to catch my words before settling back on the page.

Then my gaze drifted down again, because I'm weak and the universe is cruel. A strip of skin, lean and cut, glowed in the warm light. The edge of a tattoo curved low on his hip—fine black lines, geometric and deliberate, disappearing where no one but God and the brave would see. I swallowed hard, trying to look anywhere else. I failed spectacularly.

That's when a small green blur launched itself from beneath the cabinet.

The scream ripped out of me before logic had a chance to protest. Not dignified. Not subtle. Just raw, instinctive terror of something the size of a keychain.

Luc jerked so hard he smacked his head on the pipe. The wrench clanged against the floor. "Merde!" he barked—loud enough to startle the birds outside.

Juliana jumped, pen flying out of her hand. "¡Madre de Dios!" she gasped, then saw the culprit and exhaled, pressing a palm to her chest. The relief arrived a second before the laughter.

"What in the world—" she started.

"A frog!" I shouted, backing up like it had a vendetta.

Juliana blinked at me, then at the frog, which sat smugly on the tile. "A *ranita*, Emme." Her voice was dry again now, calm reinstalled. "Harmless."

Luc rubbed the back of his head, bewildered. "You screamed at that?"

"Yes," I said, heart still sprinting. "Because it *moved*."

Juliana looked between us, her expression a slow surrender to amusement. "You two are going to be the death of me."

Luc froze. Juliana blinked. The frog blinked back.

"I have—" I gasped, pointing like the frog had committed a felony, "—an *irrational fear* of frogs!"

Luc just stared, wrench in hand, utterly lost for words.

Juliana bit her lip, but amusement leaked through. "Irrational?"

"Yes," I said.

"Because they are small," she said.

"Yes."

"And you are not."

"Correct."

Luc's mouth did the smallest, most dangerous twitch. "You screamed like it had a knife."

"It has webby feet," I said, breathless, still pressed against the counter. "They grab."

He blinked once. "Feet."

"Yes, and they *grab*."

Rafa coughed laughter as he walked into the kitchen.

I did what any self-respecting professional woman would do in that moment: grabbed my coffee and fled.

Upstairs, I shut the door and leaned against it until my pulse quit slam-dancing. Then I opened the laptop and did the most dangerous thing: emailed my sisters.

Subject: Frog 1, Dignity 0
To: Brynn, Rayann, Annie

Cc: not Summer, not Juliette

EMME: I just had a religious experience in the kitchen and it involved plumbing and a frog. Please hold your applause while I tell you everything I am willing to admit on the internet.

BRYNN: If this isn't about a naked Frenchman, I'm unsubscribing.

EMME: Not naked. But there were abs. Impeccable line quality. I almost had an orgasm in the kitchen. Also, there's a tattoo low on his hip like a compass fell in love with a map and they had a very private child.

RAYANN: Wouldn't be the first time you orgasmed in a kitchen. Did you scream?

EMME: Yes. Wait—no. Yes, but not at him. The frog.

ANNIE: Wait, you screamed? What am I missing here?

EMME: A fucking frog. A terrifying *ranita* with devil eyes. It launched at my soul.

BRYNN: So you almost orgasmed in the kitchen and then screamed at a frog. *This* is your Roman Empire?

EMME: Please don't cheapen my journey.

RAYANN: Spill it.

EMME: The pipe was clogged. Which I'm pretty sure is a sex thing, but I didn't have time to research because then he hit his head when I screamed and cursed a lot. He was under it.

RAYANN: The frog?

EMME: No, the sink. Under the *sink*. On his back.

ANNIE: I googled, and it's not a sex thing.

BRYNN: Bored now. Are you going to fuck him.

EMME: Brynn.

BRYNN: That was not a question mark.

EMME: I noticed.

RAYANN: She just met him, for fuck's sake. Also, she's working. Also, he is her host contact.

BRYNN: And?

ANNIE: I support love and ethics and also French kissing.

BRYNN: Cute. Comedy central is calling now.

EMME: Argh. No one is kissing anyone. I came back to my room like a grown-up, drank coffee, and am going to work on contracts. I'm not going to imagine what that tattoo looks like when said Frenchman is *not* under a sink. Nor am I going to pretend I don't want to lick it. I'm very professional.

BRYNN: Sure, slut. So... how'd the view change when he *got off* the floor?

EMME: I'm signing off now.

BRYNN: Wait, did you bring a vibrator?

RAYANN: Okay. Serious now. How's the vendor list going?

ANNIE: Um, thanks for the cold shower, Ray.

EMME: Good. The vineyard and the outfitters are in if we finalize quantities by Friday. The shuttle partner can add a second run on Tuesdays. The cooper is a poet. I'll summarize for Summer in the morning—minus any hydration-related lust.

ANNIE: Proud of you. Also, I found a photo of a *ranita* that is extremely cute, and I think you should be friends. Sending now.

EMME: If you send that photo, I will come home and put your succulents in the dishwasher on *sanitize.*

ANNIE: Deleting.

BRYNN: Last chance. Are you going to—

RAYANN: Brynn.

BRYNN: —respect his boundaries and your contract? Fine. But if you don't at least touch his abs with something other than your eyes, I'm calling you to check for a fever.

EMME: I already touched them with my eyes, and then my nervous system resigned. Goodnight.

I shut my laptop and stared at the ceiling. Snow tapped the window, light but steady. The whole place had gone quiet again—too quiet. Somewhere down-stairs, the pipes were still adjusting. Maybe him too.

My body hadn't gotten the memo that we were done thinking about Luc Moreau. Every time I closed my eyes, I saw that strip of skin, the perfect V, and the tattoo that definitely has a story. It was unsettling how fast my professionalism folded.

I washed my face, brushed my teeth, and tried to cool off the kind of heat that doesn't care about logic or contracts. Then I got into bed, told myself to focus on vendor lists and timelines, not forearms and French curses.

Didn't work.

I turned on my side and watched the snow until my pulse stopped pretending it was innocent. If Luc kept fixing things around here himself, the least he could do was start doing it shirtless.

Ugh. Stop it, Emme. Get to work.

I blew out a breath, grabbed my laptop again, and opened the vendor spreadsheet—absolutely *not* imagining the view from under the sink.

Tomorrow, I'd apologize to Juliana for fleeing the crime scene. And maybe buy her a bottle of wine. Or a frog trap.

Chapter 12

Fifteen Minutes

LUC

THE MORNING ARRIVED CLEAR and sharp, the kind that didn't forgive hesitation. Snow still clung to the shadows, but the sky promised a rare gift: blue.

I found her in the great room by the fire, already working, a mug of coffee beside her laptop. She looked too bright for the hour, like the day had already surrendered to her.

Putain, moi aussi je me rendrais à elle. Fuck me, I'd surrender to her too.

"Put that away," I said.

She blinked up, distracted. "Excuse me?"

"Work. Laptop. Whatever your sister is demanding today."

"Summer isn't demanding anything. Yet."

"Then before she remembers to, we're leaving."

She frowned, cautious. "Leaving for where?"

"Outside of work," I said simply. "You've been here, but you haven't actually *been* here."

She tilted her head, studying me like I'd spoken in code. "Meaning?"

"Meaning you've seen the mountains and the lodge and whatever's on your laptop," I said. "But not the reason people fall in love with this place."

Her curiosity edged forward. "And you're planning to fix that?"

"I'm calling in a favor," I said. "You have fifteen minutes."

Her eyes widened. "Fifteen minutes for what?"

"To get ready. To see what you've been missing."

She looked at me like she wanted to argue, then closed her laptop instead. "Do I need hiking boots or diplomacy?"

"Both wouldn't hurt," I said, glancing toward the window. "Your camera. And your hat. The wind near the water doesn't care about your hair."

"The water?" she repeated, half teasing, half intrigued.

"You'll see," I said, checking my watch. "Fifteen minutes, Emme."

She arched a brow. "Bossy much?"

"No. Experienced. People who take twenty miss the boat."

"There's a *boat*?"

"Clock's ticking."

The road to the coast took two hours and most of my patience. My truck handled the mud better than I did.

Emme sat beside me, legs tucked up on the seat, head turned toward the window as if she was afraid to blink and miss something. Every few miles, she'd point out a wild guanaco or some fleeting miracle of light over the ridges.

She wasn't talking for my benefit—she was just noticing things out loud, like she couldn't help it.

I didn't interrupt. Some silences are better filled by wonder.

I didn't answer, which was answer enough. She grinned out the window, like the world had just handed her proof that it wasn't all work and obligations.

By the time we reached the coast, the sky had turned glass-bright and endless. A narrow wooden dock curved into the water, and Alejandro—a friend and guide—waited beside a small boat, his grin carrying a hint of trouble.

"Luc Moreau," he said, clapping my shoulder. "You still know how to show up with little warning."

"Bad habit," I said.

Alejandro's eyes slid to Emme and warmed. "And you brought someone worth the trip."

"She's here for business," I said.

"Of course she is," he said, like it was a punchline.

Emme pretended to inspect the life jackets, hiding her smile.

The water crossing was short—fifteen minutes, maybe less. Wind tugged at her scarf, the air sharp with salt.

Halfway across, she leaned forward, squinting toward the horizon. "What's that? Are those... rocks?"

"Could be," I said.

She watched harder, brow furrowing, then broke into a grin. "They're moving."

By the time we drew closer, the shapes resolved into neat, comic rows—black and white and impossibly self-important.

Emme gasped, then laughed outright. "Oh my God, look at them! They're ridiculously cute!"

Alejandro slowed the engine near the shore, guiding us toward a narrow strip of beach marked by a weathered post. A few penguins waddled closer, curious but unbothered by the boat.

One of them stopped at the edge of the surf and blinked up, like it had an opinion about our arrival.

Alejandro cut the engine, and the boat rocked gently in the shallows. "We don't stay long," he said. "No touching, no chasing. They come to you if they want."

Emme was already nodding, eyes wide, phone in hand like she'd forgotten how to use it. The wind tossed a strand of hair across her face, and she laughed, pushing it back with the kind of smile that makes you forget what silence sounds like.

Alejandro steadied the bow against the dock, and I stepped out first. The wood was slick with spray, the air sharp and bright. I offered her my hand. She hesitated—professional habit, probably—but took it anyway. Her fingers were cold through her gloves.

The island smelled of salt and kelp and something faintly sweet, like wet grass. Penguins called across the rocks, a chorus of absurd little voices that somehow filled the whole sky.

Emme turned a slow circle, phone half-lowered, eyes shining. "They don't even care we're here."

"They're used to people," I said.

She glanced at me, grinning. "Still feels like we shouldn't be allowed."

"We're not, most days," I said.

Alejandro chuckled behind us. "But today's a favor."

One penguin waddled straight toward us, stopped, and blinked up like it had an opinion about our footwear.

"Do they bite?" she asked.

"Only when insulted," I said.

She nudged me with her elbow. "You've met them before, haven't you?"

"Once or twice" I admitted. "Alejandro's sister used to work out here with the research team."

Her eyes lit up. "Used to?"

"It was a few years ago," I said, rubbing the back of my neck. "She's married now."

Emme's smile tilted. "You dated her."

I looked out over the water, pretending to check the tide. "Briefly."

"Uh-huh. And here I thought you didn't like people."

"Most people," I corrected.

She laughed softly, and the sound mingled with the wind and the gulls—too easy, too warm.

I looked away before I started smiling like an idiot. It wasn't the kind of thing I did. I'd brought her here to get her out of work mode, not to end up in whatever this was.

Still, watching her—kneeling near the rocks, phone in hand, hair blowing wild—I couldn't remember the last time someone looked at this place and made it feel new again.

Alejandro waved us back toward the boat after a while. "Before the wind changes," he said, which in Patagonia meant *now*.

Emme crouched to take one last photo, then straightened reluctantly. I offered my hand to help her in. She hesitated, smiling like she knew what she was doing, but took it anyway.

Her glove slipped slightly against mine—warm skin under cold fabric—and for a second I didn't want to let go.

I did, of course.

The ride back was calmer. Alejandro hummed off-key to some old song on the radio. Emme stood near the bow, hair flying, cheeks flushed from the wind. Every few seconds, she'd look back and grin at nothing in particular, which somehow made it worse.

When we reached the dock, Alejandro pointed uphill. "My house is close. You'll come for wine, sí?"

I started to say no. Emme said yes at the same time.

He laughed. "That settles it."

His home sat above the cove—whitewashed walls, tin roof, a fence meant to convince the wind to behave. His wife, Sofía, met us at the door, warm and smiling, flour on her hands.

"Pasen, por favor," she said, already ushering us toward the kitchen. The stove glowed red, the air thick with bread and herbs. She poured wine—a Malbec, dark and heavy—and handed us each a small glass.

I accepted out of courtesy. One glass, slow. Always enough to appreciate, never to dull.

The country bread was still warm, the sheep's cheese sharp and perfect. Alejandro and Sofía started trading stories before the second pour, their rhythm practiced, like they'd been waiting all week for an audience.

"Tell them about the woman with the sea lion," Sofía said, eyes dancing.

Alejandro groaned. "You'll never let that go."

Emme leaned in immediately. "Oh, now you have to."

He sighed, but the grin gave him away. "A tourist from California—nice woman, expensive camera. She saw a sea lion sleeping on the beach and decided it was a stray dog that needed help."

Emme blinked. "You're joking."

"She called to it," Sofía said, laughing. "Made kissing noises, like *'Here, puppy!'*"

"Oh no," Emme said, half covering her face.

"Oh yes," Alejandro replied. "It barked back, all teeth, and she ran so fast she lost a flip-flop. I still have it hanging in the shed."

Luc shook his head. "Souvenir or warning?"

"Both," Sofía said.

Emme was crying from laughter. "That poor woman! I mean, good instinct, terrible execution."

"Exactly," Sofía said. "We like her spirit, though."

Alejandro refilled everyone's glass. "Better than my spirit the day the truck went swimming."

Emme brightened. "Oh, this I need to hear."

"He thought the tide would wait," Sofía said.

"I calculated wrong," Alejandro admitted. "By about an hour."

"And a meter," she added.

Emme looked between them, trying not to laugh. "Did it actually float?"

"Briefly," he said. "Before it sank up to the doors. Luc helped pull it out."

Emme turned to me, incredulous. "You?"

I nodded. "Long afternoon. Mud, rain, and poor decisions."

"He cursed the ocean," Sofía said, chuckling. "In French. Very dramatic."

Emme tilted her head. "What did you say?"

"That it could keep the truck," I said.

She burst out laughing again, doubling over until tears streaked her cheeks. "You're serious."

"Deadly."

Sofía wagged a finger. "And that's how we learned not to argue with tides or Frenchmen."

Alejandro raised his glass. "Especially both at once."

We all drank to that. For a while, the only sound was the fire snapping and Emme's quiet laugh as she tried to catch her breath. I hadn't seen her this alive before—her laughter big and unguarded. It was contagious. Before I realized it, I was laughing too, a real sound, not the polite version I usually give people.

When it faded, she caught me watching her, and something passed between us. Sofía noticed it, of course—women always do—but had the grace not to say anything.

Alejandro poured another round, talking about the vineyard that bottled the Malbec. I added a comment about the oak aging, and he nodded in approval. Emme listened, smiling at how easily we slipped into it.

It was the first time she'd seen this side of me—the side that could laugh, talk wine, sit by a stove and not think about what needed fixing next.

When the laughter finally settled, Sofía brought out a plate of *alfajores* dusted with sugar and a pot of coffee strong enough to wake the dead. Emme took one bite, sighed like it was a religious experience, and immediately asked for the recipe. Sofía promised to write it down, though everyone in Patagonia seemed to make them differently and swear theirs were best.

By the time we drained the last of the coffee, the shadows had shifted across the floor. Alejandro glanced toward the window. "You'll want to head back soon. The wind changes quick after four."

I checked my watch. He wasn't wrong.

Emme stood, stretching, still smiling. "Gracias... por todo esto."

Sofía hugged her like they'd known each other for years. "You bring light into a room, *querida*. Come back when you can stay longer."

Outside, the air had cooled, the light sharpening into that blue-gold edge Patagonia saves for late afternoons.

We waved to Alejandro and Sofía at the gate, then turned back toward the road. The drive was quieter—the kind of silence that didn't need fixing.

Halfway to the lodge, Emme said softly, "You have good friends."

"I know," I said.

She looked out the window. "It suits you."

I didn't ask what *it* was. I just drove, the hum of the engine steady beneath the sound of the sea. When I glanced over again, she was asleep.

By the time the mountains came back into view, the sky had turned the color of iron. The day was closing, and the new guests would be arriving soon. But for once, I didn't feel the weight of what came next—just the echo of her laughter, still somewhere in the truck with me.

Chapter 13

Dinner for Eight

EMME

I COULD STILL FEEL the boat in my knees when we pulled into the drive at Refugio Cielo. The sky had shifted to that steel-blue pre-evening, the kind that made the mountains look closer than they were. Luc killed the engine and was already in motion—door, bags, check the mailbox, thumb the door latch—while I followed in that drowsy, satisfied float you get after a day that actually counted. Inside, the kitchen wore its uniform: orderly counters, knives sleeping on a magnetic strip, the big Dutch oven on the back burner like a patient animal waiting to be fed.

I washed my hands, grabbed the stack of plates, and started setting the big table in the great room for eight.

The long windowed wall had gone silver with evening. You could hear the wind but not feel it, which made me feel smug and lucky. I lined up cutlery, water glasses, wine glasses, the little bowls I knew he liked for salt and olives, and then went hunting for napkins.

"Drawer by the stove," Luc said without looking. He was checking the oven temperature the way some men check a pulse.

He appeared behind me with a basket of warm rolls wrapped in a towel. The smell made my stomach turn into an entire choir. "What are we eating?"

"Lamb," he said. "I started it this morning. Cabernet Franc, thyme, garlic, slow oven. Roasted carrots and potatoes. Salad if there's time."

"So, a snack." I peeked under the towel. "How many rolls are you prepared to lose to the greater good?"

"How many do you need to test?"

"Three," I said, then corrected, honest, "Four."

"Two," he said, and handed me one. "And I'm watching you."

I tore the roll open. Steam curled up like a promise. "You're cruel."

"You'll live." He returned to the stove. "What did you like best?"

"About what?"

"Today," he said, like it was obvious. He kept his eyes on the pot as he stirred, but I could feel him listening. "You've wanted Patagonia for a while. You had a few candidates."

He meant the mountains, the wind, the water. The penguins, obviously. I lifted the roll to buy time, then answered the way it arrived, clean and true.

"Your friends," I said.

He went still for a second, then set the spoon down. "Alejandro and Sofía."

"Yes," I said. "And how you are with them. Like you've already spent a thousand dinners in that kitchen and most of them ended with laughter. It was... nice to see."

He didn't move, but something shifted anyway. "That's what you liked best."

"I loved the penguins," I said quickly. "I'm not a monster. But my favorite was watching you belong to people and letting them belong to you." Maybe that was part of what made today feel different—the way this place didn't push me to the edges. The way it kept leaving space, like it expected me to stay.

He picked up the spoon like the conversation weighed nothing. "You say things like that and expect a man to stay still."

For a second, neither of us moved. Then I reached for the bread again—because touching *something* was safer.

Holy hell. Did that just turn me on? Awesome. I'll be over here combusting quietly.

"You said eight."

He blinked once, hard.

"Settings," I clarified.

"Right. Eight."

"Teresa and Mariela will be down in a few minutes. The new people are due any time. Elliot?"

Luc set the spoon on a towel. "Elvis-Elliot left this morning."

"Elvis-Elliot," I said, smiling. "We missed him?"

"He was gone before breakfast," he said. "Probably filmed his own farewell on the way out."

"Of course he did."

"Two angles," Luc said. "And a speech on the porch about 'the ephemeral nature of light.'"

I grinned. "Bet his followers will eat that up."

He didn't roll his eyes, but I could feel it in the atmosphere. "He left a note for Teresa and Mariela. They left early for the ridge."

"Did we hear our names?" called the teachers as they came down the stairs, looking every bit like women who'd wrung the last drop from their final day and were still glowing from it.

"No Juliana. *You* cooked," Teresa said to Luc with the reverence of people who had seen his food before.

"He prepared," Mariela corrected. "And then he let the oven do the rest."

"I supervised," Luc said.

I hugged them both. "You guys missed Elliot."

Mariela put a hand to her heart. "I will never forgive the universe."

Teresa took in the table and looked my way. "You really *are* here because of Vendor Relations, aren't you?"

"I'm a woman of many talents," I said.

Teresa smiled. "This place feels different tonight."

Did she mean because of me? God, get a grip. Still... maybe.

"It's because we're leaving," Mariela said, dramatic. "We are the soul of the party."

"The soul of the party is the bread," I said, reaching for the basket, and Luc gently intercepted my hand and replaced it with a pair of salad tongs like a man redirecting a toddler away from a candle.

I added the final touches to the table when Luc glanced toward the entryway.

"Juliana won't be back until morning," he said. "And Rafa's still in town."

"So just us, then." I smiled. "And whoever the wind blows in next."

As if they were summoned, the front door swung open on a gust of cold air and a chorus of new voices.

"Hello hello hello," a woman sang, followed by a man and two more voices tumbling in behind them. "We come in peace—and possibly frostbite!"

Luc's mouth twitched. "Incoming."

Four travelers spilled through the doorway, stamping snow from their boots and shaking off laughter. The man in front—about my age, tall, all grin and accent—was already halfway through a story he'd clearly started in the van. The woman behind him had the look of someone who'd long accepted that resistance was futile and loved him anyway.

Then came *her*—a drop-dead-gorgeous model type with wind-flushed cheeks and hair that looked like it had its own publicist. She radiated warmth, easy and effortless, the kind that makes you want to either hug her or add her to your hit list.

Last was a younger guy, maybe late twenties, my age. Tall and travel-rumpled, clutching a weather-beaten field bag like it contained state secrets.

They looked like people who'd been strangers at the airport and friends by the end of the drive.

"Charm and frostbite," the grinning man declared. "Mostly charm."

"Harper and Finn Dalton," the woman said, stepping forward with her hand out. "We're so sorry we're late. There were wild horses. And a standoff between an armadillo and a herd of sheep. The armadillo lost."

"Harper," Finn said, breathless and thrilled, "show them the horses."

She had her phone out in a second and then thought better of it. "Later. Hi. We're normal. I promise."

Teresa and Mariela waved from the table. Luc did introductions efficiently—names, rooms, dinner in fifteen—and I hovered, because hospitality Barbie had taken over my body. I kept telling myself I was only helping. But the truth was easier: it felt good to be useful here. Natural, even.

Zoë Moretti, it turned out, was a travel journalist covering conservation lodges across South America. Of course she was—the kind of woman who could make sustainability look like a lifestyle brand.

Nico Alvarez was a doctoral student in environmental sciences, here for a few weeks to finish his glacier research—quiet, thoughtful, the type who probably apologized to trees.

They both thanked Luc in that dazzled way people do when the reality of the place outshines its reputation.

Finn turned to me like we'd been mid-conversation for a year. "Okay, and you must be Mrs. Co-Captain."

"The *what* now?" I stuttered.

"Co-Captain," he repeated, pointing between the two of us like a magician revealing a card. "Obviously. This is your place together, right? You're very... co."

I had just stolen a sip of the Cabernet Franc in the kitchen and absolutely did not intend to be caught with it in my mouth during a sentence like that.

I spit. Not full sprinkler, but a delicate, humiliating mist back into the glass, which I then tried to hide with my entire body.

Harper slapped Finn's arm, mortified. "Oh my God, I am so sorry. He has no filter."

"I have *vibes,*" Finn said, unrepentant and beaming. "Look at them. They're doing a dance."

"We're not doing a dance," I said, helplessly laughing because of course *this* was my life now.

Luc, infuriatingly steady: "Emme is here on business."

Finn's eyebrows did a tiny drama. "Business. Uh-huh."

Harper rushed to fix it. "We've been traveling too long. Please ignore us. Your home—this—is stunning. Thank you for having us."

Luc's shoulders unhitched a fraction. "Welcome," he said. To me, quietly: "You all right?"

"I drowned gracefully," I said under my breath. "Go stir your lamb."

He went. I caught Harper's eye and we both smiled like women who understand that men will absolutely deny jealousy while setting entire stews ablaze with it.

They took their bags upstairs, promising to "de-gear and re-human." Teresa and Mariela helped me finish the table—straighten, fill, fuss—while I told them the condensed penguin version. They squealed appropriately and took turns pretending to hate me.

By the time they all returned, the room had gone honey-warm. Luc set the Dutch oven on a trivet, lifted the lid, and the table got very quiet in the universal human language of *ooooh*.

"Your home is stunning," Nico said.

Zoë rested a hand on the table, fingertips tracing the wood grain. "This table is beautiful," she said, looking at Luc. "It feels... personal."

"He built it," I said before he could. "The chairs too. The sheepskin keeps the heat from escaping."

"It's perfect," Zoë said, smiling—and, inconveniently, I think I developed a minor girl crush. The whole room felt like that to me too—lived-in, warm, quietly waiting.

We passed bread and bowls. The stew went around like gravity. The first dip of spoon to mouth did that thing—eyes closing, shoulders dropping, silent gratitude for the dumb luck of being alive and hungry at the same time.

Finn made a sound that got away from him. "Sir."

"Don't call him sir," Harper said, laughing. "He's barely tolerating us."

"I am tolerating you perfectly," Luc said in a tone that suggested this might be his personal Everest.

Finn pointed a spoon. "That accent, though—French, right? What brings a Frenchman all the way down here?"

"Finn," Harper hissed. "Personal question!" She smacked his arm, but he only grinned.

Luc's mouth twitched, polite and unreadable. "Long story," he said. "Better told another time."

"Over wine?" Finn offered.

"Over several," Luc said, and that earned him a round of laughter.

Harper took a photo of her bowl, then stopped herself. "Is it okay?"

"Photos?" Luc asked.

"If we tag you," she said. "We do an eco-luxury series—but if you'd rather not—"

"It's fine," he said. "Photograph whatever you like—just ask permission for faces first."

She nodded, then glanced at me. "You count as co-owner. Do you consent to being gorgeous in the background?"

"She does," Finn said, like a man who enjoyed getting thrown out of places.

"Finn," Harper warned.

"What? I'm supportive."

Teresa and Mariela were loving this. Every time Finn opened his mouth, they made the kind of teacher faces that mean someone is about to be assigned a reflective essay.

"So you do this full-time?" I asked, genuinely curious. "Travel and film?"

"Travel, film, edit on the road, collapse, repeat," Harper said. "We prioritize low-impact partners, local guides, places that treat the land like it's sacred, not a backdrop."

"Then you're in the right place," I said, and meant it.

Finn ladled more stew and aimed a question at me over the steam. "So how's the division of labor? You run guest relations while he cooks? Or do you charm the chef and then guest relations happens by itself?"

Luc's chair made a tiny noise as he shifted. "She does plenty," he said, soft and edged, and half the table looked at their bowls like the broth had become suddenly fascinating.

I nudged the bread basket toward Finn. "I have a niche skill set."

Harper laughed, relieved. "Great vibe here. We'll subscribe to the channel, whatever you do."

Conversation swerved into safer lanes. Teresa described their last hike with the kind of precise joy that makes you pack a bag in your head. Mariela announced that she had conquered her fear of suspension bridges and would now be unstoppable. We toasted her. The Cabernet Franc loosened into the room in a way that felt warm, not reckless; even Finn settled, as if the stew had instructed his body to behave.

Nico wanted to know about the wine. Luc, who never performed, answered in the steady tone of a man who simply liked to get things right. He spoke about the altitudes of the local vine, the lean fruit you get down here, the way Cabernet Franc holds structure without the heavy hand of Malbec. He didn't posture. He explained in a way that made it feel like a secret being saved for whoever had the patience to listen.

Harper's eyes went crescent-shaped. "I could listen to you talk about grapes for hours."

Finn elbowed her. "Ma'am, I am present."

"You'll live, sweetheart," she said.

Dessert was a calafate tart with cream that made Zoë close her eyes—apparently even perfection has a sweet tooth. Mariela asked if the recipe came with the building. Luc said no, he stole it from a grandmother who'd forgive him because he sends Christmas cards. Nico offered a family cake recipe in trade, and Luc smiled like he'd already memorized the ratios.

When the plates were mostly empty and the tea had made its rounds, Teresa cleared her throat softly. "Okay," she said to the table, "we're the boring ones tonight. We leave at dawn, and we promised ourselves we'd pack before we sleep."

"We're not boring," Mariela said. "We are paragons of responsibility."

"And we're going to miss you," I said.

They stood, and there were hugs that smelled like tea and wool. Teresa squeezed my hand. "You found a good place to stand still for a minute." And God help me, I did. I felt it in my bones—in the warmth, the laughter, the way people folded me into their orbit without asking for anything in return.

"I know," I said, and it came out quieter than I expected.

To Luc she said, smiling, "You're a beautiful soul... and a menace with an oven. Thank you."

He inclined his head like he'd been knighted by a school district. "Travel safe. El Calafate in the morning?"

"Quick stop," Mariela said. "Then Buenos Aires, then home."

"Send us a photo when you land," I said. "Proof of life."

They promised, waved, and headed for the stairs with the unhurried efficiency of women who can pack blindfolded.

Harper and Finn tried to help with plates, were forbidden, and compromised by rearranging chairs in a way that made sense only to them. Harper took a group photo in the doorway—Teresa and Mariela insisted we all crowd in—and Finn coached us into "soft smiles" like we were a yogurt ad. Luc endured it with the expression of a man tolerating a minor blizzard.

When the door to the south wing shut behind the last of them, the lodge exhaled. The fire settled. Wind stroked the eaves.

I reached for a stack of plates. Luc opened his mouth to object, then thought better and closed it. Progress.

The quiet settled around us—comfortable, familiar. Not borrowed. Not temporary. Something I could almost see myself slipping into, piece by piece.

Chapter 14

The Road to Here

EMME

"DON'T TELL ME TO sit," I warned. "It will go badly for you."

"Never occurred to me," he lied, and handed me the plates instead.

We moved around each other in the kind of easy quiet that only happens after laughter. I stacked. He wiped. I wiped. He stacked. We traded spots without speaking, which felt suspiciously like chemistry pretending to be competence.

"Hey," I said at the sink, "if you had to grade Finn on a scale of Labrador to actual human man—"

"Border collie," he said. "Trainable. Excessive staring."

I snorted. "He did assume we were... co-captains."

"Finn assumes many things."

"You were very calm."

"I was," he said. Then, after a beat, without looking at me, "You spit your wine."

"Not my finest hour," I admitted. "In my defense, I stole it. So the universe was correcting the balance."

"You could have asked."

"It was more fun to steal it."

He made a sound that might have been a laugh if you caught it with both hands.

We finished the last of the dishes. The kitchen went back to itself, like a stage after a curtain call. I dried my hands and leaned against the counter, watching him. He wiped the same square of wood twice, then set the towel down like he'd just remembered it was allowed.

"Earlier," he said, "you surprised me."

"With what?"

"Your answer." He didn't push away from the counter. He looked like he was bracing for weather that might or might not arrive. "About the day."

"Oh." I tucked hair behind my ear, a stall I hated myself for and did anyway. "I meant it."

"I know," he said. And there was something in his voice that made me go very, very still. "Thank you."

"For what?"

"For noticing the right thing," he said, and then immediately looked like he regretted saying the last three words of that sentence.

"You think I don't do that often?" I asked, light.

"I think you do it all the time," he said, not light at all. "Just not for me."

We stood there in the soft thrum of the fridge and the tick of the stove cooling and the sound of my heart being extremely annoying about it.

I pushed off the counter. "Everyone's in bed."

He nodded.

"The fire's still going."

He nodded again, slower.

"Come sit with me for a minute," I said. "No work. Just... sit."

He watched me for a second like he had to test a bridge he wasn't sure would hold. Then he reached over, turned off the last light in the kitchen, and followed me into the great room where the lodge waited, quiet and warm, the kind of place you only find on purpose.

I curled into the end of the sofa where the fire threw heat and light in equal parts. He took the other end like he needed to prove a point. It wasn't far enough to undo the fact that we were sharing the same piece of air.

"Tell me something true," I said.

He closed his eyes, just for a beat, then opened them and looked at me like maybe he'd spend one of his favours on this. "All right."

I waited. He didn't make me wait long.

"I liked watching you today," he said. "Not the photos. Not the part where you narrate for the rest of the world. Just the part where you forgot to."

I swallowed. "I'll try to do that more."

He nodded once. "Good."

We watched the fire for a while, because watching the fire is easier than surviving eye contact when your whole nervous system is doing cartwheels. The wind pressed once against the window and moved on. In the lull, a floorboard popped like a polite cough.

I turned my head then, because I couldn't not. He was still in his corner of the couch, long legs, tired eyes, that maddening mouth that didn't give anything away unless you knew how to look.

"Luc," I said.

He looked back, steady.

"Thank you for today," I said. "All of it."

He nodded once. "You're welcome."

I could have left it there. I probably should have. Instead, I tucked my feet under me and sank one inch closer to the middle of the couch, which was either nothing or everything depending on your blood pressure.

He didn't move away.

We sat like that until the fire became embers and the lodge breathed around us and the part of me that thinks in email subject lines finally shut up. He looked down at my hand, then up at me, and for once, didn't retreat behind silence.

"You asked me—what brought me here."

"To Patagonia," I said.

He nodded. "A long ride. A longer reason."

I waited. The fire cracked once, like punctuation.

"My brother, Adrien, died in a car accident four days before we were supposed to leave for our trip. *Un putain d'accident de voiture.* He was running an errand for me. For *me.*"

I inhaled.

"My boss—he was a good friend—told me to go anyway. Said I needed to heal. So I sold my apartment. Gave away the furniture. Kept what fit in a small pack. Even sold my bike."

I nodded.

"Then I flew to Texas, near the border, and bought another one in Laredo. A machine too heavy, too loud, too American. Adrien and I had already ordered bikes for our trip. We would have resold them at the end."

My chest tightened.

"Adrien was the better version of me. Younger. Smarter. Louder. He thought I worked too much. He thought he'd live forever."

He paused. The flames shifted. His profile was sharp against the light, every angle made of memory.

"I left Paris with our original plan. North to south. Mexico, Peru, Chile. I told myself I was looking for quiet. What I found was motion. That was enough for a while."

"Let me guess," I said. "You and that too-loud, too-American bike caused minor chaos everywhere you went."

"Possibly."

"I'm sure it had nothing to do with *un beau Français sexy* in the leathers."

"The *what*?"

"Don't play innocent. Women notice things."

"I was not looking for that kind of attention."

"Good thing attention doesn't ask permission," I said.

His eyes flicked toward me—startled, amused, and something else he didn't name. The breath he let out wasn't quite a laugh.

He ran a thumb along his palm, slow, thoughtful. "I left the plan behind. Met people who never asked my last name. Stayed places that had no address. Fixed roofs. Built fences. Slept under engines. I thought if I kept moving, the world would forget what I'd lost."

"Did it?" I asked.

"No." He smiled, small and unfinished. "But it made the noise bearable."

I didn't move. Didn't breathe too loud. His story folded itself between us, thin and true.

"When I reached the south," he continued, "I was supposed to keep going. There's a ferry to Antarctica in the summer. I had a ticket. But I stopped here first. This valley." He lifted one shoulder, eyes steady on the fire. "It felt... right. Not simple, but honest."

"And you stayed."

"I rebuilt a roof for the woman who owned this place before me. Then I rebuilt the kitchen. The foundation. Everything. When she decided to sell, she said I should keep it. I didn't argue."

I let out a breath I hadn't noticed holding. "So you traded motion for stillness."

He considered that. "Maybe not. Building is still movement. Just slower. More deliberate."

I smiled faintly. "So you didn't get lost. You built your own map."

His eyes met mine then, direct and careful. "Something like that."

The room went quiet again, but it wasn't empty. It was the kind of quiet that felt shared.

After a while, I said softly, "Adrien would've liked it here?"

Luc's voice was a murmur. "He would've filled it with noise."

"Then maybe he'd forgive the quiet," I said.

That earned me the smallest smile—half gratitude, half surrender.

Outside, the wind slipped along the glass and went on its way. The fire leaned low. I wanted to say something comforting, something true, but everything that came to mind sounded like a postcard. So I didn't.

Instead, I sat there with him until the last flame faded into coal, and the world settled around us in that fragile, wordless truce you only find when two people finally stop pretending they aren't broken in the same place.

Chapter 15

No Blueprint for This

LUC

BY BREAKFAST, THE LODGE was awake and pretending it had always been easy to live here.

The stove clicked twice before it took the flame. I set water to a slow boil and turned the hand crank of the grinder to the notch it knows by heart. Outside, the wind moved down the valley in long, tired breaths that carried powder from the eaves and made the pines nod like elders humoring a joke. The new guests arrived in bursts of energy and colored jackets, finding their seats as I put plates on the long table.

"Buenos días," I said, to the room at large.

The chorus came back at me—some bright, some sleep-heavy. The coffee was doing its work. I poured a mug for the grad student and handed another to the wife who took photos of steam. By the time I reached Zoë's place by the window, she had pushed her sunglasses into her hair and was watching me the way city people watch the ocean: attentive, hungry, a little proud to be near something they can't make behave.

"What's your story, Luc?" she asked, like we were not strangers, like the question weighed the same as cream or sugar.

I put a bowl of berries down without touching the table. "Long," I said.

"Intriguing." She leaned forward, elbows on wood. "I like long."

I gave her the half-smile I used for scaffolding that would hold, dishes that would not. "Then you'll like the Andes."

She laughed and said something to the wife, and whatever else she meant to say to me stayed in the air. Not my business.

Emme came in with the last tray—bread still warm, the apricot jam that never set properly—and slid it onto the table with a competence that made people sit up straighter. Morning fit her. I had learned that already.

She wore a navy sweater that fit her snug in a good way. Hair up. Smile on.

Hard on.

Putain, mec. Ressaisis-toi. Fuck, man. Pull it together.

Zoë angled her body toward her. "What's his deal?" she asked, not quietly enough to be private, not loudly enough to pretend she didn't mean me to hear.

Emme looked at me once, quick, then at Zoë . "A complicated one."

That should have been the end of it, but Zoë repeated the phrase softly, as if she liked the taste of the syllables. Comp-li-ca-ted. She made it sound like a dare. I poured more coffee. Emme's knee brushed the chair as she moved past me and that was the only part of the room that found my pulse.

Guests discussed their plans for the day. All the normal things. I gave the usual warnings and the truer ones, which are about not pretending the mountain cares about your schedules. "Back by three," I said.

"Four," Zoë challenged.

"Three," Emme added, same tone as a second rope on a bridge. "No later."

Zoë rolled her eyes, cheerful, already enjoying the boundaries she planned to push. She put her sunglasses back on like a curtain drawing itself. By nine-thirty the lodge was light and quiet, the kind of quiet that can fool you into thinking it belongs to you.

Emme stood at the edge of the great room with her laptop hugged against her chest. "Still good to go over the contract?"

"Yes," I said. "Now."

We set up by the fire because that is where people tell the truth, and because the table was still warm from the morning. She sat on the sofa with her legs tucked under, laptop open to a page that wore my name too cleanly. I took the chair opposite. Between us: documents, a pencil, a bowl with two last strawberries pressed against the side where someone had left them.

"We'll go line by line," she said, voice brisk, professional, unfairly calm in a way that made me want to push and agree at the same time.

"Line by line," I said.

We started with staff rotation. She proposed a small roster of bilingual guides for high season, with two on-call locals for winter, signed to fair contracts that would make my former colleagues in Paris stop pretending Patagonia was hobby work.

"Yes," I said. "But no one works both avalanche training and night watch in the same week."

She typed. "Agreed."

Sustainability clauses next. Composting, greywater commitments, local sourcing in a radius we negotiated like cartographers. The numbers pleased me. I had, at twenty-two, argued for the same numbers on a project that built penthouses with trees no one watered. This, at least, was honest.

"Partnership listing," she said. "Wilder Horizons added to your site and signage. Your brand added to ours. You retain final creative control of your imagery."

"Final," I repeated, to hear the word in this room. "I approve text."

"You approve text." Her mouth tugged once. "We'll argue about commas later."

"I don't argue about commas."

"Good," she said, making a note. "Because I win those."

We went on like that, small turns in a road that felt like the right one. There's pleasure in precise agreements with someone who understands the materials you're building with. I didn't say that. I told her we should raise the maximum group size for shoulder season. She countered with tiered pricing that would make the right kind of people feel smart and the wrong kind feel bored. We met in the space that opened between those choices.

Then we reached the paragraph she had marked with a pale yellow flag, the color the map makers use for caution.

"Digital infrastructure," she read. "Wi-Fi installation in the common areas and office, with limited guest access during specified windows. Redundancy with a second satellite for weather outages. A small equipment closet behind the office wall."

"No."

She looked up. "No discussion?"

"That is the discussion. No."

Her fingers rested on the keys. "Luc—"

"This place lives because people put their phones down," I said. "Because they remember they have hands."

"They don't forget that because there's a password," she said. "They forget because they're afraid of the quiet."

"Exactly."

She breathed in. "You aren't afraid of their quiet," she said, softer now. "You're afraid of yours."

"Don't do that," I said, sharper than I meant. "Don't name things you don't have to carry."

She closed the laptop gently. The sound was not loud but it changed the air. "You can say it's about beauty and unplugging, and it is. But it's also about control. If there's no signal, you control what gets in. You decide when the world can find you."

"It's my lodge."

"I know." She held my gaze. "But you also don't send the lodge on a pack trip every time someone shows up with questions you don't want to answer." A breath tightened her shoulders for a second before she smoothed it away, like the words cost her more than she meant to show.

"You think this is about questions?" I stood without knowing I would, the chair moving back just enough to be a fact. I paced because there are conversations you can't have sitting down. "You bring a signal here and they'll drag their offices into the firelight. They'll make calls in the doorway and cry into the snow about deadlines. They'll check out of the day while they're still inside it."

She tilted her head. "Like me?"

That found the place I hide. It knocked once, politely. Then it put its hand on the handle.

"You're different," I said—too fast, too certain. The words came out like defense, not truth.

She didn't move, didn't blink.

I exhaled a breath that wasn't laughter. "You watched me for forty-eight hours and decided you have the math."

"I watched you for forty-eight hours and *listened*," she said. "And last night you told me a piece. I am not asking you to stop loving the quiet. I'm asking you to let people reach the lives they promised to return to."

"I promised no one," I said, and it came out rough, the truth not proud of itself. "That is the point."

"No," she said, just that word, but she made it sound like a bridge that held. "That's the armor."

The window clicked as the temperature shifted. A knot in the wood of the mantel popped like an old hinge. Outside, something shed snow in a hush. In the fire, a half-burned log went from sullen to bright, as if reminded of its job.

"You'll lose people if they can't check in," she went on, quieter. "Not just our clients. Your scientists. Your volunteers. Your next-*you* who comes down the road with a pack and a reason not to say."

I shook my head, the movement too large for the room. "Tu ne comprends pas," I said—*you don't understand.* My hands opened as if the air needed translation. "Je ne veux plus perdre. Je ne veux plus sentir." *I don't want to lose anymore. I don't want to feel.*

Her eyes softened—barely—but enough that even the fire seemed to pull back to give her space to hear me. She looked up at me with calm that wasn't performance. "Alors arrête de te cacher derrière ton silence." *Then stop hiding behind your silence.*

All the sound went out of the room and I could hear the things I usually outrun. "You understood that," I said, but it wasn't a question.

"Every word," she answered. "In more ways than one."

I saw how she had listened last night: not like a tourist, not like a witness, but like someone learning how to carry something without telling it how heavy it was allowed to be. I saw her making space for noise I had refused to assign to myself. I saw the lodge as it might be with a signal that didn't turn it into an airport, and me as I might be if I stopped using blank places on a map as a kind of lid.

Her fingers curled slightly at the edge of the table—not pulling back, not reaching, just bracing, like she felt the shift before I made it.

I saw this all in less than a second.

The only movement I trusted was forward. I crossed the space in two strides because there was nothing useful left at a distance. I wasn't careful and I wasn't careless. I was decided.

Her hands were on her knees, palms down, as if she were bracing for weather. I reached for one; she turned her hand and gave it to me. The heat of her skin traveled up my arm like a truth that didn't need an argument. She stood when I asked without words. The laptop slid farther down the table until it met the bowl with the two strawberries and stopped there, quiet against the glass.

"You're shaking," she said. It took me a moment to realize she meant me.

"I don't do this," I said. "Here. Now."

"That's already changed."

I didn't think. Didn't calculate. Didn't care. I caught her face in my hands and kissed her like I'd run out of options.

She made a sound—soft, startled—and I chased it, mouth hard, then careful, then hard again because control was gone and I didn't want it back. Her lips were warm and slick and real. She tasted like tea and salt and the kind of need that doesn't wait for permission.

Her fingers curled into my shirt. That was all it took. I pressed her against me, deepened the kiss, broke it, found it again, rougher. Breathing was something that happened somewhere else.

I wanted to memorize her with my mouth. Every sound, every catch of breath, every time she leaned closer instead of pulling away.

When I finally drew back, her breath still hit my cheek. My pulse was a noise in my ears. I should've let go. I couldn't.

She didn't look away. Not once. Not when I touched her, not when I broke, not when I let her see exactly what she'd done to me. Her breath hit mine like a yes she didn't need to speak.

I caught her hips, lifted her, and carried her upstairs. My lips never left her mouth.

Chapter 16

French Twist

LUC

THE WORLD NARROWED TO her taste, her weight, the pulse hammering in my chest. The bedroom door gave under my shoulder and hit the wall. The sound vanished into the noise of our kiss.

I didn't set her down. I laid her onto the bed, the mattress groaning under us. Light sliced through the blinds—stripes of gold, shadow, and breath.

Her hands were everywhere—hair, back, skin. When her palms met bare flesh, a shudder hit hard enough to blur the edges of thought. "Mon Dieu, Emme."

She arched. Control died. I yanked her shirt off, found her throat with my mouth, tasted salt and skin. She cried out—short, sharp—and it detonated in my gut. Her fingers went for my jeans, brushed the edge of the tattoo on my hip. I flinched. She saw. Didn't ask. Instead she bent and traced the lines with her tongue. Everything inside me broke.

She paused there—just for a second—the tip of her tongue lingering against the ink like she was memorizing it before she moved on.

"Luc," she breathed. "Please."

I stumbled to the drawer, found the condom by feel, tore it open, turned back. She was waiting—hair wild, lips swollen, a halo in the dim light. I rolled on the condom, came back to her. Hooked her leggings and underwear, dragged them away. She opened for me, and I lost the last of my reason.

"Look at me," I said.

Her eyes met mine as I pushed inside. No gentleness, only truth. She gasped, nails digging into my arms, back arched. I held still, buried deep, the world reduced to heat and pulse. Then I moved. Hard. Fast. The bed hit the wall in rhythm. Her cries came short and rough. I marked her throat with my mouth; she locked her legs around me, drew me deeper.

"Don't stop," she whispered.

Couldn't. Didn't. Everything else—silence, past, control—burned away.

"Emme." Her name came out half-prayer.

She shattered around me, and I followed, a roar torn from somewhere I'd kept closed for years.

After, I stayed where I was, face buried in her hair, our hearts still running. Her hand slid to my hip, resting over the compass. Her fingers stilled there, not curious—certain—like the mark meant something she didn't need to ask.

I eased out of her, slow, careful, and reached for the edge of the blanket. She made a small sound—content, not complaint—and I pulled it over us before settling back.

"Well then," she sighed. "If I'd known Wi-Fi was your undoing, I'd have brought it up days ago."

I huffed a laugh against her shoulder. "You would've weaponized it."

"Maybe," she murmured. "But only for good."

There was a smile in her voice that I felt before I heard. She kept her face angled toward the ceiling, but the corner of her mouth softened in a way that didn't match her teasing.

I don't know how long we stayed like that—long enough for my pulse to steady, for the fire to fade to coals, for the air to remember what quiet was.

Her fingers traced lazy lines over my back, nothing meant, everything said.

She spoke first, very quietly. "Not just the Wi-Fi."

"No," I said. "Not just the Wi-Fi."

The words sat there between us, heavier than they sounded.

I didn't move. She didn't either. Outside, the snow kept doing what it always does—falling, not caring who's watching.

I turned my head toward the glass. "I don't want the lodge to become a station," I said. "I don't want it to lose what makes it quiet."

"It won't," she murmured. "We can zone the signal—lounge and office only. Program it to shut off at night. No ads, no public network. You decide the schedule; I'll write the note that explains it."

I looked at her. Not her face—her posture. Shoulders loose, no defense. The quiet confidence of it struck me harder than the plan itself; she wasn't trying to win—she was trying to meet me where I lived.

She believed I'd come around on my own.

That kind of patience hits harder than any argument.

"And if people abuse it?"

She tilted her head. "Then you can be a tyrant about it for a while."

I almost smiled. "You think that's my default?"

"No," she said quietly. "I think it's your shield."

"You would like that."

"I'd like you to trust yourself," she said. "And me." Her voice dipped on that last word, soft enough that it felt less like a request and more like a promise she hoped I'd believe.

The words hit clean. Tight. Like something lining up the way it should. Trust isn't a feeling—it's structure. You get it wrong, things crack. You get it right, they hold.

"What else," I asked, my voice not quite steady, "would you insist on?"

Her mouth curved. "Windows that open in the guest rooms."

"They do."

"Then curtains that don't fight the light."

She hesitated, then: "And a line on your site—one sentence—that tells the truth about the kind of stillness this place offers."

"What sentence?"

"Something like: *Not simple, but honest.*"

It reached back into last night and touched my shoulder. I nodded before I knew I had.

"Zoë asked this morning," she said, changing the subject without really changing it. "What your story was."

"And you said?"

"A complicated one."

"That sounds like something a person says when she is planning to leave it at that."

She watched me. "I can say something simpler if you want."

"What is the simpler thing?"

She didn't blink. "You're a good man who thought solitude was a wall and finally realized it's a door."

It landed. Harder than she probably meant it to. She didn't look away after she said it—not even for a heartbeat—and something in her stillness felt like an invitation.

Mon Dieu. Maybe she knew exactly what she was saying.

I looked at her the way I look at blueprints when I don't trust the measurements. The line held.

I nodded once. "We'll try the signal," I said. "On your terms."

Her smile held relief, not triumph. Her shoulders eased, not all the way, but enough that I could see how tightly she'd been holding that moment. "On *your* terms," she said. "*And* mine."

"And yours," I agreed. We included a trial period because that is how builders breathe. Ninety days. Review at sixty. Cut it at thirty if the lodge felt wrong.

The air tightened between us.

She held my eyes, steady.

Whatever we'd said, it was already binding.

She nodded as if that was the answer she'd expected—and hoped for. "Good."

She shifted closer, voice lower now. "Luc."

"Yes."

"This place is extraordinary," she said. "Not because it's hard to get to. Because it asks for truth."

I could've told her that buildings keep what we hide in them.

I could've told her I wasn't looking for truth—just somewhere that stayed still.

Instead, I reached for her. Some things don't need blueprints.

I kissed her again. Long. Hard. It was an acknowledgment. It was a line drawn with a steady hand. I could feel the moment she kissed me back not as a reply but as an agreement—our terms, the ones we had written and the ones we hadn't. The world didn't narrow this time; it widened and made room.

I set my hand at the back of her neck, her skin warm under hair that had fought me all morning.

Her fingers found my ribs, light and sure.

We didn't rush it. Didn't fake it.

When we finally eased apart, her breath came uneven, mine not much steadier.

She touched my jaw where the stubble had scraped her and smiled like she'd just confirmed something she already knew.

"Three o'clock," she said, a glance toward the clock. The light had softened; snow blurred at the edges like it was exhaling. "Your guests will be back by then, demanding applause."

"They'll settle for soup."

"We'll give them both."

Her laughter was low and easy, the kind that lived somewhere under my ribs.

Chapter 17

Too Hot to Steep

EMME

T HE KNOCK OF PIPES broke the quiet, a low reminder of how fast time moves when you stop counting it. Luc glanced at the clock again, then back at me. "We have twenty minutes before they roll in."

"You saying that like it's a challenge?"

His mouth curved, small and knowing. "Like it's logistics."

He pulled me up with him, efficient even now, and steered us toward the bathroom. Steam rose before the water hit full heat. "Together," he said simply. "Saves time."

I laughed. "Always the practical one."

"Practical now," he murmured, guiding me under the spray. "Longer next time."

The words slid through the sound of the water—quiet, certain, like a promise disguised as planning.

We moved fast, hands helping more than lingering, though every brush of skin made the clock irrelevant.

When the water finally stopped, he reached for a towel and wrapped it around my shoulders, then found one of his flannels hanging on the hook. "This will do," he said, pressing it into my hands.

"Smells like cedar," I said.

"That's me."

He kissed my temple, brief and grounding. "Go. Before I forget why we're hurrying."

I hurried to my room at the other end of the hall and changed fast—black leggings, a soft henley, and Luc's flannel pulled back on over it. Sleeves rolled. Collar open. My hair was still damp, so I twisted it into a loose knot at my neck and pretended it looked intentional.

Engines. Laughter. The shuffle of boots on stone. The vans were back. I bolted downstairs, determined to look busy before anyone came through the door. No questions, no knowing looks.

Within seconds, my laptop was open and my feet were propped on the table by the fire. Luc was already at the counter, sleeves rolled, refilling kettles. The domesticity of it—his steady hands, that composed expression—made the afternoon's chaos feel like a fever dream.

I tried to focus. Numbers. Projections. The Wi-Fi clause. None of it mattered when the door handle clicked and the cold rushed in—a rush of life pouring back into the quiet. I closed the laptop on purpose this time and stood slowly, stretching like someone who'd been at it for hours.

Old habit—look busy before someone asks why you weren't.

A practiced yawn. The picture of productivity.

Harper came through first, camera slung cross-body, cheeks flushed the color of glacier berries. Behind her, Zoë and Nico spilled in like warmth in human form.

"Home again," Finn announced, sweeping his knit cap from his hair. "We bring stories, mud, and possibly divine enlightenment."

Zoë rolled her eyes, unwrapping her scarf. "Mostly mud."

They looked radiant—wind-bitten, grinning, alive in that way only travel can manage. Luc stepped out from the kitchen, and for a heartbeat our eyes caught. Nothing overt, just an instinctive check-in—but it felt like the room noticed.

Zoë's voice carried from the common room. "Luc! You'd have loved the ride out to the springs. Our guide swore the horses could smell tourists." Her glance flicked to me—assessing, curious, maybe something sharper.

I knew that look—the quick math, the quiet comparison. I'd lived through enough of them to recognize the opening steps. Did I subconsciously put on his shirt so she'd notice? *No.*

That's ridiculous. You're not in high school, Emme.

"They can," Luc said, deadpan, and she laughed.

"I'll help," I said quickly, escaping toward the kitchen to... do *something*. Anything. My pulse had gone unreliable again.

I poured water over the tea leaves, pretending to be fascinated by steam. He came in behind me while they stripped their gear, and when his arm brushed mine, it was nothing—and everything—all at once.

Don't read into it. You've imagined "more" before.

When we carried the trays out, the group had settled around the fire. Nico was halfway through describing their guide—a weathered man with a voice "like smoked leather and regret." Harper sat cross-legged, already transferring footage from her camera.

"You should've seen the view," Zoë said, spreading her hands wide. "Blue pools like spilled sky. I almost baptized myself."

Nico grinned. "She did. The horse sneezed."

Laughter filled the room, easy and bright. I eased onto the arm of a chair, watching the play of it—the way travel stitched strangers into brief, messy families.

Luc passed around mugs, efficient as always. Zoë touched his wrist lightly. "Have you heard the legend they tell up there? Two serpents—how the world began."

She leaned forward, warming to the story before anyone asked. "Apparently, the Mapuche people believed there were two giant serpents—Kay Kay, who ruled the sea, and Treng Treng, who ruled the land. Kay Kay woke one day angry at humans for forgetting their place and started to flood the earth. Whole valleys disappeared under water."

Nico jumped in, ever the academic. "And then Treng Treng rose from the mountains to protect the people. He lifted them higher and higher, creating the ridges and peaks so they wouldn't drown. Every time Kay Kay sent a wave, Treng Treng pushed the land up farther. That's how the Andes were born, or so the story goes."

Zoë nodded, eyes bright. "Our guide said the people who survived weren't the strongest—they were the ones who listened. They learned when to climb and when to wait."

"Sounds familiar," Harper said, smiling over her mug.

"Right?" Zoë added. "Balance. Water and earth. Movement and stillness. The world always needing both." She shot Luc a teasing glance. "You'd be the mountain in this story."

"Stable or stubborn?" Nico asked.

"Same thing," Zoë said, grinning.

Luc's mouth twitched, but his gaze flicked to me before he could hide it. Zoë noticed. I saw the flicker of confusion—hurt maybe—and tucked my own reaction behind a polite sip of tea.

The story lingered, warm as the fire. Conversation shifted back to trail mishaps and the kind of laughter that only happens when everyone's finally dry.

Luc slipped back into the kitchen, already setting the kettle on for another round. I followed, grateful for the excuse to move. The noise from the common room softened behind us, replaced by the hiss of steam and the quiet clink of mugs cooling in the sink.

"Second wave?" I asked.

He nodded, reaching for a clean pot. "They'll want something to go with it this time."

"What are we serving with the tea?"

"Tortas fritas," he said, pulling a bowl from the shelf without hesitation. "Fried dough—simple, a little sweet, a little salty."

"Of course it's fried," I said, finding a towel to line a plate. "You're trying to seduce your guests through carbs."

"It works," he winked, already measuring flour. His movements were methodical, practiced—every gesture efficient enough to be comforting. It was easy to forget that not long ago, those hands had been anything but calm.

The kettle whistled. He poured, and for a few quiet seconds, the world shrank to steam, flour, and proximity.

That was when Juliana appeared in the doorway, framed by the low light from the fire behind her.

"¿Todo bien?" she asked lightly, but her quick gaze said she already suspected the answer.

"Tea and tortas fritas," Luc replied without missing a beat. "We thought they might be hungry."

"Always," Juliana said, stepping in. Her eyes flicked once to my collarbone—to the unmistakable flannel that wasn't mine—and back up again. Not judgment, just confirmation.

"Smells good," she said, and reached for a towel, efficient as ever. "I'll take these out when they're ready."

"Gracias," Luc said.

Juliana gave a small, knowing smile—half amusement, half approval. "I'll tell them ten minutes," she said, and slipped back through the doorway, leaving behind the faint scent of rosemary soap and certainty.

Luc watched the door close, then looked at me.

"She knows," I said quietly.

"She's observant."

"That's one word for it."

He stepped closer, voice low. "Come here."

The kiss hit hard—steady hands, rough intent. My knees nearly gave.

"I like you in my shirt," he said against my mouth, the words more breath than sound. "Mais ce qu'il y a dessous me plaît encore plus." *But what's underneath pleases me even more.*

No one had ever said it like that—without claiming, without apology, just wanting. It hit somewhere old.

He didn't move, didn't let the moment slide past. His forehead rested against mine, breath warm, grounding, like he knew exactly what he'd touched.

Chapter 18

Gravity, Briefly

LUC

THE LAST MUG HIT the drying rack with a soft click. The fire in the common room had dropped to embers. The last of the laughter drifted down the hall and vanished into the wind.

Emme closed her laptop and rubbed the bridge of her nose. The glow from the screen cut a faint blue line along her cheekbone. "Dinner's at eight," I said, like we hadn't spent the afternoon breaking every rule between us.

"I'll be here." She hesitated, fingers brushing the cuff of the flannel she still wore. Then she nodded once and left.

The quiet she left behind was heavier than before.

Juliana came in a minute later, drying her hands on a towel. "Everyone's happy," she said.

"Good."

We cleaned side by side, the scrape of porcelain and the slow drip of the faucet marking time.

"Emme leaves tomorrow?" Juliana asked, not really asking. Her tone was level, but the space after it carried a whole conversation.

"Sí, that's the plan."

Juliana folded the towel neatly, eyes on her work. "Plans change." Her accent softened the words, but the intent was hard as stone. She left the towel folded with surgical precision before walking out.

I looked up, but she was already gone.

The clock over the pantry ticked too loudly. I reached for it, stopped halfway. No point silencing something honest.

Boots hit the tile behind me. Rafa. "Jefe, you got a minute?"

"What broke?"

"The gutter on the north roof froze again. I can't get the pipe to drain."

"It'll be worse by morning," I said, already grabbing my gloves and reaching for my coat.

"Thought you'd say that."

The air outside hit like a warning. The world was colorless—just wind and white. The cold had weight to it, the kind that burned instead of bit. My breath turned to vapor, curling away before I could finish a thought. Metal groaned somewhere above us, an old hinge complaining to the gust.

We set the ladder and climbed into the kind of cold that gets into your teeth. Rafa went first, muttering about bad timing. I followed, wrench clipped to my belt, mind nowhere near the roof. I was still seeing Emme at the table, her hair caught by firelight, that tiny line between her brows when she's deciding what to type next.

"Careful," Rafa said. "It's slick."

"I've got it."

Another lie. I didn't have anything under control except a list of excuses to keep her here. If the contract wasn't settled, she couldn't leave. A pathetic logic, but it had teeth.

I crouched by the pipe, set the wrench, and twisted. The metal screamed, sharp enough to make my teeth ache. Ice cracked but didn't give.

Rafa steadied the ladder, watching. "Careful, jefe," Rafa called. "Roof's slicker than it looks."

"I've got it."

"Sure you do." The sarcasm was mild, but his grip on the ladder tightened anyway.

The wrench slipped. Once. Twice. I swore under my breath, tried again, too rough.

"Easy, jefe," Rafa warned. "You'll strip the valve." His breath fogged in the air, the wrench biting against the joint. "You want me to finish it?" he asked. "Or you still proving something?"

I eased off, jaw tight. My gloves were slick, and the sound of her laugh kept cutting through the wind. Her smile. It shouldn't have hit the way it did, but it lived somewhere under my ribs now, refusing to leave.

Rafa exhaled, long and slow. "Let me swap with you."

"No. I've got the angle, I said. "Just keep the ladder steady."

Snow shifted under my boots. I adjusted, leaned farther out. The wrench slipped first. Then my footing. The sound tore through the wind—metal against metal, boots scraping for purchase, the hollow thud of snow giving way. The world tilted.

For a heartbeat, nothing existed except the sound of wind and the shock of weightlessness. Then the ground came up fast.

The landing wasn't loud; it was internal—a crack that traveled up my leg and turned the air metallic. The taste of iron hit my tongue. Snow filled my collar, melted fast against the heat of my skin. Somewhere close, the ladder rattled, then went still.

"Luc!" Rafa's voice broke through the ringing in my ears.

I tried to sit. Bad idea. The pain wasn't sharp; it was *bright*, blooming from my ankle to my teeth.

"I'm fine," I lied.

Rafa jumped down beside me. "Don't move."

"Trust me, I'm not going anywhere," I said.

He peeled back my pant leg. Pulled off my boot. His hiss told me enough. "Broken, jefe."

Snowflakes landed on my glove and melted instantly. Fragile things never lasted long out here.

Juliana's shout carried from the doorway. She reached us fast, coat half-zipped, eyes wide. "What happened?"

"Roof bit back," Rafa said.

"Ambulancia?"

"Hospital's closer," I managed. The words came thin through clenched teeth.

Rafa nodded and sprinted for the truck. Juliana helped me upright, her grip stronger than her frame suggested. Every step was a small explosion.

Then a voice behind her—steady, cutting through the cold.

"I'm coming."

Emme.

My coat over her shoulders, her own boots, hair loose, cheeks flushed from the wind.

"You don't have to," I said.

"Yes," she said. "I do."

No arguing with that tone.

"Juliana, I need my wallet."

She was already moving—snatched it from the counter, grabbed a blanket and pillow from the back of the couch, and tossed them to Emme. Then she looped a towel around her arm. "For the ankle."

Emme grabbed what she needed.

"I'm phoning ahead," Juliana said, already dialing. "You need to get your head checked too."

Head, pride, priorities—take your pick.

Wind slipped through the open door, carrying the smell of snow and woodsmoke. Emme dropped to her knees beside me, steady hands, steady breath.

Rafa slid the truck to the edge of the path, door already open. Juliana braced my shoulder while I climbed into the back seat, swearing through my teeth. Emme followed without being asked. I leaned against the door while she slid a pillow beneath my ankle, steadying it on her lap, then pulled the blanket over me. She snapped her seat belt hard, all business.

The commotion must've carried—Harper and Finn ran out onto the porch, jackets half-zipped, concern written all over their faces.

"Everything okay?"

"Todo bien," Juliana said, which was a lie and everyone knew it.

Finn held the door to keep it from swinging in the wind. Harper offered to grab a thermos like that would help.

Rafa gunned the engine. Snow kicked up behind us as the truck lurched forward.

"Drive fast," Emme told Rafa.

He did.

Snow whipped across the windshield in horizontal streaks. The tires fishtailed once before catching. The pain was steady now, a rhythm I could measure against the engine.

Emme's hand found mine. "Breathe," she said.

"I am."

"Liar."

Her thumb moved once across my knuckles. I didn't realize I was shaking until she stilled it.

"Tell me how bad," she said.

"Bad enough."

"On a scale of one to you-trying-to-hide-it?"

I almost smiled. "Somewhere around 'don't tell the guests.'"

"Too late." She rolled her eyes. "You're supposed to be the careful one."

"Guess I'm learning balance."

"That's one way to call it."

Rafa glanced back. "We'll make it in thirty. Roads are slick."

"Fine," I said, though my vision was starting to gray at the edges.

Emme saw it. "Hey. Reste avec moi, Luc." *Stay with me.*

"I'm here."

"You better be. I'm not letting you die in a pickup truck. Too cliché."

That earned a laugh that turned into a groan. "Noted."

Silence stretched between us, filled only by wind and the low grind of tires. She didn't let go of my hand. I didn't ask her to.

Outside, the landscape blurred into white on white. Inside, it was heat from the vents and the scent of her shampoo—something clean and sharp that cut through the antiseptic smell of fear.

"I'm not finished with the contract," she said suddenly.

I turned my head. "You should be."

"Maybe I want one more day to double-check the clauses."

My pulse hitched. "That so?"

"Depends," she said. "You planning to add any mysterious new terms while I'm distracted?"

"Could be."

Her smile cracked through the worry. "Then I'll need to stay close to supervise."

Before I could answer, a jolt of pain shot through my leg, stealing breath. She tightened her grip again. "Almost there," she whispered.

Through the windshield, the first hospital lights bled into the snow—small, steady, impossibly far. Rafa down-shifted, the truck growling as it fought the hill.

Emme leaned closer. "Ça va aller." *You'll be okay.*

I wanted to believe her. I wanted to believe the part where she stayed close.

Snow hammered the glass harder, like it was trying to erase the road entirely. We climbed the last turn; the lights grew brighter, the edges of the building sharp against the white. Rafa swore softly in Spanish, easing the truck into the lot.

Emme turned to me, her voice low. "Don't move until they tell you to."

"Wasn't planning to tango," I said again, though it came out thin.

"We tangoed just fine a few hours ago." She winked, but the light didn't quite reach her eyes.

Her thumb brushed my cheek—checking for color, or proof I was still here. "You scare the hell out of me," she whispered.

"Join the club."

The tires crunched to a stop. The hospital doors slid open ahead of us, throwing a rectangle of sterile light into the cab. Everything beyond it smelled like disinfectant and inevitability.

Rafa cut the engine. "¿Listo?"

Emme reached for the door handle, already halfway out into the snow. "Ready," she answered. Then to me: "Don't go anywhere."

"Wasn't planning to," I murmured, but she was gone before the joke landed.

The cold rushed in through the open door, sharp enough to make me gasp.

Juliana's voice echoed in my head—*Plans change.*

The doors ahead of us waited, bright and unflinching. I had no idea which plan would survive the night.

Chapter 19

Clause Thirteen

EMME

T HE HOSPITAL SMELLED LIKE bleach and lemon peel, bright and endless under flickering lights. Rafa was left behind at the admissions desk, murmuring Spanish to a woman with a keyboard older than both of us, while I trailed Luc's gurney through the automatic doors.

A nurse tried to stop me. "Family only."

Luc's voice was quiet but carved from iron. "She's family."

Her brows lifted. I felt the heat crawl up my neck, but she waved me through. "Two minutes."

The hallway swallowed us—machines hissing, phones ringing, the faint static of snow against the windows.

Luc's jaw was locked tight, his knuckles white around the blanket edge.

"You're good at sounding like an authority," I said.

He winced when the gurney bumped. "I am an authority. On bad ideas."

"Then you're overqualified for this."

He huffed something that could've been a laugh, and for one second it loosened the grip the night had on my chest.

The nurse parked him in a curtained bay, asked questions in rapid Spanish. My Spanish was decent, not perfect, but panic improved fluency. I answered for him until the nurse raised a brow at our back-and-forth.

"You two sound like newlyweds," she said.

Luc and I said, in perfect unison, "We're not."

Her grin said she didn't believe either of us.

When she left, I adjusted his blanket. "You could've corrected her."

"I tried once." His smile was lazy, faint. "Didn't take."

"You mean with me or with marriage?"

"Both."

I shook my head, pretending the blush was from the hospital heat. "You need to stay still."

"I need a new contract," he said. "Clause twelve: Wilder Horizons provides one Emme for risk management."

"Clause twelve-B," I countered, "said Emme is not responsible for consequences of idiotic French behavior."

"Clause twelve-C: Emme provides physical therapy."

"Clause twelve-D: No shower supervision."

"Denied," he said solemnly. "Shower supervision ensures full recovery."

I pressed my lips together, half to hide a laugh, half to breathe. "You're insufferable."

"Optimistic."

"Sedated."

He turned his head toward me. "Not yet."

The curtain stirred with a gust of antiseptic air. Another nurse slipped in, frowning at the monitor, then at the two of us. "Vitals," she said, pretending not to notice our joined hands.

When she left, Luc exhaled. "She likes me."

I glared at him. "You're impossible."

"Jealous?"

Maybe. The thought flashed so fast it startled me. I ignored it and focused on the rhythm of his breathing instead.

Minutes later the doctor came, X-rays in hand, all polite gravity. *Fracture. Immediate surgery.*

The words dropped through me like ice water. Luc went very still.

"They'll prep you right away," he said, translating. "It's a clean break. You'll be fine."

Luc looked at me, not the doctor. "Stay until it's done?"

"As long as it takes."

He caught my wrist again, thumb brushing the inside of my pulse. "Clause thirteen," he murmured. "You stay."

"I'll bill you for overtime."

"Worth it."

The orderly appeared; she had to pry his fingers from mine. I watched them wheel him away, the green curtain swinging back and forth until it stopped moving, and then I couldn't seem to breathe.

Rafa leaned back in the plastic chair, arms folded, gaze steady. "If anyone can argue a bone into healing faster, it's Luc."

A short, shaky laugh escaped me. "You're not wrong."

He gave a small nod, the kind that carried more weight than words. "He listens to you. That's good. Not many people get through."

The truth of it snagged something low in my chest. I swallowed. "I need to message my sisters."

Silence settled between us, broken only by the hum of the vending machine and the faint squeak of a gurney down the hall. My phone felt slippery in my hand. I typed out the group chat before I could think too hard about it.

Wildlings Chat

ME: Quick update. Luc's in surgery. Broken ankle, nothing worse. I'm staying a few days to help.

SUMMER: Are *you* okay? What happened?

ME: Fell off the roof.

JULIETTE: *He* fell off the roof, I hope?

BRYNN: Juliette.

JULIETTE: You know what I mean.

ME: Correct. He fell off, not me. I was finalizing the contract.

JULIETTE: That's a relief. When are you coming home?

ME: TBD. Depends on how soon they let him hobble.

SUMMER: Contract signed.

RAYANN: Sympathy, Summer.

BRYNN: Don't marry him on morphine.

SUMMER: What does that mean? Is there something I need to know?

BRYNN: He's hot, I'd fuck him at least.

EMME: Oh my God

ANNIE: But if you do, livestream. I'll handle the playlist and vows.

BRYNN: They have subscriptions for that.

RAYANN: Brynn!

ME: Monsters. I love you.

ANNIE: Love you too. Keep him away from ladders. Or roofs. Or gravity.

I laughed out loud, and Rafa's mouth twitched while he murmured updates to Juliana.

When I ended the chat, the screen glow faded, leaving only the glass doors and the snow beyond—soft edges, gray light, everything turned to watercolor. I told myself the ache in my chest was just exhaustion.

Hours later, the recovery nurse let me back. Luc was pale but breathing evenly, his left leg wrapped in white plaster, his lashes dark against the pillow. Machines blinked slow and steady.

I sat beside him, took his hand, tracing the ridge of his knuckles.

He stirred. "You stayed."

"I signed the supervision clause."

His mouth curved. "Shower?"

"Tomorrow we renegotiate terms."

It was nearly two in the morning when Rafa pulled the truck up to the lodge. Snow glittered under the headlights, thick and soundless. Juliana met us at the door, hair twisted up, robe over her flannel pajamas.

"Todo bien?"

"Cirugía exitosa," Rafa said. *Successful surgery.*

Juliana touched Luc's arm. "I'll stay as long as needed. Guests are asleep."

Between the three of us, we got him upstairs—slow, careful, graceless. His room was still warm from the woodstove Juliana banked earlier. I peeled back the covers while she adjusted pillows.

When he finally sank onto the bed, I tucked the blanket around his cast. "Comfortable?"

He cracked one eye. "Clause eighteen: nightly audit of pain levels."

"Clause nineteen," I said, smoothing the sheet. "Penalties for noncompliance."

His grin was small but real. "What kind of penalties?"

"Creative."

Rafa lingered in the doorway. "I'll be back early."

"Gracias," I said.

Juliana closed the door behind them, and the silence felt enormous. Outside, the wind picked at the eaves.

Luc reached for my hand again. "You should sleep."

"I will." I climbed onto the bed beside him, careful of the cast, and rested my head on his shoulder. His skin smelled like soap and antiseptic, underneath it the faint cedar of his jacket.

He exhaled slowly, heartbeat steady under my ear. "Juliana isn't going to help me in the shower."

"Thank God," I murmured, and felt him smile against my hair before sleep pulled me under again.

I woke to the sound of wind howling through the chimney. The room was gray with dawn. The fire had burned to embers, and the cold had teeth again. Luc was propped on one elbow, phone in hand, expression sharp.

"What's wrong?"

He didn't answer right away. The light from the screen made his eyes look almost silver.

"Storm system. It's shifting," he said finally. "It's worse than the forecast. They've issued blizzard warnings for the entire region."

I pushed upright, heart kicking. "How bad?"

"Roads will close by midday. Maybe sooner." He glanced at me. "Your flight—"

"Already canceled," I said.

He blinked. "You what?"

"I called last night."

"Why?"

"Clause thirteen," I said softly. "I stay."

The wind slammed against the window hard enough to rattle the glass. Somewhere below, a door banged open. The first flakes spiraled sideways, thick and fast, erasing the mountains beyond the lodge.

Luc looked at me, jaw tightening, every bit the man who watched the weather like scripture.

"We're not going anywhere," he said.

Outside, the world disappeared in white.

Chapter 20

Stillness, Redefined

LUC

THE WIND STARTED BEFORE dawn, a low hum in the rafters like a throat clearing before a storm. A faint metallic rattle trembled through the roof, the sound a lodge makes when cold bites deep into the nails holding it together. I woke to it, air sharp enough to taste, ankle stiff as hell beneath the blanket. The room was a cold blue, snow plastered to the glass until the world looked half-erased.

Beside me, Emme still slept, one arm curved over her head, hair spilling across the pillow.

Mon Dieu... so damn beautiful.

I brushed her cheek, then reached for my phone on the nightstand. The signal wavered, then steadied long enough to show a red band crawling across the radar.

Blizzard warning. Moving fast.

Putain, c'est grave.

The floorboards creaked under the first step I dared take.

She stirred. "What time is it?"

"Too early," I said. "And too late to outrun what's coming."

She pushed up on an elbow, eyes narrowing as I turned the screen toward her. "That wasn't in yesterday's forecast."

Outside, the wind thickened into a low howl. Then—two quick knocks below, muffled by distance, followed by voices and the thud of boots. Rafa.

"He made it up early," I said.

Emme was already pulling on her sweater, hair falling loose as she moved. "I'll go down. Need help before I sit your ass back down off that ankle?"

Autoritaire. Merde, pourquoi ça me plaît autant?

Bossy. Damn, why do I like that so much?

After she steadied me to and from the bathroom, I told myself I'd stay put. That lasted maybe thirty seconds.

The sounds from below—boots stomping, laughter, the low rumble of Rafa's voice—itched under my skin. I had guests, a lodge, a job to do. I wasn't about to let someone else shoulder it while I hid upstairs.

I found my flannel pants, pulled on the nearest thermal, and braced on the crutch. The first step sent a lightning bolt up my leg. The second one hurt worse. By the third, the pain had blended into rhythm—thump, curse, thump—until I reached the landing. The bannister was colder than it should've been—chill seeping through the wood as if the storm had already found the grain.

The smell of coffee and toasted bread hit first. Juliana was already there, moving easily around the kitchen—hair pinned back, sleeves rolled. She must've been up since dawn, setting out soft cheese, jam, and the honey Rafa left on last week's run. Guests hadn't come down yet, but the place already smelled like comfort. The bread still carried the warmth of the basket, a faint yeasty sweetness that cut through the cold edge of the room.

Then the door opened again and wind followed Rafa inside—white flakes, wet boots, a breath of cold. He stamped the snow off and set down two crates.

"Necessities," he said, shaking off his gloves. "Gas canisters, first aid restock, bread, candles—and more tape for Luc's ankle he's pretending doesn't hurt." He looked up then, taking in the crutch under my arm. "Good timing."

"Appreciate it," I said. "Check the generator before you leave—it's been coughing."

"Already on it."

Juliana slid a mug toward him. "Coffee first."

Emme was there too, sleeves pushed up, helping him unpack. She checked expiration dates, sorted tins, lined up what needed inventorying. Efficient as hell.

Then she looked up and saw me. "Luc Moreau! What did I say about staying upstairs?"

"That I wouldn't," I said, gripping the banister.

Rafa huffed a laugh. "Stubborn as ever."

"Temporarily," I said.

Juliana rolled her eyes and pointed toward the nearest chair. "For the next forty-eight hours, you're grounded. Doctor's orders. Mine."

Emme crossed the room and gestured to the seat. "Sit. Before I find rope."

I leaned in close. "*Tu es coquine, toi.*" A little kinky, aren't you?

Death glare.

I lowered myself carefully, trying not to wince. Rafa produced a carved wooden cane from under his arm—sleek, hand-burnished, the handle shaped like a condor's head.

"From Bariloche," he said, pride in his voice. "Figured you'd need something with personality."

Emme took it before I could. "Perfect. It'll look great mounted on the wall after he breaks the other ankle."

I grinned up at her. "*Dominante.*"

"What was that?" The look she gave me could've peeled paint. Worth it.

"Nothing you'd disagree with," I said.

Juliana glanced toward the stairs as footsteps sounded—first one guest, then another. They arrived in pairs, drawn by the smell of breakfast and the low hum of voices. Relief crossed their faces when they saw me upright, if only in a chair.

Zoë came first, wrapped in an oversized blanket. "So the rumors were true," she said, grinning. "Owner down, storm incoming—this trip just got even more interesting."

"Glad I could provide material," I said.

Behind her, Harper and Finn appeared—Harper perfectly put-together even in wool socks, camera already in hand, and Finn wearing his sweatshirt inside out, gripping the gimbal-mounted camera he never seemed to put down.

"Morning," Harper said, giving the bandage a once-over. "Juliana said that ankle went through major surgery. You're either made of steel or still high on painkillers."

"Try telling him that," Emme said.

Finn tilted the lens toward me. "You want us to film the rehab montage or wait until you can limp more heroically?"

"Wait," I said. "Give it another twenty minutes."

Nico was the last to join, hair damp, eyes softer than usual. The man moved like someone who'd slept well and sinned better. Zoë looked up, caught his eye, and immediately found her coffee fascinating.

I leaned toward Emme. "He got laid."

Her head snapped toward me. "Luc."

"I'm injured, not blind."

Her lips twitched. "Behave."

"I'm sitting. That's halfway there."

Zoë poured coffee, her camera already clicking toward the windows. "If the light holds, I might actually get a storm shot worth publishing."

"Call it *Man Down in Patagonia*," Finn said, waving his hand like a director pitching a scene. "A survival story featuring one injured host, a world-class snack spread, and four women who make crisis management look hot."

Harper smacked his shoulder. "Ignore him, he's delirious."

"Too late," I said. "I think he's branding it."

Juliana set out plates—toast, soft cheese, and honey—and the group clustered near the stove. Outside, the wind was starting to lift snow sideways, a white curtain smudging out the trees.

Harper's curiosity finally broke. "What did they have to do to fix it?"

"Plate and four screws," I said. "Simple fix."

Finn whistled. "Four screws? That's two more than the GoPro mount on my drone."

Harper rolled her eyes. "He's been comparing everything to drone parts lately."

"It's called *re-la-ta-bil-i-ty*," Finn said, chopping the air with mock seriousness. "Hashtag human connection."

Nico poured himself coffee, unfazed. "I take it we're about to be buried for a while."

"Not unless someone wants to help me shovel out," I said.

Emme didn't look up from the kettle. "You. Not happening."

She moved through the kitchen with that quiet efficiency that made everyone else unconsciously match her
rhythm—checking mugs, stacking plates, collecting the
supplies Rafa had brought.

"Generator's steady," Rafa said. "Propane full."

"Pantry's fine for a week," Juliana added.

"Good," I said. "Let's keep it that way. Last thing we
need is anyone deciding to ski out for snacks."

Finn raised his hand. "Define snacks."

"Anything not nailed down," Emme said without
missing a beat.

Laughter circled the room, soft and fleeting. Outside,
the wind had picked up a pitch that set the windows
humming. Rafa and Juliana exchanged a look—one Luc
had learned to recognize.

"Go," I said. "Road'll be worse in another hour."

Rafa hesitated. "You sure?"

"Positive. We're stocked. Generator's fine. Guests are
in good hands." I nodded toward Emme, who didn't
glance up but gave the faintest smile.

Juliana squeezed my shoulder on her way past. "You're
lucky I like you, Moreau. Next time, stay off roofs."

"I'll put it in writing," I said.

The guests called out thanks as she gathered her coat
and scarf. Harper told her she should open her own

lodge; Zoë agreed, calling her the heart of the place. Juliana just laughed, brushing off the praise like snow from her sleeves.

"Gracias, but he built the heart of this place long before I arrived," she said, eyes flicking to me just long enough for the words to land.

Rafa and Juliana disappeared into the white, their figures swallowed by wind.

By noon, the light had gone flat, a white so complete it erased the horizon. The generator coughed, held steady, then stuttered again.

The power blinked, came back, blinked again. A low boom rolled through the valley—snow shifting somewhere high, the kind of sound that settles in your ribs before it reaches your ears. Then everything died—the lights, the hum, the steady heartbeat of the place. The silence that followed was total.

For a beat, no one breathed. Then the wind hit the walls, a deep, low groan that reminded us the mountain was still out there.

Nico was the first to speak. "What can we do to help?"

"Keep warm," I said automatically, then caught the look on his face—steady, serious. The others were watching too. These weren't people who wanted to sit idle.

"All right," I said, shifting forward. "We've got back-up heat from the fireplaces and the kitchen stoves. The great room's the warmest—it'll hold most of the heat once we get a few fires going. Emme, take the kitchen. You'll need a steady burn for cooking."

She nodded, already moving toward the pantry.

I pointed to Nico. "You and Finn—firewood. There's a stack under the eaves on the north wall. Bring in as much as you can before it ices over."

Finn gave a mock salute. "Roger that, Captain Crutch."

"Zoë," I said. "You're good with details. Books, games, anything from the cabinets. Keep people occupied."

She smiled. "Distraction duty. Got it."

Harper was already pulling candles from the drawer. "We'll get these around the room—less tripping, more ambiance."

The generator tried to kick back once, coughed, and died again. Emme glanced up from the counter, lantern light catching the curve of her cheek. Calm. Grounded. "We'll make it work," she said, and somehow everyone believed her.

The air grew softer as the first flames caught—wood crackling, light flickering across the stone. Heat rose fast in this place; the lofts and upper rooms would stay tolerable so long as we kept the great room fire burning. My room had its own fireplace; the others didn't, but the venting system I'd built would carry enough warmth through the floors to keep anyone from freezing.

"See?" I said as Finn and Nico came back in, arms full of wood. "Not our first storm."

"Yeah," Finn said, dumping the logs with a grin. "But probably our best view."

I tried to get up, but my body had other plans. Pain pulsed in my ankle like a second heartbeat.

"Sit," Emme said, appearing beside me with a candle in hand. "You're no good to anyone limping into walls."

I wanted to argue, but her tone made refusal feel childish.

She crouched, adjusted the pillow beneath my leg, and looked up. "Better?"

"Yes." I watched her tuck stray hair behind her ear, fingers quick and steady. "You've done this before."

"Crisis management?" she asked. "Family specialty."

The candlelight trembled between us, throwing gold across her throat. "Careful, *ma belle*," I said softly. "You keep taking care of me like this, and I'll have to find a way to return the favor. Properly this time."

Chapter 21

Pressure Systems

EMME

B Y LATE AFTERNOON, THE storm had swallowed
the world whole. Wind screamed down the chimney; snow clawed at the windows. The fire hissed and
roared in turns, the air thick with resin and smoke.

I moved through the great room on instinct—redistributing blankets, securing shutters, setting candles
where their glow could hold the edges of the storm at
bay. Every small act steadied me. The rhythm of care.
The ritual of control.

Finn cracked jokes while pretending not to shiver.
Harper filmed everything until her battery died. Zoë and
Nico flirted so loudly over instant soup packets that even
the storm paused to eavesdrop.

Luc sat in the corner of the couch, ankle bound, shoulders braced like he was fighting an invisible tide. Watching him watch me did something strange to my pulse. He looked equal parts exhausted and dangerous—like a man trying to wrestle calm out of chaos—until his eyes drifted shut.

When everyone wandered toward the kitchen, I stayed back. Someone had to mind the fire, and I didn't mind the silence.

Laughter carried from the next room—Zoë, Finn, Harper, and Nico arguing good-naturedly over a board game near the wood stove. Dice clattered, mugs clinked, the sound of people determined to out-shout the storm.

After a while, I slipped into the kitchen, refilled the kettle, and brewed two mugs of tea. No one noticed; they were too busy accusing Finn of cheating. I slipped back into the great room, the warmth of the cups seeping into my palms.

He stirred as I approached—the soft rasp of wool, a low breath through his nose.

"Tea," I said, setting the mug beside him. "If you're pretending to sleep, at least do it hydrated."

His eyes opened, that small, crooked smile finding me. "You run a dictatorship."

"A benevolent one." I folded onto the rug across from him, candle between us. Firelight flickered up the planes of his face—cheekbone, jaw, the scar at his temple that looked older than the mountains outside.

For a while, we didn't speak. The storm handled the conversation: wind in the rafters, snow hissing against glass. I liked the sound of it—nature reminding us who was in charge.

Then he said softly, "Tell me about Paris."

I should have expected it. My comfort with the language always gives me away eventually. But the question landed deeper than it should have.

"You assume I was in Paris," I said.

"Your French is too good for anywhere else."

I smiled. "A year there. Internship with Maison Delaurier—interior architecture and spatial design. All white walls and impossible expectations. The creative director liked to say minimalism is what's left after you've stripped away everything that makes you comfortable."

He chuckled low. "I know of them. Sounds... pleasant."

"It was hell." I smiled despite myself. "But the beautiful kind. Paris taught me precision. I learned how to draw silence into a space, how to make a room feel like it's breathing. Every line mattered."

The memory unfolded easily now: narrow streets slick with rain, coffee so bitter it tasted like ambition, the metallic smell of the Seine at dawn. "I shared an apartment with two other interns. We lived off croissants we couldn't afford and heat we never turned on. I thought if I worked hard enough, I could build a life there."

He watched me like he could see the reflection of that city flickering behind my eyes. "What made you leave?"

I hesitated, caught by the familiarity in his tone. "You miss it," I said.

"Sometimes," he admitted. "I worked there for years, but I never really belonged to it. I grew up just outside the city—in a small town where everything closes by eight and everyone knows your name."

Something in his voice softened the space between us. "That's not so different from where I grew up," I said, smiling faintly. "Except mine came with humidity and mosquitoes instead of baguettes."

He laughed quietly, the sound low and warm. "We might have crossed paths, you know. You, chasing design deadlines; me, chasing permits and clients. Same city. Different dreams."

"Maybe," I said, smiling a little. "I loved it there. But life had other plans. My dad got sick."

The words came out thinner than I meant. "Cancer. I flew home, but not soon enough to stop feeling like I was too late." I exhaled, steam curling into the candlelight. "After that, the company became ours—me and my sisters. Wilder Horizons wasn't supposed to be forever for me, but it was something to hold onto when everything else fell apart."

Luc's expression softened. "He'd be proud."

"Maybe." I met his gaze. "Or worried."

His voice gentled. "You built something from loss. That's not easy."

I looked into the fire. "Neither is staying still."

He was quiet for a long moment, gaze fixed on the flames. "The lodge was that for me," he said finally. "After my brother died, I needed to make something that lasted. Something that didn't disappear when he did."

The words landed between us—unpolished, raw.

He shifted, wincing slightly, and I wanted to reach out without making it pity. Maybe that's what drew me to him from the start: the restraint under his control. A man who knew the cost of composure.

"You've been married," I said quietly.

He nodded once. "Two years. We were young. Thought we'd figured out the world."

"And?"

"The world had other opinions."

I smiled without humor. "It usually does."

He looked at me like he could see past the practiced calm. "You sound like someone who's been through her share of opinions."

"Maybe," I said. "Maybe I just stopped asking for them."

Something flickered between us—recognition, maybe, or the relief of not needing to explain every scar.

"Your sisters?" he asked after a moment.

"We all had lives—or at least plans—before Dad died," I said, turning the mug in my hands. "None of us really pictured running the company. Summer's the oldest. She was engaged back then. He hated Florida, couldn't wait to leave. She let him go instead—traded the life she wanted for our father's dream. For us."

He studied me over the rim of his mug. "You gave up your dream too."

"Yes," I said. "But no. I don't feel resentment the way I probably should. I loved Paris, but I love what I do now. It's different, but it feels like mine."

"The others?"

"Juliette was always the business mind—sharp, fearless, already running board meetings in her head by the time she was ten. She's our CEO now. Brynn and Rayann—identical twins, my favorite kind of trouble. When I was little, I used to pretend we were triplets even though they'd already had their own little universe. And Annie's the baby. Sweet. Less jaded, maybe. Our mom died giving birth to her."

I stared into the fire. "She carries that absence like an invisible inheritance. Not guilt exactly... more like a shadow she keeps trying to walk out of."

The fire sank to coals. I reached to feed it, wax spilling from the candle's rim. Light caught in his hair and painted everything softer.

"You should rest," I said.

"So should you."

"If I stop moving, I'll hear the wind."

"Maybe that's the point."

I turned toward him, heat rising from the hearth and somewhere lower too. "You always this philosophical on painkillers?"

"Only around you."

My laugh caught halfway between amusement and ache.

When our eyes met, something in the air stilled. He sat back on the sofa, ankle stretched toward the fire, one arm draped over the cushion like he hadn't moved in hours. The storm outside roared against the windows, but the sound barely reached us.

I found myself watching the way the light traced his throat, the way his breath slowed when mine did. The space between us wasn't far, but it felt loaded—like the room remembered what already happened between us, and neither of us dared speak it aloud.

He leaned forward again, forearms braced on his knees, eyes steady on mine. The fire threw our shadows together on the floor.

"Come here," he whispered.

The words shouldn't have undone me, but they did. My pulse caught, a flutter low in my throat. I rose onto my knees, the rug soft under my shins, my palms braced on his thighs for balance. Every breath between us turned into invitation.

He caught my other hand, our pulses syncing in that fragile space where wanting turns dangerous. His fingers slid into my hair, tilting my face toward his.

The first kiss tested ground. The second surrendered it.

The house around us faded.

From the kitchen came bursts of laughter and the clatter of dice—Zoë, Finn, Harper, and Nico deep in some fierce board-game standoff near the wood stove. Their voices rose and fell with each dramatic play.

That sound—normal, ordinary—wrapped the lodge in a sense of safety. Life still happening just out of sight.

Beyond that small circle of light and noise, the world narrowed to firelight and breath. To him.

Luc's hand found my waist, pulling me closer until I was half-balanced against his knees. Then he lifted, guiding me easily into his lap.

The blanket slipped from the back of the couch. He caught it, wrapped it around us both, his palm settling at the small of my back.

He smelled of cedar. Flannel. Firelight.

His body was warm against the cold pressing through the walls.

The kiss deepened—not a rush, but a slow pull that gathered strength the longer it lasted. His hand slid up to the nape of my neck, thumb tracing the place just below my ear.

Not possession.

Something quieter. More dangerous.

I melted into him, one hand braced on the cushion beside his hip, the other pressed against his chest. His heartbeat thudded hard and steady beneath my palm, a wild rhythm that matched my own.

God, this man.

He groaned, low in his throat, and the sound went straight through me. His tongue traced the edge of my mouth, and I opened for him before I could think better of it.

My fingers fisted in his shirt.

I wanted closer. To climb fully into his lap. To forget everything but the heat of him.

But the bulky cast on his ankle mocked me. A ridiculous, infuriating reminder that reality still existed.

A small sound escaped my throat—half laugh, half plea.

He understood. His eyes found mine, dark and glassy with want.

"I know," he said, voice roughened by restraint. "Believe me, I know."

His gaze dropped to my mouth. Then lower.

He didn't pull me onto his injured leg. Instead, his hand slid from my neck down my arm, leaving a line of heat that made breathing feel optional.

His fingers brushed the hem of my sweater.

Don't stop.

He shifted, tugging the blanket up and around us until it formed a cocoon of soft wool and shadow. His hand moved beneath, fingertips tracing slow, burning circles against bare skin.

The fire snapped. I drew in a breath that broke halfway, my body arching to chase his touch. The cuff of his flannel brushed my ribs each time he moved, a reminder that the world still existed outside the small, secret space he'd made of us.

"Dis-moi... c'est bien?" he murmured against my throat, voice gravel and heat. *Tell me... does that feel good?*

His palm flattened over my stomach, moving lower, the heel of his hand pressing where want had already started to ache.

My pulse thudded in my ears. The storm outside might as well have been another planet. Every shift of his fingers felt like a question I was answering without words.

His fingers didn't fumble. They were sure and knowing, this touch a confident echo of the kiss we'd just shared. The pad of his middle finger stroked over the silk of my panties, a slow, maddening circle that mapped the damp heat already blooming there. The fabric was a flimsy barrier, and I bucked against his hand, a silent, desperate plea.

A low, approving sound rumbled in his chest. "I know," he breathed again, as if reading the frantic script of my nerves.

He hooked a single finger under the elastic edge and tugged, the delicate silk yielding with a soft whisper. Then, his hand was on me, skin to skin, and the contact was so electric, so shockingly intimate, that I had to bury my face in the crook of his neck to stifle a moan.

His palm stayed firm against me, heat steady, grounding.

No rush. No hurry.

Something slower.

More devastating.

Every motion felt intentional, like he was learning me by touch alone.

For once, I wasn't the one in control. Every decision in my life had been deliberate—measured.

But this? This was surrender. And somehow it didn't feel like losing.

His middle finger slid through my slickness, gathering the evidence of my want, painting it back onto my skin in a slow, deliberate glide. He traced my opening, circling, teasing, learning the shape and rhythm of my need without ever quite giving me the pressure I craved.

"You're so ready for me," he whispered, his voice thick with an awe that was more arousing than any dirty talk. His thumb found my clit, applying a perfect, circling pressure that made my thighs clamp around his leg.

Even now, he was careful—measured.

He built things for a living, but the way he touched me felt like preservation, not construction. As if breaking me would ruin him too.

Then, finally—*for the love of all things holy*—he pushed inside.

It wasn't a thrust, but a slow, inexorable filling. One thick finger, sinking into me, stretching just enough to make me gasp. He held it there, buried to the knuckle, letting me feel the fullness, the intimate possession. My inner muscles fluttered around him, a helpless, involuntary response that drew a ragged groan from him.

"*Putain,*" he gritted out, his forehead dropping to my shoulder.

He began to move, a lazy, deep rhythm that was all about the sensation of being filled and emptied. His thumb never stopped its gentle, persistent circles on my clit, the dual stimulation building a coil of pleasure so tight, so intense, I thought I might shatter. Every stroke was a promise, every retreat a torment. The soft fabric of his pants brushed my inner thigh, a gentle contrast to the slick, deliberate slide of his touch.

"Tu me rends folle." *You drive me crazy.*

My breathing became a series of ragged pants against his neck. I could feel the sweat-slicked skin of his throat under my lips, the pounding of his pulse a wild drum-beat against my tongue. The world had narrowed to this: the hidden, deliberate motion under the blanket, the scent of our shared arousal, the ragged sound of our breathing.

"Look at me," he commanded, his voice a husky whisper.

I forced my eyes open, meeting his darkened gaze. The intensity there, the raw, unfiltered hunger, was my undoing. His finger curled inside me, finding a spot that made me see stars, and his thumb pressed down just so.

Mother of God don't stop.

I'd been touched before, wanted before—but never like this.

He wasn't trying to take; he was trying to know. And that was somehow far more dangerous.

The climax ripped through me, silent and seismic. My body locked around his hand, a wave of pleasure so over-whelming it stole my breath and my sight. I trembled against him, my cry a silent, open-mouthed gasp against his skin as he worked me through it, his movements gentling until the last shiver subsided.

Slowly, carefully, he withdrew his hand. His gaze held mine as he brought his fingers to his mouth and, without looking away, tasted me.

Sweet fuck, this man was sinful.

And God help me, I already knew I'd want him again—not for the heat, but for the quiet that came after it.

After that, everything softened—the fire, the air, the edges of the room. The tension drained from my body until the world narrowed to firelight and the weight of his arm around me. Outside, the storm kept testing the walls. Inside, something far more dangerous had already found a way in.

Chapter 22

Worth Every Fracture

LUC

THE FIRST THING I felt was weight.

Not pain. Not the dull throb of my ankle. Her. Emme lay against me, her back tucked into my chest, hair tangled against my throat. Morning pressed the house into a silence I'd almost forgotten—no generator hum, no crackle from the fire, only the slow rhythm of her breathing against my ribs.

We'd made it upstairs somehow. I remembered the meal—soup, wine, the flicker of candles when the power still refused to return—and then her hand on my arm as

I'd leaned on the railing. After that, warmth and exhaustion.

And, admittedly, a generous dose of pain meds.

She shifted in her sleep, a small, unconscious motion that stirred heat where restraint should have lived.

I should have moved—checked on the guests, done something that looked like control—but I didn't.

Instead, I watched a lock of her hair rise and fall with my breath.

C'est dangereux, whispered the part of me that still knew how to build walls. But the rest of me—what she'd touched last night—stayed very, very still.

When she finally blinked awake, she smiled like the world hadn't ended, and whispered, "Power's still out?"

"Of course it is," I said, my voice rough. "Patagonia's idea of humor."

She sat up, hair a mess, eyes bright. "We could try the stove again. Or—"

Her gaze fell to my ankle, wrapped and elevated. "Or you could stay put, and I'll handle it."

That tone—firm, unarguable—made me want to argue anyway. "I need a shower," I muttered.

"No hot water."

"I'll manage."

"You won't."

First out of bed were her legs—bare, purposeful—pulling on the sweatshirt she'd borrowed the night before.

"I'll heat some water," she said. "Don't move."

It wasn't a request.

"I'm not helpless," I muttered.

"No," she said, finding her socks, "you're concussed with pride. Stay put."

Her footsteps faded down the stairs—the hiss of the gas stove followed, then the scrape of metal, the clatter of the kettle. The smell of burning dust from an unlit burner drifted up the hall. It smelled like every storm that had ever cornered me here.

I stared at the ceiling, told myself to wait—didn't.

The crutch leaned against the wall, the floor cold through the boards beneath my feet, but the ankle felt steady enough—or maybe that was the pain meds lying to me.

By the time I reached the bathroom doorway, sweat was sliding down my spine. Every step made the joint throb harder, the edge of the cast biting skin.

"Luc, I swear to God if you're—" Her voice rose from the stairs before I reached the doorway.

"I'm fine," I said. Not convincingly.

She appeared in the doorway, a bowl of steaming water in her hands, jaw tight, eyes bright with fury trying to disguise fear.

"Unbelievable," she said. "You lasted what, three minutes?"

"Four."

"Congratulations. Sit down before you fall down."

She adjusted her grip on the bowl, shook her head, and exhaled hard. The steam ghosted between us. "Next time I tell you to stay put," she said quietly, "listen."

"I built this house," I said. "I can survive a trip to the bathroom."

"You built it to survive storms, Luc. Not you."

I should have protested again, but the way she carried that bowl—like a commandment—every argument dried in my throat before it formed.

Following her out of the bathroom, each step thudded a reminder—pride dragging weight where strength should have been. I eased down on the edge of the bed near the table.

She tested the water with her fingers, gave a small nod. "Close enough."

Crossing to the bedside table, she set the bowl down, and grabbed a clean towel and a bar of soap from the bathroom. "We'll make this work."

"You don't have to—"

"I know."

She knelt between my knees and wrung out the cloth, steam fogging the air between us. The first touch was at my throat, warm and deliberate. She didn't rush. Didn't tease. Just... *tended*.

For a man who's spent half his life fixing things, it was fucking disarming to be the one being fixed.

She moved to my shoulder, my chest, the slow circles tracing where salt had dried on my skin. My pulse refused to behave. Her fingers lingered a second too long each time she dipped the towel back into the bowl.

When she reached my abdomen, I caught her wrist.

Her eyes met mine—steady, knowing.

"Luc," she said quietly. "Let me."

Steam blurred the edges of the room, carrying the clean bite of soap and melted snow. The house held its breath. No hum of power, no noise but ours.

Her eyes stayed steady, calm where I wasn't. I still had her wrist, fingers locked out of habit more than will. Control had always been my armor; now it felt like sand leaking through a cracked plate.

"Luc," she whispered again, softer this time, and it cut through everything.

A tiny breath caught in her throat before she spoke, like she wasn't sure if I would.

My hand released before my mind caught up.

She didn't look away. The cloth slid lower, over my stomach, heat trailing behind each pass.

As she continued downward, her movements slowed. Steam and breath tangled in the air between us.

She hesitated—just long enough for the silence to thicken—then brought the cloth even lower, around me, careful, steady, thorough.

The heat of it made my pulse trip.

She didn't just wash—she studied me. Every pass grew slower, her thumb tracing the line of my ribs as if counting them, needing to feel the rise that proved I was still breathing.

Only when she was sure I wouldn't flinch did she trade cloth for skin.

Bare. Deliberate. Slow.

Her fingers moved with the same focus she gave to everything she cared about—maddening, precise, reverent.

When her hand wrapped around my cock—hard, waiting—the sound that came out of me wasn't language.

"Luc," she breathed—half warning, half wonder.

She cupped my balls, her touch impossibly gentle, and the sheer, fucking tenderness of it was what undid me completely. I'd been all sharp corners and broken parts, yet she touched me like I was still intact.

She gave a quiet, almost nervous laugh—just a breath of it—like she couldn't believe the effect she was having.

The towel fell away. Her head lowered.

A rough groan ripped out of me—sharp, involuntary.

Then her mouth was on me. A wet, shocking heat. Her tongue, flat and firm, dragged slowly up the entire length of my cock before she took me deep.

I could feel the tickle of her hair against my bare stomach and she held my thighs in place.

She didn't just take me in; she worked me. Her tongue swirled tight around the head, then traced a slick, relentless path along the most sensitive vein underneath. Every flick was a promise, every slow, sucking pull dragged me closer to the edge. Her lips created a tight, wet seal, moving up and down in a rhythm that was selfless, filthy intent.

And with every dirty thing her beautiful mouth did, my body remembered how to feel. How to come alive.

Pleasure coiled, tight and urgent, in my spine. The need to let go—to fall into that abyss—was a physical ache.

But it was wrong.

Too one-sided. Too passive.

I was the one being fixed. *Mon Dieu*, I needed it.

But I needed to fix her, too.

To meet her.

In this.

"Stop," I rasped, the word breaking loose before I could catch it. My hand found her hair—not to push, but to cradle.

She stilled instantly, looking up, her lips swollen, her eyes questioning but steady.

"Come here," I breathed, tugging gently.

My hand slipped into the drawer, closing around the foil packet.

Understanding dawned in her gaze. She moved, a fluid shift in the morning quiet, and I guided her over me, my hands on her hips.

The ankle's throb kept me present. It made everything slower. More real.

"Like this," I murmured, my voice rough. "I need to see you."

She nodded, the movement small but sure, matching my steadiness with her own.

She settled over me, knees bracketing my hips, and took me in hand. When she sank down, it hit like recognition—something my body had been waiting to remember.

A soft, choked moan escaped her, her head tipping back, and I watched, mesmerized, as the pleasure washed over her features.

"Putain que t'es belle."

Her hands settled on my chest for balance.

When she began to move, it wasn't fast.

It was steady. Certain.

Like we were finding the same rhythm instead of chasing it.

The house stayed silent around us. Every sound belonged to us now—her breath, the soft drag of fabric, the rough pull of mine.

My hands roamed her body, learning the curve of her waist, the weight of her breasts, the frantic beat of her heart.

I was pinned, broken, and yet I had never felt more powerful than in that moment, watching her find her pleasure atop me, using my body to fuel her own.

Her eyes found mine, and it hit deep—too much, too close, almost painful.

"Regarde-toi," I whispered, my thumbs stroking the damp skin of her thighs. *Look at you.*

Her breath caught—half sob, half surrender. "Oui," she whispered, the sound shaking.

The rhythm faltered, then found its way back, sharper now.

I felt her tighten, the tremor in her legs giving her away as she gazed down at me with her beautiful emerald eyes.

I held them.

The pull in me answered hers, steady, certain.

This wasn't a race.

It was a collision—two currents meeting at the same breaking point.

When it hit, she went quiet—mouth open, body arching, breath caught somewhere between a cry and a prayer.

Then it took me too, a deep rush that burned everything clean—the pain, the fear, the weight I'd been carrying for years.

I caught her against my chest. Exhaled her name into her skin while the last tremors shook through us.

For a while, the only thing that moved was our breathing, slow and even. Morning crept in, turning the walls gold.

She rested her head on my shoulder, her hand over my heart. I held her there, tracing small shapes along her back without thinking.

The bowl of water cooled beside us; the power was still out, my ankle still a mess.

But in that quiet, it felt like I'd stopped fighting myself.

Putain de bain.

Worth every fracture.

Somewhere below, the world outside my room had the nerve to keep turning. Footsteps. A burst of laughter from the hall. The muffled thud of boots on stairs.

Emme sat back, flushed and trying to remember where her clothes had landed. I reached for her hand, stopped halfway, and pretended it was to adjust the blanket.

Outside, someone called her name.

She dressed quickly, pressed a quick kiss to my jaw, whispered, "Stay put," and was gone.

I listened to her voice drift through the hall—clear, steady, already in motion. The leader again. The part of her the guests saw, the one I was supposed to let walk away untouched.

My pulse hadn't gotten that memo.

I dragged myself upright, the blanket slipping to my waist, and looked out. From the window, the world looked freshly built. Snow draped the pines in clean lines, sunlight glancing off the ridge.

She'd been gone only a few minutes, but the room felt too still once she left

Finn was the first outside, jacket unzipped, throwing a test snowball at Nico. Nico retaliated immediately. Within seconds, the entire group was laughing, ducking, and firing back.

Emme stepped out a moment later, boots crunching on ice, coat unbuttoned. She tried to mediate, failed spectacularly, and grabbed a handful of snow. Her throw caught Nico square on the shoulder. Her laugh carried all the way up to my window.

Finn, the traitor, used a cooking pot as a shield. Someone toppled a half-built snowman, and judging by Nico's outrage, it was now an international incident.

I caught myself smiling. Then the ache behind it hit harder than the ankle ever could.

She belonged in motion—out there, bright against the white, alive in a way I hadn't been for years. I belonged here, watching from behind glass.

The house had survived the storm. I wasn't sure I had.

Chapter 23

Holding Patterns

EMME

TWO DAYS SINCE THE world went white.

Two days of melting snow for water, rationed candles, and pretending not to notice the silence coming from the man who refused to stay still.

The storm had left its signature—snow pressed against the windows, trees bent and glittering.

Inside, the house smelled of smoke and damp wool, of people who'd waited out a storm together. Luc's crutches leaned against the wall beside him, defiant as their owner.

"Again," he said from the sofa, gesturing toward the breaker box.

"It's humming."

"Not right."

His voice was clipped, the patience scraped out of it. The generator had sputtered to life that morning, coughing in short bursts. Each time it failed, he went still—like he could will it back to life through silence.

I crouched by the panel, toggled the switch he'd described. The light flickered, steadied, and for a heartbeat the Refugio breathed again—electric hum, refrigerator drone, the small miracle of heat pushing through vents.

Luc exhaled. It wasn't gratitude; it was surrender. "Leave it. That's enough for now."

When I turned, he was staring at the pale curve of the cast, jaw tight, eyes unreadable.

"You should rest."

"I've rested for forty-eight hours."

"And complained for forty-seven."

That earned me a ghost of a smile. Then it was gone.

By afternoon, the silence shifted. Not gone, just waiting.

Finally, a low rumble carried through the valley, distant engines crawling toward us. Juliana and Rafa arrived just before dusk, headlights carving gold through the snow.

Juliana burst through the door first, scarf half-undone, cheeks flushed. "We thought we'd have to dig our way in."

"You nearly did," I said, hugging her.

Rafa stomped snow from his boots, grinning at the revived lights. "You kept the place alive, *jefa*. I'm impressed."

"Because someone wouldn't sit still," I said, watching Luc.

"Control issues," Rafa corrected, glancing toward the man on the couch.

Yeah, a forehead Post-it that said DON'T BE STUPID had crossed my mind.

Luc nodded once, all restrained courtesy. "Good to see you both made it."

Juliana crossed to him, eyes narrowing. "*Estás de mal humor.* You're grouchy. How's the ankle?"

"Fine," he said—an obvious lie.

"Mm-hm." She smacked his shoulder lightly, the gesture pure mother hen. "Try sitting still for once, *mi amor*. The world won't end if you rest."

His jaw worked once, like he was swallowing a retort he didn't have the energy to voice. "I'm resting," he muttered. "Just not good at it."

I caught the twitch at the corner of his mouth—humor fighting its way through pride.

That night we cooked real food again. Pasta boiled in actual water from actual pipes. The power held steady at last; lights glowing amber against the timber beams. The lodge felt alive in a way that made my chest hurt.

The lights flickered once, just enough to remind me how fragile that feeling was.

Rafa leaned back in his chair, wineglass in hand. "My son learned to ski on a hill so flat, you had to push yourself with the poles. Every time he stopped, he'd yell, *'Look, Papá, I'm flying!'*"

Juliana snorted. "You mean falling."

"Semantics." He shrugged. "We celebrated like he'd conquered Everest."

Juliana waved a fork. "That reminds me—my sister once had to amputate a cast during a blackout. With nail scissors."

Harper blinked. "You're kidding."

"She's a nurse," Juliana said, proud and horrified at once. "One patient. One flashlight. Forty-five minutes. It looked like she fought a raccoon."

Luc huffed a laugh, low and genuine. "Remind me not to get injured near your family."

Laughter rippled through the table, the kind that left cheeks sore and ribs aching.

Then Harper lifted her glass, eyes bright. "Oh, I've got one. There was a crazy storm last spring. Lightning hit the power line right outside our cabin. Finn thought the roof was coming down."

Finn groaned. "Don't you dare."

"Oh, I dare." She grinned. "He sprinted outside in his boxers, waving a broom, yelling that he'd 'fight the fire with honor.'"

"It was a reasonable response," Finn muttered, burying his face in his hands.

"Reasonable?" Harper laughed. "You threatened thunder."

The laughter started again, easy and unguarded.

Zoë leaned forward, eyes dancing. "I've got one, too. Last month I tried to film a storm for my travel channel. I was going for *mystical and moody.*"

Nico raised a brow. "And instead?"

She sighed. "A gust of wind flipped my umbrella inside out, smacked me in the face, and the video went viral as 'woman loses fight with weather.'"

"You won in spirit," Nico said, deadpan.

"Oh sure," Zoë shot back. "The spirit of public humiliation."

Even Juliana laughed, wiping at her eyes with the corner of her sleeve.

I hadn't meant to add to the chaos, but something in the room—maybe the wine, maybe the relief—loosened my tongue. "Once," I said, "during a tropical storm in Belize, I accidentally trapped myself in a supply closet with a bottle of tequila and a wedding cake."

Every head turned.

"I was attending a conference, and we crashed a wedding," I explained. "Storm hit, lights went out, doors blew shut behind me. The cake survived. I did not. By the time maintenance found me three hours later, I was drunk, covered in buttercream, and giving the cake motivational speeches."

The table went still for a heartbeat, then erupted. Even Luc laughed—deep, helpless, the sound rough from disuse. The sound startled *him*. I saw it in the quick stillness that followed—like he hadn't expected laughter to come out of him.

For the first time in days, it felt like everyone could finally breathe.

By morning, the Wi-Fi stumbled back. My phone lit up with a flood of pings—emails stacked like snowdrifts.

SUMMER: Status update on Refugio contract. Confirmation?

SUMMER (again): Luc Moreau signature still pending. Need response ASAP.

Of course. Not "Are you alive?" Not "How's Luc?" Just the contract. Classic Summer—human triage by priority level.

JULIETTE: Tracking the storm. You alive or currently buried under paperwork?

Paperwork? No. A six-foot-two Frenchman with a limp? Absolutely.

BRYNN: Please tell me you saved the wine.

Priorities. At least one Wilder sister had them in order.

ANNIE: Checking in. You okay? How bad was it?

Oh, baby sister. Thank God someone in this family still leads with empathy.

I reread Summer's messages until the letters blurred. We'd agreed before the storm. He'd said yes—had even printed the final draft. Then came the roof, the fall, the morphine, the silence.

The screen's glow faded against the morning light.

"Something wrong?"

Luc's voice pulled me back. He was at the desk, laptop open, posture too formal.

"Just catching up."

"On contracts," he said, not asking.

"I still have a job."

"You also nearly froze to death."

"And yet somehow survived. Lucky me."

His gaze held mine, steady. "It can wait." But he didn't look away, not right away—like he recognized the kind of overwhelm you can't hide behind a screen.

I set the phone facedown. "Fine."

But the unease stayed—a small, sharp thing under the ribs. I hated that he saw it, hated that he might be right.

Then Zoë's voice cut through the air, bright as sunlight after rain. "I've already got the title for my article—*Refugio Cielo: Resilience at the End of the World.* You'll be famous, Luc."

He gave a dry laugh. "That's exactly what I was hoping for. Fame."

Nico grinned from the window seat. "We'll come back next year—less blizzard, same wine."

The morning blurred into motion—phones charging, flight apps glowing, the soft murmur of logistics replacing laughter. Harper spread maps across the table, Finn counting hours between connections. Zoë bartered for an extra night near the airport "in case Patagonia changed her mind again," and Nico promised to send her the best empanada place in Buenos Aires.

I should've been doing the same—checking flights, making my own plan to leave. But every time I looked at my phone, the thought of going felt heavier than it should've.

I helped Harper confirm her flight, checked Zoë's transfer to El Calafate, made sure Finn and Nico had enough gas to reach town. Every time I opened my own airline app, I found something else that needed doing first.

Luc noticed.

"Your turn," he said finally, leaning on his crutches near the desk. "Flight booked?"

"Soon."

He arched a brow. "That means no."

"I thought I'd wait until everyone else was sorted."

"Always the caretaker."

Because he wasn't wrong.

I bristled. "It's called being responsible."

"It's called stalling."

I busied myself stacking the leftover paperwork. "You shouldn't be up."

"I'm fine."

"You're not."

He jerked away when I reached for him, breath sharp through his teeth. I felt the flinch—the quick shadow crossing his face before he locked everything down again.

"Don't do that," I said.

"Do what?"

"Pretend you don't need anyone."

He froze. For a heartbeat, the mask slipped—enough to show the exhaustion beneath.

"I don't," he said. "And you have a plane to catch."

That one landed clean. Precise.

I folded my arms. "You're kicking me out."

"I'm reminding you you've got a job waiting. The contract, remember?"

His tone softened, but it didn't help. "Florida needs you. The lodge needs what you planned. Wait too long, and the rest of the world moves on without us." He said it carefully, like each word had to be measured to keep from cracking open something he didn't want me to see.

"So you'll sign?"

He met my eyes. "I'll sign. But you don't need to babysit me through recovery. You've got deadlines waiting." But the way his fingers tightened around the crutch told a different story—like letting me go cost him more than he'd allow in his voice.

I looked down at my phone. My thumb hovered over the screen longer than it should have before I booked a flight for the next morning.

He turned back to the window, already pretending the conversation was over. "Another storm's coming," he said quietly. "If you don't leave at dawn, you won't leave at all." He didn't look at me when he said it. He watched the ridge like the answer was hiding there, not in the space between us.

I glanced toward the window. The sky had already shifted—bruised clouds gathering again over the ridge. He wasn't exaggerating.

If the flights grounded again, I'd be trapped another week. Trapped with him.

The message beneath it was clear: *go before I ask you to stay.* His knuckles whitened on the crutch, the only part of him that betrayed how close he was to breaking his own rule.

I nodded, because anything else might have broken the thin line holding us both upright.

By late afternoon, the last guest vehicles idled at the drive, tires crunching on ice. Guests waved from windows; Juliana wiped her eyes; Rafa loaded the final crate of supplies. And then it was just us again—the moun-

tain, the low hum of power, and the steady drip of thawing snow from the eaves.

It was aftermath.

The world outside was already changing—drip by
drip, thaw by thaw. Tomorrow I'd leave, and the mountain would keep its secrets.

Maybe that was the point of storms: they show you
what breaks and what refuses to.

I wasn't sure yet which one I was.

Either way, I'd find out tomorrow.

Chapter 24

No Promises

EMME

THE SILENCE FELT HEAVIER now that the power was back and Luc's guests were gone. The fire crackled quietly in the hearth, one last pulse of warmth in a space already cooling.

It felt cavernous here without voices. No Juliana clattering pans in the kitchen, no guests tracking in snow. Just the tick of heat through old pipes and the whisper of wind finding seams in the wood. We'd sat by the fire with the last of a lentil stew, a half-empty bottle of red between us, shoulders brushing once in a while, saying almost nothing. The quiet wasn't uncomfortable—just full of everything we didn't want to unpack.

When the bowls were empty, we cleared them together in silence. He stayed downstairs, stoking the fire, moving slow and deliberate, like tending the embers gave his hands something to do.

I went upstairs, the sound of the fire fading behind me. My suitcase waited in the corner, half open.

I folded another sweater and smoothed it flat in the suitcase. The wool carried the scent of cedar and Luc's soap. I told myself it was laundry detergent. I told myself a lot of things tonight.

And I told myself that fucking him was a lapse in judgment, not a declaration.

Bullshit, Emme.

Outside the window, a faint light flickered from the direction of Martín's cabin, blurred by the falling snow. He'd helped shuttle the last group to the airport before sunset. Tomorrow he'd come back for me on his way to town.

I zipped the main compartment and set the folder with the signed contract on top. Sent, received, backed up twice. *Wilder Horizons thanks you for your efficiency.* I could almost hear Summer saying it. Professional closure, clean and tidy.

Emotionally, the folder didn't cover much.

My reflection caught in the dark window—hair tied up, thermal sleeves rolled, face I didn't quite recognize. The mirror caught the dull drag of exhaustion—deeper than sleep could touch.

The bed behind me was still neatly made, untouched. *His* room carried the ghosts of our intimacy; mine just held the echo.

The lights hummed back to life, polite and impersonal, like the house had already moved on without me.

I'd left the window cracked to clear the air, but the cold pushed in anyway—sharp, invasive, honest. I sat on the edge of the bed, palms pressed to my knees, listening to the drip of melting snow and pretending the thin air was what burned in my chest.

Tomorrow, Martín would drive me to the airport.

Tonight, I would pretend packing was progress.

I'd barely set the suitcase by the door when the knock came—soft, almost polite. Too polite for everything we'd been.

When I opened the door, Luc was there, cast showing beneath soft gray sweatpants, one hand steadying him on Rafa's cane, the other holding my scarf—folded neat, like he hadn't wanted to let it wrinkle.

"You left this." His voice was even, but the pause after it wasn't.

I took the scarf, fingers brushing his. Warm skin. Cool air. Familiar pull. "Thanks."

"Martín's leaving earlier than planned for town," he said. "Roads will crust over by dawn. You should go with him." He kept his eyes on the hallway, not on me, like looking too long might undo whatever resolve he'd stitched together.

"You sound like you want me gone."

"I sound like someone who doesn't want you stuck halfway down the pass."

"Touché."

The corner of his mouth lifted, almost a smile. The kind that used to undo me.

"I'll be up early to see you off."

"You don't have to—"

"I know."

He shifted on the cane, closer than he needed to be. His breath hitched—barely there—but close enough that I felt the effort it took for him not to close the rest of the distance. The lamplight caught the edge of his jaw, warming his skin. The faint trace of soap and smoke clung to the sleeve of my shirt—his, not mine.

"Luc—"

He met my eyes before I could find the rest of the sentence. A flicker crossed his expression—quick, unguarded—the kind of look he usually shut down before anyone could catch it.

He exhaled first. "Get some sleep, Emme."

I nodded, though neither of us moved.

Please don't walk away.

The silence filled up between us, thick and breathing.

He reached out, brushed a strand of hair from my shoulder, and let his hand fall. His fingers hovered a moment near my collarbone—like whatever he meant to say lived in the space he couldn't cross. Then he turned, the cane tapping softly as he walked down the hall.

The door clicked shut.

I stood there with the scarf in my hand, heart still stumbling. It still held his warmth, faint and foolish as the scent that refused to fade.

Better this way. That's what I keep telling myself, anyway.

I didn't even bother pretending to sleep.

I'd tried—turned the pillow, pulled the blanket up, scrolled through my phone like that would make the night shorter. My carry-on sat half-zipped by the door, neat lines and folded certainty pretending to be control.

Through the cracked window drifted the smell of woodsmoke and frost, the mountain's quiet exhale after too many days of holding its breath. The air was heavy with that damp chill that promised morning ice.

I opened the weather app out of habit. A single snowflake icon blinked beside the word *light.* Nothing alarming.

"Normal for Patagonia," I whispered into the dark.

Sure. Totally normal.

Somewhere outside, snow sloughed from a branch with a soft *whump.* The roof answered with a low creak, the sound of the mountain shifting in its sleep.

I stared at the ceiling until the shapes blurred, willing logic to keep pace with want.

He'd said he'd be fine. Maybe he would.

Maybe I would too.

It didn't feel true tonight.

It was still dark when I woke. The time of morning even spirits rejected.

I dressed by habit—layers, scarf, my ride-or-die leather boots fished from the same carry-on that got me this far. Every motion was deliberate, like if I moved softly enough, the morning might forget to stop me.

I started down the stairs with my suitcase, metal wheels thudding against each step. Halfway down, Luc appeared at the bottom, one hand on Rafa's cane, the other reaching up.

"I've got it," he said.

"You don't—"

He tried anyway. The suitcase tilted, his balance wavered, and a muttered curse slipped out before I could finish the sentence.

"Exactly," I said. "You've got a broken ankle, remember?"

He steadied himself, jaw tight, and I carried the bag the rest of the way down. His jaw flexed; the corner of his mouth almost softened. Almost.

The lodge was warm and dim downstairs, a single lamp over the counter throwing soft gold across the kitchen. Luc had already been busy, the smell of coffee and toasted bread curling through the air, a coat slung over the back of a chair.

"You're up early," I said.

He glanced over his shoulder, cast shifting as he reached for a thermos. "So are you."

"I didn't really sleep."

"Didn't think you would."

He poured the coffee into two travel cups and slid one across the counter without asking. It was exactly how I liked it—black, splash of cinnamon, no sugar.

"You guessed right," I said.

"Didn't guess."

I wrapped my hands around the cup. The warmth bit pleasantly at my palms.

While he packed a breakfast for me to take on the road—homemade bread, dried apricots, a handful of almonds in a napkin—I paced near the window, watching for headlights through the dark. The world outside looked unreal, sky and snow blurring together in one endless shade of blue-gray.

"Martín should be here any minute," Luc said.

Right on cue, two beams of light cut through the trees. The distant growl of the truck drifted closer, Gitana's bark echoing off the hill.

Luc reached for his coat. "I'll walk you out."

"Luc, you don't have to—"

He gave me that half-smile again. "Je sais, Emme." *I know.*

The door groaned against the cold when he opened it. Frost bit the porch railings, the air sharp enough to sting. Martín climbed out of the truck, beard dusted white, calling out a quiet *"Buenos días."*

He moved quickly, hauling my suitcase into the back while Gitana wagged her tail from the passenger seat. Luc slipped her a treat.

He stood beside me, shoulders squared against the wind. "Safe travels."

"Try not to climb anything."

"No promises."

The laugh that escaped me fogged the air between us. For a heartbeat, it felt like we'd paused the world right there.

All he had to do was ask.

I leaned in for a hug and got a sideways one instead—his arm around my shoulder, mine brushing the edge of his jacket. Warm, quick, gone too soon. He held his breath when he let go. I felt that more than the hug itself.

"Take care of yourself," I said.

"You too."

He stepped back as I climbed into the truck. His posture didn't move with the cold—only with me pulling away. The door shut with a hollow thud, sealing the moment between us.

Martín shifted into gear, tires crunching over the frozen drive. I kept my eyes forward until the lodge disappeared behind the hill, biting the inside of my cheek until the sting gave me something else to feel. I didn't have to look back to know he stayed on the porch longer than he should have; I could still feel the weight of him long after the road bent away.

Gitana pressed her nose to the window, breath fogging the glass.

"Buena chica," Martín murmured, voice low and affectionate as he scratched Gitana's ears. Even without the words, I understood—*good girl, she likes the cold.*

"A ti también," I said—*you do too.*

He grinned. "Me gusta... sobrevivir más." He tapped his chest, then the steering wheel. *I like surviving it more.*

We rounded a switchback where the ridge rose steep and white, snow stacked high like layered pages in a story not finished.

A sound rolled through the valley—a deep, distant thunder that didn't belong to the sky.

Martín's hands tightened on the wheel. "Nieve vieja," he said, nodding toward the ridge. Even with my limited Spanish, I caught the meaning—*old snow settling, nothing to worry about.*

I wanted to believe him.

Except the sound it made wasn't small. A low, muted crack rolled down the valley—too heavy, too deep to match the shrug Martín gave it.

The rumble faded, but my breath kept catching, like the mountain was still holding it for me.

Outside, the landscape looked perfectly still. Too still. We kept driving.

Chapter 25

No Signal

LUC

I MUST HAVE FALLEN asleep on the couch after she left.

The fire had died to a soft orange bruise in the hearth, the room dim except for the gray push of early light through the windows. My neck ached from the angle, my ankle throbbed in its cast, and for one suspended second I forgot why the house felt wrong.

Then it hit.

Too quiet.

The kind of quiet that wasn't peace, but vacancy.

I sat up slowly, the blanket I pulled over me sliding to the floor. The cold beneath it felt undeserved.

The mug on the table still held the last traces of the coffee I'd made for her before dawn—her cup, not mine. My hand hovered above it like she might still be sitting there. Ridiculous.

Juliana wasn't here yet. No pans clattering. No hum in the kitchen.

It wasn't just the silence—it was the way it settled in my chest, heavy and uneven, as if the whole place exhaled without her and didn't quite know how to breathe again.

Like she'd been holding up more of the place than I'd realized.

I told myself getting her out early had been the smart call. It should've settled something in me. Instead, waking up without her left the air tilted, like the house knew something I didn't.

I crossed the floor to the weather station mounted beside the window, rubbing sleep from my face. The screen glowed faint blue, numbers scrolling in patient indifference.

Barometric pressure had dipped.

Fast.

Faster than it should have.

I blinked hard, refreshed the satellite feed. A band of cloud that was supposed to move east had stalled over the ridge instead. The frost line hadn't budged even though sunrise should have lifted it.

"Light snow" had quietly updated to "moderate."

I refreshed the page.

Then again.

And again.

Each identical screen felt like a warning I couldn't interpret, a pattern I should've recognized but didn't want to name.

The predictions stubbornly held.

I should have been able to look at the data and shrug it off. Patagonia shifted moods like a temperamental child—unpredictable, often dramatic. But something in the tilt of the numbers crawled beneath my skin. The back of my tongue tasted metallic, that old warning tang I'd learned not to ignore.

Not danger yet.

But not right.

A soft crackle broke the air.

The radio on the counter sputtered to life, Rafa's low voice spilling out in a string of static and consonants.

I grabbed the receiver. "Rafa?"

"Estoy llegando." *I'm coming up.* A beat of snow-muted silence. "Oí un retumbo al amanecer."

A rumble.

My stomach dropped.

"You sure?" I asked, though I already knew what he meant.

"Viejo," he added, tone hardening, "nieve vieja moviéndose."

Old snow shifting.

I pressed the heel of my hand to my brow. The room felt smaller. The mountain outside felt bigger.

"I'll try Martín," I said.

The call didn't even ring. Straight to no signal.

I tried again.

Failed again.

Then Emme.

Nothing.

Just "attempting reconnection" flashing like a taunt.

I swallowed against the heaviness creeping up my throat, a slow clot of dread. Maybe they were already on the far side of the pass. Maybe the signal was only catching the weather. Maybe—

Maybe.

I hated that word.

By the time Rafa pushed through the door, stamping snow from his boots, I'd already tried the phones a dozen more times.

"You feel it too?" he said, unwinding his scarf.

"Something's off."

The words felt too small for the pressure building in my ribs, the kind that only ever came before something broke loose on this mountain.

He nodded once, solemn. "No me gusta." *I don't like it.*

Neither did I.

Outside, light was barely breaking over the ridge, a thin gray slash across the valley. The wind hadn't picked up, but the cold had teeth.

I moved toward the door, intention already set.

"¿A dónde vas?" *Where are you going?*

"I'm going after them."

Rafa looked pointedly at my cast. "¿Con qué pierna, jefe?" *Which leg?*

I ignored him and shifted my weight forward any-way—stupid, stubborn, instinctive. Pain shot through my ankle. My balance faltered; the cane clattered against the floor. I caught myself on the table, breath ripping sharp through my teeth.

Rafa swore under his breath. "Stop. Luc—stop."

"I shouldn't have let her go," I said, voice low, nearly a growl.

"You let her leave safely," he corrected. "With Martín. Before the roads ice. That was the right call."

It didn't feel like the right call.

He stepped closer, tone leveling. "If the ridge moves, we'll hear it."

The words landed like a promise.

Or a warning.

"Or feel it," he added.

What he didn't say sat louder than what he did: I wasn't in any shape to run.

My jaw tightened. He wasn't wrong. That didn't make it easier to stand still.

I stared out the window, pulse thudding in my throat like something trying to escape. The valley stretched wide and white, peaceful in a way that didn't match the low hum in my chest.

"I'm not waiting," I muttered.

"You have to," Rafa said. "If you go now, you'll slow down anyone who can actually help." He placed a steady hand on my shoulder. "We wait for a sign."

"I don't want a sign," I said through clenched teeth. "I want—"

Her safe.

Here.

With me.

Not on a road I suddenly didn't trust.

Rafa must have seen it in my face, because his grip tightened.

"Luc."

I didn't turn. Couldn't.

The air outside shifted. It was subtle, a faint rearranging of cold and quiet, the kind of shift you only notice when you've lived long enough in a place that teaches you to listen with your bones.

A faint tremor threaded through the floorboards—a vibration more felt than heard. It rolled through the soles of my feet, up my calves, a low humming pressure like the mountain testing its own weight.

I froze.

Rafa went silent beside me.

Then it came.

A low, rolling thunder that didn't belong to the sky.

Deep.

Awful.

Ancient.

The birds outside burst from the trees in a frantic scatter.

Rafa whispered the word I didn't want to hear.

"Avalancha."

I closed my eyes.

Emme.

The sound kept rolling.

And then—

it hit.

***

EMME

The first jolt threw my shoulder into the door.

Shit—ow.

Snow slammed across the windshield in a blinding sheet, Martín swearing under his breath as the wipers scraped useless arcs, the sound rattling straight through my teeth. Gitana whimpered once—high, sharp, scared.

Holy hell, I feel you, sweet girl.

I reached back, fingers finding her fur—soft, trembling, trying to anchor both of us.

And then the world disappeared into white.

"Sin visibilidad," Martín muttered, leaning forward as if it would help him see better. The headlights barely reached the hood; everything beyond it swirled in a chaotic veil.

Another jolt. Harder this time.

Oh my God. "Martín?"

The truck fishtailed, corrected, fishtailed again.

"Is that—?" I started.

But what I was seeing didn't make sense.

The ridge to our right... shifted.

Not a collapse. Not a slide. Just a subtle, sickening ripple through the slope, like the mountain had inhaled. The ground vibrated faintly, as if something enormous beneath the snow had shifted its weight.

Ohh, that's bad.

"Martín?" My voice sounded thin.

His eyes flicked to the ridge and widened. "Mierda. Desvío. ¡Desvío!" *Off the road!*

He wrenched the wheel left.

Too late.

The avalanche hit like a blunt-force roar—snow, pressure, light obliterated. The truck surged upward then sideways, metal screaming as something tore—a sound that cracked through my skull like lightning. Air punched out of my lungs. Gitana's yelp cut off. My seat belt yanked hard across my chest as the world tilted, slammed, shifted again.

Then—

Silence.

Not real silence. The wrong kind.

The air thinned fast, turning dry and brittle, every inhale scraping like cold glass down my throat. Thick.

Compressed. Cold enough to taste metal when I bit my lip.

Snow pressed against every window, turning the truck into a half-buried tomb.

My breath fogged the air so fast I couldn't track the seconds between inhales.

"Martín?" My fingers shook as I reached for him.

He groaned. Alive. Thank God. Dazed, but conscious. His hand twitched toward the wheel.

"Gitana?" I twisted, heart stuttering hard enough to make my ribs ache. I reached back again, smoothing her fur—damp with fear, but warm. Terrified but alive.

Okay.

Okay, breathe.

One breath. Then the next.

I checked myself—head buzzing, lip coppery. I swallowed, the taste sharp and metallic, grounding me in a way nothing else could.

Breathe, damn it.

I pulled my phone from my coat. No bars. Not even a flicker. The screen dimmed, then lit again with a single, half-delivered message—frozen mid-send:

LUC: Call me when you...

(no delivery)

...get down the pass.

The words blurred once before they sharpened.

We weren't getting down anything.

The mountain had swallowed us whole.

Chapter 26

The Line Holds

LUC

T HE LAST OF THE avalanche's thunder still rolled
through the rafters when the radio shrieked.

Static. A clipped voice. More static.

Then—

"...possible vehicle involved..."

My heart stopped. Started again. Wrong.

Not peace.

Not silence.

Vacancy.

I snatched the receiver so fast Rafa startled.

"Say that again," I barked, breath shaking so hard I
heard it.

I pressed the button hard. "There were two people on that road. And a dog. Gray Hilux. They left before sunrise."

The channel clicked open. "...kilómetro treinta y siete... off the pass... snow event... units en camino..."

My grip tightened on the receiver until the plastic creaked.

Thirty-seven.

They'd be at thirty-seven.

"Luc." Rafa's hand closed on my shoulder, steady and useless.

I didn't look at him.

Couldn't.

"Silence isn't peace without her," I whispered, not realizing the words were out until Rafa froze beside me.

Another burst of radio static.

My pulse thudded so loud I almost missed the next burst of static.

A second voice came through—sharp, commanding.

"Desplegando la grúa con gancho. Repito, el camión con gancho está en camino." *Hook truck is on the way.*

Rafa cursed low.

My breath stalled in my chest for a beat too long.

The hook truck.

For buried vehicles.

For people buried.

I was already moving.

"Luc—wait—your leg—"

I didn't hear him.

Didn't feel the pain.

I shoved past him, out the door, snow hitting my face like needles. Rafa was right after me, grabbing my arm just before I face-planted on the steps.

"Fine," I snarled, pulling free. "I'm going."

"I'm driving," Rafa snapped, the tone of a man who'd buried bodies on this mountain.

I didn't argue—couldn't—words bottlenecked behind a tight, burning inhale.

We slid into his truck. Snow sprayed behind us as he floored it down the road, the tires digging for grip.

The radio in the truck crackled again.

"...*vehicle confirmed...*"

"...*partially buried...*"

"...*matches the reported Hilux...*"

My hand slammed the dash before I realized I'd moved.

"Jefe," Rafa said quietly, "my brother trained these men. Ellos van a hacer su trabajo." *They will do their job.*

I couldn't answer.

There was no air left.

All I saw was her.

Hair tangled, lip bleeding, breath fogging a window she couldn't open.

Hold on, Emme.

Hold on.

Hold on.

***

EMME

Everything was white.

Not snow—pressure.

Weight.

Cold packed so tight against the windows it looked like frosted steel.

My breath came out shallow, fogging the air faster than it could fade.

"Martín?" My voice wavered, thin.

He groaned. Alive.

Barely.

Gitana whined in the backseat, curling against my hip, her fur trembling.

"It's okay, baby. I know. I know."

My wrist throbbed from where I grabbed the seat as we slid. My head rang with the echo of impact. The copper taste in my mouth got sharper when I swallowed.

Focus.

Breathe.

Check him. Check the dog. Check the air.

I tried the window again.

It didn't even shiver.

We were sealed in.

My phone flickered.

One half-delivered text still glowing:

LUC: Call me when you... get down the pass.▢

My throat closed.

We weren't getting down anything.

And then—

A distant metallic clank.

Faint. Rhythmic.

Gitana lifted her head.

"Oh God. Someone's here."

I pressed my forehead to the frozen glass.

Snow pressed back.

"Luc," I whispered, even though he couldn't hear me. "Please."

***

LUC

We reached the staging point at the base of the pass. Emergency trucks. Flashing lights. Road authority crews already strapping chains onto tires.

And the hook truck—its arm lifted high, the steel hook swaying like a pendulum.

Before Rafa could put the truck fully in park, I was out the door.

"Luc!" he hissed, diving out after me.

I limped fast, half-hopping, half-stumbling, grabbing for the handle on the hook truck. One of the operators tried to block me.

"You can't—"

"She's there!" I snapped. "Let me in or move."

Rafa stepped in behind me, voice dropping into the tone Patagonian men didn't ignore.

"His woman is in that truck. Let him come. Mi hermano los entrenó." *My brother trained them.*

The operator's eyes flickered. Recognition. Respect.

He stepped aside.

I hauled myself into the cabin of the hook truck, cast slamming the step, pain ripping up my leg.

I ignored it.

We roared up the mountain, chains grinding over ice, diesel choking the air. I held the dash with one hand, the radio with the other.

Static.

Then—

"...clear visual on the vehicle. Roof exposed..."

My eyes stung. I blinked once, twice, forcing the world back into focus.

The truck curved around a drift and suddenly—

There it was.

A lump of snow.

A smear of metal.

Martín's truck.

My pulse went silent.

***

EMME

The pressure in the cab felt thicker.

Martín's eyes kept slipping shut.

"No, hey—hey—stay awake." I shook him gently with my good hand. Pain shot up my wrist.

Gitana whimpered.

My chest tightened.

Air felt wrong.

Thin.

The metallic clank got louder.

Something thudded against the roof.

Snow shifted.

Then—

A sliver of light.

I gasped so hard spots danced in my vision.

Voices.

Spanish.

Urgent.

Hands pounding the door.

And then a shout:

"La mujer—conscious!"

I closed my eyes. Relief hit like pain.

***

LUC

I vaulted out of the hook truck before it stopped moving.

"Luc—careful—" Rafa called, but I stumbled into the snow, nearly dropping from the shock to my ankle. I grabbed a shovel out of someone's hands and clawed at the snowpack.

Men dragged me back.

"Déjenme—let me—"

"Stand back—stand back!" someone shouted.

The hook arm swung again.

Snow tore away.

Metal screeched.

Then I saw her.

Her fingers first—shaking, white-knuckled around the seat.

Then her face—pale, eyes half-closed, blood streaked across her lip.

Her breath fogged fast-fast-fast.

Too fast.

Her gaze lifted.

Found me instantly.

"Luc?"

My casted leg wobbled, and I caught myself on the doorframe.

"Chérie—yes—I'm here," I rasped, voice breaking open. "I'm right here."

They pulled her out gently, sliding a blanket around her shoulders. Her body trembled violently.

I reached for her without thinking.

She collapsed into my chest like she'd been waiting her whole life for that exact angle.

***

EMME

Warmth.

Not heat—him.

His coat.

His arms.

His breath shaking against my hair.

"Oh," I whispered, voice cracking. "You're here."

He cupped the back of my head, pulling me in tighter.

"Don't talk." His lips brushed my temple. "Just breathe."

I felt him tremble.

Luc didn't tremble.

***

LUC

They tried to take her from me.

I didn't let go until the EMT physically guided her onto the stretcher. Even then I kept my hand on her shoulder.

Martín was loaded first—unconscious now, face gray.

Emme's breath hitched.

"Focus on me," I said, brushing my thumb along her jaw. "Not him. You. Stay awake."

"My wrist..." she whispered.

"We'll fix it."

"You hit your head?"

"A little..."

"Emme."

"I'm fine."

"You're not."

Her lips parted like she wanted to argue.

Instead she whispered: "I knew you'd come."

My voice cracked on the next inhale.

The EMT tried to block me.

"Sir, you can't ride with—"

I stepped past him.

"Try to stop me."

He didn't.

Inside, the doors slammed shut. The siren wailed.

Emme lay strapped to the stretcher, face pale, whole body shaking. I sat beside her, gripping the rail with one hand and her hand with the other.

Her fingers curled weakly into mine.

I brought our hands to my mouth.

"Je suis là." *I'm here.* "Je ne te laisse pas. Pas toi. Jamais toi." I wouldn't leave her. Not her. Never her.

Her lashes fluttered.

"Luc..."

"Respire."

I stroked her cheek with trembling fingers.

"Respire pour moi, mon cœur." *Breathe for me, my heart.*

She inhaled. Slow. Shallow. Trying.

"Good. Again. That's it. Stay with me."

The EMT checked her vitals.

"BP dropping. She's going into shock."

Non. Non—mon Dieu—non.

I gripped the rail to steady myself and bent close enough that my breath warmed her cheek.

"Emme," I breathed, the word catching. "Stay with me."

My voice cracked.

"I can't lose you."

Her fingers twitched against mine.

"I'm here," she breathed.

I bowed my head over her hand.

The siren drowned everything else.

They tried to pull her away from me at the doors.

Rafa caught me when my cast nearly gave out, his arms locking around my ribs.

"Let her go, jefe," he murmured. "They'll take care of her. She's safe."

Safe.

Alive.

Breathing.

But not with me.

The doors swung closed.

I stood there with snow melting in my hair, my hands shaking like I'd been left on a battlefield.

The silence after the siren rang in my skull.

But this time—

It wasn't empty.

She came back.

She was inside those doors. Alive. Breathing. Fighting.

And the line held.

Chapter 27

The Shift

EMME

THE HOSPITAL DOORS WHOOSHED open like they were exhaling for us, releasing a blast of over-heated air that stung my nose and made my eyes water. The fluorescent lights were cruel after the blue dimness of the mountain. I flinched at the brightness, blinking hard as the lights stabbed at the edges of my vision.

"BP dropping—she's borderline shock," one medic called as they pushed my gurney through.

Martín was beside me for only a second. His bed veered left—mine veered right—two different teams peeling off with clipped urgency.

Words blurred past me — hypothermia protocol, cold exposure, something about rapid vitals — none of it sticking, all of it too much.

Luc didn't let go of my hand until they physically made him.

"Señor, necesitamos espacio—hay que estabilizarla," the nurse said firmly. *We need space—we have to stabilize her.*

"I'm staying with her," he snapped, voice frayed and dangerous. His grip tightened on my fingers, like he could anchor me by sheer force of will.

Another nurse stepped in, eyes soft but firm. "Señor, we'll take care of her. Let us work."

My vision blurred for a moment—lights and faces and rushing air smearing together. "Luc—" I whispered, my voice paper-thin.

His face dropped close, breath shaking.

"I'm here. I'm right here."

His thumb swept over my knuckles. "Stay with me, Emme."

Then the nurse gently pried his hand from mine. "Sir, please—we have to move her."

His leg buckled under the cast when he tried to follow. Rafa caught him—strong arms locking around his ribs from behind. "Jefe," he murmured, voice low and steady. "They've got her. She's safe."

I'm safe.

I'm alive.

I'm breathing.

But he's not with me.

The last thing I saw as they pushed me around the corner was Luc being lowered into a wheelchair he refused to sit in, hands shaking, eyes locked on me until the doors swung shut between us.

A nurse rolled me straight into a curtained bay, lowering the rails with a practiced snap. Warm blankets fell over my shoulders, then another across my lap. Someone removed my boots. Someone else wrapped a blood pressure cuff around my arm.

The world narrowed to beeping monitors, warm hands, efficient voices.

I heard them speaking, but it all sounded underwater, like the storm had crawled inside my skull and settled behind my ears.

Stay awake.

"BP dropping earlier, now stabilizing," a nurse said. "Let's keep her on the monitors until the numbers hold."

An IV went into my arm before I could process the needle. Warm fluid slid in. My hands shook anyway.

Someone dimmed the lights.

Someone tucked the blankets closer.

Someone placed a warm pack between my palms.

Relief slammed into me so abruptly I had to blink hard, eyes burning—warm hands, steady voices, the quiet certainty that I was safe and being cared for.

My throat tightened.

A nurse rested a hand on my shoulder.

"You're safe now, querida. He got you out, yes?"

I couldn't speak. I just nodded.

And when the room finally settled, when the beeping evened into something soft and steady...

My phone vibrated violently beneath the blankets—the first bars of signal I'd had since the pass.

I opened it to panic. The screen lit up with missed calls and messages stacking on top of each other like an avalanche of their own.

SUMMER: EMME???

SUMMER: Your plane landed an hour ago. You weren't on it.

RAYANN: Are you safe?

BRYNN: Why are you not answering?

JULIETTE: I called the airline. They can't confirm if you boarded.

ANNIE: Please answer. PLEASE.

I swallowed hard and typed one word.

ME: Avalanche.

The chat detonated.

BRYNN: I beg your WHOLE ASS pardon???

JULIETTE: Elaborate. Immediately.

SUMMER: Were you IN IT?

ANNIE: Oh my God oh my God oh my God—

ME: Freak weather through the pass. We got caught on the road.

ME: We're at the hospital. Stable. Exhausted.

ME: Luc's here too.

SUMMER: We're booking flights.

BRYNN: Say the word.

JULIETTE: Could this have been prevented??

ANNIE: I can meditate at you? I don't know I'm panicking.

ME: No. Really. Everyone's okay.

ME: Just cold. Shaken.

ME: Alive.

BRYNN: That's not the comforting flex you think it is.

JULIETTE: Is Luc okay?

ME: ...he saved me.

BRYNN: So yes. Excellent.

SUMMER: Emme. Listen. You're taking time off.

SUMMER: You can rest here or stay there. Just tell us where you want to be.

I didn't answer. Not yet.

A knock at the curtain snapped me out of the chat. A young doctor with kind eyes stepped inside.

"Señorita Wilder? Martín is stable. Mild hypothermia, concussion, but responding well. He'll stay overnight. His sister is on her way."

Relief hit me so fast it made me dizzy.

"And your... hmm, friend," he added gently, "is ready for discharge once his films finish uploading."

Friend.

Right. My throat tightened around the word.

A soft tug on the curtain pulled me back. A nurse peeked in. "Señorita Wilder? You're stable now. Vitals good. You can sit up."

I did. Slowly.

She reached for the IV line at my elbow. "I'm going to disconnect you, but I'll leave the catheter in just in case."

A quick pinch of cool air, a click, and the bag was no longer tethered to me.

"Your friend would like to see you," she added, gentle smile curving at the edge. "He's... very insistent."

She guided me only as far as the next bay over—just a few steps, my legs trembling a little from the adrenaline drain.

Luc was there.

He sat on the exam table—one leg elevated, cast exposed, hair still damp from melted snow—his skin gone gray, eyes rimmed red, jaw clenched hard enough to make a muscle tick beneath his beard.

He looked up when I walked in, breathing out like someone finally let him surface.

And God—

the way his whole body eased... it hit me low and hard.

His gaze dropped to my wrist, where the IV had been taped. His jaw clenched.

"You scared the hell out of me," he murmured.

That raw, unguarded thing in his eyes that he never let anyone see. Not guests. Not staff. Not even Juliana.

Only me.

The doctor lifted the film to the light. "No new fracture, but significant stress. You're lucky. You need rest. No weight-bearing for several days."

Luc exhaled through his nose, jaw tightening. "I'm fine."

"You're not fine," I said softly. "You're here."

His eyes flicked to mine, something like apology threading through them.

"You were out there," he murmured, voice low enough that only I could hear. "I wasn't staying behind."

My stomach didn't just flip—it dropped straight through the floor.

My throat tightened. There was nothing to say to that—not anything that wouldn't undo me—so I just breathed, steadied myself, and nodded.

Then the world rushed back in.

We signed papers, thanked too many people, and met Martín's sister, who hugged me like she'd known me for years. She kissed Luc's cheek, teary and grateful. He looked like he wanted to sink into the floor.

Rafa was waiting near the doors, shoulders dusted with snow, worry carved into his whole posture. "Listo?" he asked, gaze flicking over Luc's limp and the lingering IV tape on my arm.

"Gracias," I told him, and meant it. He'd been with Luc when the avalanche hit, gotten him to the pass, kept him steady, and driven through the storm without hesitation.

He shook his head, embarrassed. "You scared the hell out of us."

My knees wobbled, a delayed tremor rolling through me now that everything had stopped moving.

"Juliana said if I didn't bring you back in one piece, she'd make me scrub the chimneys."

Luc groaned quietly. "If she makes you scrub the chimneys, she'll make me help. Please don't give her reason."

Outside, night had fallen. Only scattered snow swirled across the parking lot under buzzing yellow lamps.

Rafa unlocked his truck and opened the back door for us. Cold slapped me instantly. Luc's jacket was around my shoulders before I could protest, heavy and warm and smelling faintly of pine soap and smoke.

"Luc—"

"Don't argue," he said.

But it wasn't gruff. It was quiet. Pleading, almost.

He helped me into the truck even though he was the one limping. Every time I tried to steady him, he pushed my hand away, stubbornly insisting he wasn't the one who needed help.

Rafa drove us back—slow, careful—the heater filling the cab with soft warmth. Luc had wedged himself into the back beside me, his arm anchored around my waist, pulling me against him like his body could shield me from the rest of the night. His breathing steadied little by little, each exhale brushing my cheek.

When we reached the lodge, Rafa parked close to the entrance and hopped out to open the door. Luc stayed within arm's reach the entire time we crossed the threshold, as if I might disappear again if he blinked.

Once inside, he insisted I shower first. "Get warm," he said. "I'll make something hot."

I wanted to say he needed the shower more. I wanted to tell him to sit. To rest. To stop pushing himself.

But the look on his face—determined, grounding, protective—made it impossible to refuse.

The water helped. A little. My hands still shook when I stepped into the hallway, wearing borrowed sweatpants and one of Luc's softest sweaters. My luggage...everything is lost in the truck for now.

He was in the kitchen, leaning against the counter, stirring something in a pot even though he looked like he could barely stand. The faint crackle from the woodstove reached me a beat later; he must have lit a fire while I was upstairs. The room was already warming, a soft, rising heat brushing my skin as I stepped in.

His head snapped up when he heard me.

His eyes swept over me like a touch. "Better?" he asked.

I nodded.

He exhaled like he'd been holding that breath since the pass.

He guided me into a chair with a quiet nudge, then moved around the kitchen with slow, deliberate motions—setting soup in front of me, sliding over a mug of tea, draping a blanket he'd warmed by the stove around my shoulders.

Then he took my hands.

He turned them gently, thumb brushing over a fresh bruise like he was afraid to make it worse. The careful way he held me—steady, focused—said everything he didn't.

I didn't realize I was crying until he brushed his thumb under my eye.

"Hey," he whispered. "Tu vas bien. Tu es en sécurité." *You're okay. Safe.*

He sat beside me, close but still careful, as if one wrong breath might shatter whatever fragile thing had formed between us. The fire crackled softly. The whole lodge felt hushed, listening.

"Emme," he said, voice gravel-soft. "I need to say something."

I didn't move. Couldn't.

He exhaled, a ragged sound. "Not even a week ago, you walked into my lodge. You were... so beautiful. So genuine. I knew instantly—it was you. The piece I didn't even realize was missing."

His fingers tightened around the edge of the table, knuckles white.

"And I didn't know what to do with that. I told myself to be logical. To give you room. To not hold on too tight."

He swallowed, the motion thick.

"But today—" His voice broke. "Today I felt the weather shift. I knew something was wrong and I still let you go."

I sat completely still, heart throbbing against my ribs.

The silence stretched.

Too long.

Long enough that I saw it happen—his face tightening, his shoulders drawing back, the warmth in his eyes shuttering at the edges.

His gaze dropped, the line of his shoulders going stiff, like he was bracing for impact. That slow retreat of his—God, I knew it by now.

He started to look away.

I reached out before I could think.

My hand closed gently around his wrist.

A simple touch. Small.

But it stopped him like a hand to the chest.

His breath caught, quick and sharp. His eyes lifted to mine, guarded but wide open.

"Don't pull back on me, Luc," I said quietly.

Not an answer.

Not yet.

Just a stop—*don't shut me out.*

For a second, neither of us moved. I could almost feel the shift happen, like the ground steadying under my feet again.

He stood slowly, limping, and helped me upstairs. The house was silent except for the boards creaking under our feet and the low hum of the fire dying behind us.

At my bedroom door, he paused.

"I'll be down the hall." he said. "You need rest. And space."

I didn't think. I just reached for his wrist.

Warm skin under my fingers.

A pulse jumping.

"Stay," I whispered. "With me."

He didn't move. Didn't breathe.

Then—very carefully—he nodded.

He settled beside me on top of the blankets, body angled toward mine, close enough that I could feel his warmth but not touching unless I moved first.

His voice dropped to something so soft it barely existed.

His fingers brushed the inside of my wrist—right where the hospital tape had been. A silent check. A silent promise.

"Sleep, Emme. I've got you."

His heat, his breath, the solid weight of him beside me—it pulled me under fast. And as sleep swallowed the edges of the world, one thing settled in hard:

Tonight altered us.

And there was no walking it back.

Chapter 28

Aftershocks

EMME

T HE FIRST THING I felt was warmth.

Not from the blankets, or the pocket of warmth we'd made under them, or even the soft glow of early light edging around the curtains. But from him.

Luc lay beside me, still asleep, his breaths slow and even. One hand rested above his chest, the other tucked near where our bodies met. His hair was a mess, dark and soft, falling into his eyes. The lines of fatigue were deeper today—etched from the effort it took him to pretend he hadn't been hurting.

But he was here. With me. Breathing. Warm.

Oh God. This is real.

We survived all of it. The avalanche. The rescue. The storm. Each other.

Gratitude hit me like altitude—sharp, sudden. Too much before coffee.

I eased onto my elbow and just watched him—a man who looked carved out of strength and stubbornness, somehow soft in sleep. His lashes twitched. His brow smoothed. Something in my chest pulled tight, like the room had shifted an inch closer.

When he finally blinked awake, confusion flickered across his face—then cleared the second he saw me.

"Morning," he rasped.

"Hi," I whispered.

We stayed tangled for a while, still in last night's clothes, my face tucked against his chest. If he'd asked me to stay there all morning, I would have.

Instead, he made the world's worst attempt at a covert escape and tried to sit up like I wouldn't notice.

"Luc."

He ignored me. Tried again.

His ankle shut that plan down fast.

I caught his arm before he could muscle through whatever stabbed at his ankle. "Doctor's orders. No weight. And don't give me that expression—you are *not* charming your way out of medical protocols."

He absolutely was trying.

And then—like the universe had been waiting for this exact moment—a knock sounded downstairs, followed by Juliana's unmistakable voice.

"¡Sé que estás despierto, y más te vale no estar sobre ese tobillo, Luc Moreau!" Juliana's voice carried up the stairs: *I know you're awake, and you better not be on that ankle.*

I shot him a look. "Told you."

Luc groaned softly, rubbing a hand over his face. "She has excellent timing."

"And she's right," I muttered.

He shifted again—this time not out of stubbornness, but grim practicality.

"I need to get up," he admitted quietly. "Bathroom."

"Okay," I said, pushing the blankets back. "Hang on."

I grabbed his cane from where he had leaned it against the wall last night. Luc took it, but not before catching my wrist and brushing his thumb across the little half-moon bruise there.

His eyes flicked up.

Worried.

Too perceptive.

"We'll talk about that later," I whispered. "For now, just—don't fall over."

He smirked. "I've survived worse."

"I don't need you reenacting anything."

He rose slowly, carefully, using the cane exactly the way the doctor instructed. No weight on the injured ankle. He managed to make it across the room with only one sharp inhale when the pain caught him off-guard.

By the time he returned, he looked pale, exhausted... but his jaw stayed set, the stubborn line of a man refusing to yield. I helped him back into bed, adjusting pillows behind him until he gave a grudging, "Merci."

"I'm going to shower," I told him. "And then I'll help you get cleaned up too."

His gaze slid to mine, and something warm passed between us.

"I'll hold you to that," he murmured.

I rolled my eyes even as my stomach flipped. My suitcase was still somewhere in the wreckage of Martin's truck, which meant I had exactly nothing to change into.

I stepped into the hallway first.

"Clothes are in my room," Luc called after me, like he'd known I'd reach that conclusion eventually.

I walked down to his doorway. The familiar scent of cedar and warmth slid over me as I stepped inside. His dresser sat against the far wall, top drawer open just enough to invite trouble. I pulled out a pair of soft joggers and a long-sleeved thermal that looked worn-in and comfortable and very him—then grabbed a second shirt and joggers for him too, because stubborn or not, he needed a change of clothes as much as I did.

Arms full, I padded back to the guest room.

Luc watched me from the bed, eyes tracking every move. I set the clothes down neatly across the foot of the mattress and headed to the tiny bathroom.

"I'll only be a minute," I said.

"Take your time," he murmured, voice rough enough to follow me through the door.

Steam filled the cramped space in minutes. When I finally stepped out, wrapped in a towel barely big enough to qualify as one, I pushed the door open and felt a rush of cooler air lick across my skin.

Luc looked up.

And stilled.

His gaze traced over me slowly, reverently—hesitant for half a second, then not at all.

Not even close.

"Rafa will let us know about your things," he said quietly. "The road crews probably moved the truck, but everything inside will take time to sort."

When the towel slipped from my fingers, his eyes followed the movement, slow and intent, the heat of it skating across my skin.

"You're staring," I said without looking at him.

"I would apologize," he murmured, voice rougher, deeper, "but you're naked, and I'm not sorry."

I put on my bra, tugged his shirt over my head, and felt the shift in the room. The air changed, his expression tightening with something that wasn't lust, even though that was absolutely there.

Not to mention the instant boner.

His gaze caught on the bruises and didn't move. Not even a breath.

The small ones on my shoulder.

The darker one on my hip.

The ghost of a seatbelt burn at my ribs.

His jaw tightened. "Emme..."

"I'm fine," I said, tugging his joggers over my hips and rolling the cuffs until I could see my toes again. "Really."

His mouth pressed into a line. Not buying a word of it.

I climbed onto the bed, kneeling near his uninjured side so I could adjust the blanket over his cast. His thigh brushed my knee. We were close enough that the warmth between us felt like its own gravity.

"Look at me," I said softly.

He did.

God, he did.

Like I'd asked for the whole sky.

"My body's okay," I said. "I promise. Nothing broken. Nothing they're worried about. But my brain..." I exhaled slowly. "It's still catching up. Everything that happened—it's like my thoughts are playing catch-and-release."

His hand came to my knee, thumb brushing once, grounding. "C'est normal. C'était beaucoup." *It's a lot.*

"It was," I whispered. "And I'm... processing. But you staying with me last night? That meant everything, Luc. I didn't realize how much I needed you there. Not until you were."

His throat bobbed. Something flickered across his face—too naked to hide, too quick to pretend I hadn't seen it.

"Emme," he murmured, voice low with something that felt dangerously close to devotion. "I wasn't going to leave you."

I believed him.

Maybe too much.

But for the first time since the avalanche, my chest loosened enough to breathe.

He squeezed my knee lightly. "My turn," he said. "Help me shower. I'll behave."

I arched a brow. "Will you?"

He smiled, slow and sinful. "I'll try."

"You won't."

"No," he admitted, gaze raking over me again. "Probably not."

And for the first time that morning, heat curled low in my stomach in a way that had nothing to do with fear and everything to do with him.

By the time we made it downstairs—Luc leaning on me and muttering about dignity—Juliana already had coffee brewing, a pan heating on the stove, and the kind of energy only women built for crisis could summon.

Rafa came in a moment later, boots half-laced, snow melting in his beard, radio still clipped to his vest.

"Morning, jefe," Rafa said to Luc as he stepped inside, tapping snow from his boots. "Storm left a few more gifts outside. I'll take care of them."

Luc eased himself into a chair, his hand tightening on the cane before he let it go. "News?"

Rafa exhaled into his palms, thawing them. "Road crews pulled Martín's truck out at first light. Looks rough, but she's still in one piece."

A knot I hadn't realized I was holding eased in my chest.

"And Gitana's fine," Rafa said with a shrug. "Martín's sister spoiled her so much already she may never come back."

I exhaled a sigh of relief.

He turned to me. "Emme, tus maletas are in the back of my truck. Frozen solid, pero vivas. I'll bring them in once I can feel my fingers again."

Frozen luggage I could work with. I needed the small victories.

Something loosened under Luc's ribs—his shoulders dropped a fraction, a breath leaving him like he'd finally let go of something sharp.

"Gracias, Rafa," he said quietly. "Really. I owe you."

Rafa shrugged like it was just another Tuesday. "You'd do the same, jefe."

Luc set his hand on the table, jaw tightening as he pushed to stand. Juliana caught it instantly and swatted his hand with a towel.

"Sit."

"I am sitting."

"Sit better."

Juliana and Luc volleyed at each other so fast I could barely track the insults. That kind of rhythm didn't happen overnight. Rafa chimed in with his own commentary, and I realized—maybe for the first time—how protective they were of him.

And how protective they were... of me. The realization hit soft and unexpected, like warmth spreading through cold fingers.

Juliana kept shooting me subtle looks. Assessing, but not judgmental. Softened. Like she was gauging if I was steady, if I was shaken, if I needed something I hadn't asked for.

She wasn't the only one watching me. Luc's gaze tracked me every time I moved.

When I reached for a cutting board, Juliana snapped her fingers.

"No."

"I can chop onions—"

"No."

"I can stir—"

"No."

"I can breathe—?"

A long look. Then: "Maybe."

I threw my hands up and backed away from the stove like it was a federal crime scene.

Luc's mouth twitched.

I glared at him.

He didn't stop looking at me.

Eventually the chaos settled into a steady rhythm—coffee pouring, bread crackling in the toaster, Rafa's radio buzzing as he went out to clear fallen branches, Juliana muttering about reorganizing the pantry "because someone will be absolutely useless for the next week."

When she stepped outside to yell something at Rafa, the kitchen finally went quiet.

Luc shifted in his chair, weight tipped to his good leg, eyes fixed on mine.

His voice softened, threaded quietly through the bustle between us. "About last night..."

I froze, the moment dropping between us like a stone in water.

"You didn't scare me," I said before he could continue.

"I didn't want to make you feel trapped," he murmured. "Or like I expected anything from you. I just—" His throat bobbed. "When I thought I'd lost you... I needed you to know why I pushed you away. What it was really about."

I leaned in, fingers closing around his, cedar warm on his skin. "Luc. I'm not shying away."

Something loosened in his expression. A muscle eased, like he'd been holding a breath for hours.

"I feel something real for you," I whispered. "And I didn't want to leave. I've never felt that before. I'm always itching to get home, get the work finished, reset for the next trip. But with you... I wanted to stay."

Luc went still, the kind of still that told me he'd heard every layer of what I'd just admitted.

"But I'm also feeling overwhelming gratitude for simply being alive, and that doesn't mix cleanly with clarity. I'm not taking my thoughts too seriously today. I think we both need... space in our heads."

His eyes softened.

Not disappointment.

Relief.

"Thank you," he whispered.

Before I could say more, my phone buzzed.

The nurse from the hospital was checking in. She couldn't tell me much—privacy laws—but she confirmed Martín was stable, monitored, and expected to recover. No complications. No need for me to worry.

I exhaled so sharply the room blurred for a second.

When I hung up, Juliana reappeared and practically herded me to the couch.

"No more kitchen. Rest."

"I'm fine."

"You survived a truck accident in the snow and a night that would kill most people. Sit. I'll start the fireplace."

Luc chuckled as he levered himself up, cane in one hand, and crossed the room with that stubborn mix of pain and pride. He lowered himself into the chair beside the couch, close enough that I could feel his warmth.

I grabbed a pillow and tossed it at him. He caught it and held it against his ribs like he needed the anchor.

Most of the day blurred in that warm, slow way where time didn't move so much as stretch. I curled up on the sofa with tea I wasn't allowed to get myself. Luc sat across from me, sketching out ideas for the lodge—cabins, upgrades, pathways, new safeties, guest experiences, expanded winter packages.

We talked through it together.

Unit by unit.

Step by step.

What we wanted for the partnership.

What the future of Refugio Cielo might look like.

And every time his hand brushed mine over the papers, something low in my stomach tightened.

By late afternoon, Juliana was upstairs prepping rooms, Rafa was radioing in a string of small repairs, and the house had begun to hum again. She came back long enough to tuck the blanket around me. "Rest. I still need to finish up before I head home. My sister's birthday dinner is tonight."

I had almost forgotten I wasn't the only one with sisters until my phone rang.

ANNIE flashed across the screen.

"Oh boy," I muttered.

Luc smiled. "La petite cheffe?"

"My tiny gremlin of a sister? Yes."

I answered. Annie didn't even say hello.

"Emme Wilder, I'll be there tonight."

I blinked. "What—"

"Nope. Save it. I need to see your face. And Luc's face. And the lodge. And you're not going anywhere without one of us."

"I haven't decided when I'm going home yet."

"That's why I'm coming."

I pinched the bridge of my nose. "Annie, this isn't—"

"It is absolutely necessary. I'm landing around dinner. I have a ride. Tell Luc I like empanadas."

She hung up.

Luc raised a brow. "Everything okay?"

I sighed. "Annie's coming."

He nodded once, not surprised. "Good," he said quietly. "Your family loves you."

He looked away, his jaw working once—like he wasn't sure he should have said it aloud.

I wasn't ready for how much I needed to hear it.

Chapter 29

Elle Veut (She Wants)

LUC

THE LODGE EXHALED THE second they left. Stillness settling into every beam and floorboard.

Juliana and Rafa loaded the last supplies, checked the kitchen, and triple-confirmed that we didn't need anything before heading down the mountain. Juliana hugged Emme tight, whispered something fierce against her ear that I pretended not to hear, then tapped my cast twice and told me not to be an idiot. Rafa promised he'd be back in the morning to help with repairs.

When their truck pulled away and the sound of the engine disappeared into the trees, the quiet that settled inside Refugio Cielo was total. Still. A silence that made the walls feel closer, the air thicker—one that put pressure behind my ribs.

A silence where nothing was left to distract us.

Putain, merci mon Dieu.

The fire was the only movement in the room, flames shifting slow and steady, painting the stone hearth in warm amber. I sat in the leather chair beside it, leg propped, hands idle. In the reflection of the hearth glass, I watched Emme—lit from below, her edges sharpened in firelight and shadow. Her hair caught the glow, molten at the ends, her profile sharp and soft at once. For a second, in that light, she looked almost breakable—a glass edge in gold.

But then her chin lifted, spine straightening, and the truth settled in my chest: she wasn't breakable. She was bracing. Preparing. Choosing.

There was steel under the softness, a steadiness in her spine, in the sure lift of her chin, in the way she held her gaze like she'd decided she was done hiding. Beautiful, yes—beautiful in a way that hollowed me out. But not fragile. Never fragile.

She rose from the couch, smoothing her hands down her thighs like she needed a second to settle her body back into itself. She moved to the kitchen, quiet but intentional, and returned with two glasses of wine—one for her, one for me. She set mine on the table beside me, then perched on the edge of the sofa, close enough to catch the firelight, far enough that neither of us could pretend any of this was casual.

She sipped slowly, eyes fixed on the fire. Her shoulders rolled back, the subtle shift of someone locking something into place inside herself.

And then she stood again.

No hesitation this time.

Something in her stance shifted—her weight sliding forward, her body moving with the slow, deliberate prowl of someone who'd stopped second-guessing herself. The stem of her glass dangled loose between her fingers, her gaze locked on mine like she was finished pretending anything less than truth lived here.

The distance disappeared inch by inch.

She stopped in front of me, the fire wrapping itself around her like a confession waiting for breath.

"Luc," she said softly.

The way she said my name felt like the moment a storm gives way.

For a second, neither of us spoke.

The fire cracked. My heartbeat felt too loud in the silence.

"Luc," she said again, quieter. "Can I...?"

She didn't need to finish. I opened a hand, and she stepped between my knees, close enough that the heat of her body erased the fire entirely. I slid my palm up her thigh, stopping where her shirt brushed her skin—warm, alive, trembling. Not with fear. With anticipation.

She exhaled shakily, fingers threading into my hair, her thumb brushing the edge of my jaw. And God, I almost broke right there.

"When the truck went under, I thought—I thought that was it," she whispered. "I wasn't ready for it to end. Not like that. And all I could think about was you. Not my sisters. Not work. You."

Everything inside me went still—my pulse dropping into a single heavy beat, the world narrowing to her mouth and her breath.

I lifted my hand, thumb brushing her cheek, slow and deliberate, like rushing would break something neither of us wanted broken.

"It's not ending," I said, voice rough. "Not here. Not now. And not because fear says so."

Her breath fluttered against my mouth, but her eyes didn't flinch. Didn't run.

I slid my hand to the back of her neck, my fingers threading into her hair, guiding her closer, foreheads touching.

She sank into my lap slowly, straddling me with careful precision so she wouldn't hit my cast, settling against me with a soft, involuntary gasp. My hands dropped to her waist—not pulling. Holding. Proof.

"I need to say something," she said, voice unsteady. "And I'm afraid if I don't say it now, I won't."

"I'm here."

Her fingers brushed my cheek, then slid down the line of my throat—a slow, studying touch, like she was learning me by feel.

"When that snow hit, I thought my story ended. And I don't know what to do with all of this yet—how big it feels, how sure it feels, how fast it's moving. It scares me. I don't trust myself when I'm terrified."

"You don't have to," I said. "Not now."

"But I feel this," she breathed, pressing her forehead to mine. "I feel you. I feel safe with you. I feel like myself. And I want this. I want you. Not because I almost died. Not because everything fell apart. But because I see you. And it's so much bigger than I know how to hold right now."

My hands tightened on her waist, a sharp, involuntary grip—like my body decided before I did.

"And I see *you*," I said, voice scraped raw. "And I want—putain, Emme... je veux tout. *I want everything*. Not your body in a storm. Not the pieces you ration out to the world. I want all of you. The whole thing."

Her breath hitched. Her thighs tightened around me. Her lips parted—not in surprise, but in permission.

The kiss didn't lunge or rush. It unfolded—warm, deliberate, her mouth learning mine with a patience that burned hotter than hunger. Her hands slid into my hair, her mouth opening to mine, her body pressing closer, heat blooming between us like wildfire catching dry brush.

I slid my hands under her shirt, palms gliding up the warm line of her spine. She arched into the touch, a soft sound catching in her throat that went straight through me.

I broke the kiss long enough to breathe against her mouth.

"Tell me what you need."

"You," she whispered. "All of you. Now. No hesitation."

My thumb brushed the underside of her breast, slow and reverent, a pilgrim at the altar of her. She shivered—a full-body tremor—her hands tightening on my shoulders, nails pressing half-moons of desperate promise into my skin.

"Then come here," I said, my voice gravel-rough with a need I'd kept caged.

I lifted her—awkward and tangled, but together—and shifted us down onto the thick rug in front of the fire. I moved carefully, my ankle barking a warning, but I didn't stop. Couldn't. She came with me without hesitation, lowering beside me with intention written in every line of her body. Not passive. Not waiting. With me—fully.

Her hands slid under my shirt. Not tentative. Claiming. She pushed the fabric up, her palms running over the hard lines of my stomach, the sharp edges of ribs, the hammering pulse under my skin. And when her mouth hit my neck, it wasn't gentle. It was teeth. Heat. A brand. A mark that said mine without the word ever spoken. My restraint—the walls I'd welded shut—snapped clean.

Clothes became a problem. A barrier. Unacceptable.

"I need my wallet," I growled.

"I know where it is," she said—breathless, certain—her fingers brushing my jaw before she stood.

She crossed the room in three quiet steps, heading straight for the console table by the door—where I always dropped my keys, my wallet, my knife.

A soft rustle. A clink.

Then she was back, the foil packet pinched between her fingers, her gaze locked on mine like the world had narrowed to this choice.

"This okay?" she murmured.

My answer was a single, rough exhale. "Oui."

We stripped our clothes off in rough, breathless pulls—my shirt ripped over my head, the tie of her bottoms fumbling beneath my hands until it gave. Skin hit skin. Hot. Urgent. The fire was nothing compared to what burned between us.

She pressed the condom into my palm. I tore the foil open with shaking fingers, rolled it on quick, her gaze never leaving mine—steady, hungry, certain.

Her thighs locked around my hips, pulling me under her. Her hair dragged across my stomach, a dark, silken brush of heat, and she rose over me—slow, controlled, unhurried. She took her time. Every inch deliberate. And when she lowered herself onto my cock, it was maddening. Slow. Deep. All-consuming. She wasn't hesitant. She was choosing. Every second of it. Her eyes locked on mine, watching me come apart.

She leaned in close, her breath shaking against my ear. "Don't hold back. I need to feel alive."

That was it. The breaking point.

I stopped thinking.

My hands gripped her hips first, then slid up—mapping her, appreciating her shape. The cut of her waist under my palms. The hard curve of muscle over bone. The heat of her inner thigh. When my mouth found the pulse at her throat, she gasped—sharp, broken—and her whole body tightened around me.

The fire lit her from behind, throwing shadow and heat across her skin. She moved—slow at first, then harder, searching for something only she could feel. Everything narrowed to the drag and slide of her body against mine. Heat. Pressure. Breath. Nothing else existed.

This wasn't survival.

This was choosing.

Two people reaching for the same thing at the same time and not hiding it anymore.

Claiming.

Not ownership.

Something deeper. Something I didn't have words for. Devotion, maybe—not in words, but in the way her hands steadied on my chest, trusting me to hold her through the tremors.

Her rhythm broke—sharp, uneven, desperate. She chased the edge hard, breath tearing out of her, a high, tight sound building in her throat. And then she came apart, her back bowing, her fingers digging into my shoulders like I was the only thing holding her to the earth.

"Luc—"

She said my name like it was everything she had left. A plea. A prayer. A warning.

I caught her hips, holding her there, locked tight against me. "Look at me," I said, rough and low, my thumb lifting her chin until her eyes opened. "I want to see you."

And she did—eyes blown wide, dark and wrecked, trusting me with everything she wasn't saying. That was it. The end of any restraint I had left.

I drove up into her—deep, hard—a final surge that ripped through both of us. Heat detonated behind my ribs, blinding, brutal, unstoppable. I held her through it, my body locked inside hers, arms wrapped tight around her as the tremors took us. She shook against me, breath breaking against my throat, and I stayed with her—steady, anchored—until the world stopped spinning and all that was left was the sound of our breathing in the firelit quiet.

Slowly—carefully—I shifted us to our sides, my arms caging her in without trapping her, keeping her pressed to the heat of me while my ankle protested in quick, sharp pulses. I pressed my forehead to hers, breath mixing, brushing the damp strands of hair off her cheek with the back of my fingers. Gentle now. Steady. The opposite of what we'd just torn through.

She was here—warm against my chest, breath damp on my throat, her thigh tangled with mine like she didn't intend to move. Real in a way that cracked something open in me.

Et putain... it wrecked me all over again.

"I'm coming back," she said, voice shaking but sure. "I need to go home in a few days. I need to think somewhere quiet, somewhere familiar. I want to choose you with a clear head. You deserve the real answer—not the storm-version of me. But I'm not running from you."

My throat tightened hard. I swallowed, thumb sweeping across her cheekbone, slow.

"I won't ask you to stay," I said. "Mais je serai là quand tu reviendras." *I'll be here.*

Her smile wobbled, faltering and rebuilding in the same breath. "Good. Because I'm not done with you."

My chest drew tight—like my heart recognized some-thing before my mind did. "Très bien." *Good.*

The fire cracked behind us—sharp, loud in the quiet.

That's when it hit me.

The world could come apart again.

The storm could come back.

"Ouais. On choisit ça—yeah. We're choosing this."

Whatever comes next—

we're already in it.

Chapter 30

Wildcard in the Snow

EMME

THE WOODSTOVE HAD BEEN burning for hours, turning the kitchen into a pocket of steady, amber heat. Luc sat at the small table near the window, his injured ankle propped on a second chair like the doctor demanded, though the rest of him radiated *deeply annoyed with medical restrictions.*

Which meant I was the one moving through the kitchen—reheating dinner, checking the timer, pretending I didn't hear every quiet direction he tried (and failed) to disguise as "helpful notes."

"Don't let it boil," he murmured.

"It's not boiling," I said, even though it was *very* close.

He lifted a brow.

Of course he knew.

"You'll want to stir that once more," he added, voice maddeningly calm.

"And you'll want to remember I'm not totally hope-less in the kitchen," I countered.

A slow, wicked heat slid over his face. "You weren't too bad an hour ago either."

Heat curled low in my stomach; my breath stuttered.

God—he really wasn't supposed to say things like that with his voice doing that.

"Keep that up and I'm putting dinner on hold," I said, trying for light and landing somewhere closer to a purr.

Luc raised his hands like he was surrendering, but his eyes were already burning with the kind of promise that made my knees consider mutiny.

I laughed and shook my head. "Forget it. Annie's on the way."

Luc let out a breath like he wasn't quite ready to let the teasing end.

I brought the plates and linens over to the table so he could set things from his seat. He took them from me carefully, fingertips brushing mine, and I leaned down to give him a slow kiss—warm, unhurried, still tasting like the wine we'd opened earlier.

The table glowed in the firelight.

Two glasses half-filled.

Candles flickering.

Dinner sending up curls of rosemary and garlic into the air.

The whole room felt like a place caught between comfort and something dangerous—the quiet realization that walking away might already be impossible.

And now we were waiting for Annie—my wildcard baby sister who could charm a border control agent into giving her free snacks.

Luc tracked me as I crossed the kitchen, the reflection of the fire caught in his eyes, his expression somewhere between calm and something unguarded flickering through his eyes.

Outside, the wind shifted, brushing against the windows.

Night pressed in.

The kind that made the lodge feel even smaller, even warmer.

Then my phone buzzed across the counter—sharp, loud in the quiet.

ANNIE: Incoming Call

Luc's gaze flicked to the screen, then back to me with that quiet, perceptive tension he never admitted to.

I answered and hit speaker, propping the phone on the counter so I could keep moving at the stove.

"Emme? EMME—hi—okay, okay, hi!" Annie practically shrieked over the wind. "We're definitely close. Or lost. Or close to being lost. Unclear."

I heard a male voice in the background, warm and older.

Annie lowered her voice to a dramatic whisper. "Emme, this driver? He's, like, devastatingly sweet. And older. And wearing a sweater that could fix my whole life."

I pinched the bridge of my nose.

Of course she would land in a foreign country and immediately seduce someone's grandfather.

"And everyone here knows exactly where we're going," Annie continued, louder again. "Did you know your boyfriend is basically famous? People just say 'Luc Moreau' and the locals are like, 'Oh, sí, por acá.' *Yes, this way.* Like he's Patagonia royalty."

Luc froze mid-breath.

Uh, oh. Boyfriend?

My cheeks warmed.

Annie barreled on.

"Wait—hold on, I'm telling him he's an angel."

She switched to fluent, rapid-fire Spanish—teasing, flirting, apologizing, probably all at once. The poor man laughed so hard I thought he might miss the turn entirely.

Luc's brows climbed.

I shook my head. "Don't ask."

And just like that, the warm, suspended bubble he and I had been floating in all evening thinned around the edges.

Annie was almost here.

And nothing stayed simple once she entered a room.

Twenty minutes later, headlights swept across the snow outside, bouncing off the lodge windows in quick, jittery flashes. Luc shifted in his chair, straightening like he could somehow stand guard from across the room.

I pulled open the front door just as the van lurched to a stop.

The wind hit first—cold, sharp, carrying that particular Patagonia bite that made my lungs seize for a second. The driver climbed out slowly, probably exhausted from being flirted into oblivion, and then Annie tumbled out after him like she'd been ejected from the side of a cliff.

"OH MY GOD," she gasped, clutching the door. "Is this altitude? I think I'm dying. My lungs are crisp. My knees are lying to me. Why does the air feel like skinny jeans?"

Patagonia wasn't even remotely high-altitude.

But this was Annie.

Her hair was a wind-wrecked snarl.

Her cheeks were violently red.

Her jacket was half-zipped, her scarf trying to migrate upward like it wanted to escape.

She attempted to drag her suitcase, except it immediately rolled backward down the slight incline of the walkway.

She spun. "No—no, you come BACK!"

The suitcase did not come back.

I almost laughed.

Almost.

Because then she saw me.

She froze mid-grab, her hand half-extended toward the runaway suitcase, eyes locking on mine like she'd been searching for them in the dark for hours.

Something in her face cracked—quietly, cleanly. The bravado, the jokes, the altitude drama... they all fell away.

"Emme," she whispered.

Not shouted. Not teased.

Just said my name like a prayer she hadn't wanted to admit she needed.

And then she ran.

Full sprint.

No balance. No coordination.

Just raw, terrified relief.

She collided with me so hard my ribs protested, arms wrapping around me in a grip that wasn't comedic at all. Nothing about it was funny. Her breath hitched against my shoulder as she pressed her forehead into me like she needed to physically confirm I was real.

A small tremble.

A soft sniff she tried to swallow.

No theatrics.

Her arms locked around me, fierce and shaking, like her body refused to let go even if her mind tried to play it cool.

I closed my eyes and held her just as tight, grounding myself in the reality that—after everything—my little sister was here. Warm and in my arms.

Her voice cracked, barely audible. "You scared me," she whispered into my collarbone.

I swallowed. "Yeah," I murmured back. "Me too."

The wind roared around us, but for a moment, the world went very still.

"Okay, okay, inside," I said finally, pulling back enough to look at her face. "You're going to freeze to death before you even see the lodge."

"It's not cold, it's *aggressive*," Annie wheezed, grabbing her runaway suitcase with both hands. "This air needs therapy."

I laughed—actually laughed—and looped my arm through hers to drag her toward the door. The driver gave me a kindly, exhausted wave that said *your sister is a hurricane, good luck*, and then he climbed back into the van like he needed a nap and possibly a prayer.

The moment we crossed the threshold, the warmth from the woodstove rolled over us in a thick wave—heat, rosemary, garlic, and that quiet glow the lodge always settled into at night. Annie stopped dead the second the warmth hit her face.

"Holy—" she breathed. "This place is *cozy-cozy*. Like... magazine cozy."

Then she saw Luc.

He was still at the table—ankle propped, posture straightening as we stepped inside. Firelight flickered across his face, sharpening the lines of his jaw, making his eyes look darker than they really were.

Annie froze.

Tilted her head.

Then leaned in close to my ear, whispering behind her hand even though she was not remotely subtle:

"Oh my God, Emme. You didn't tell us he looks like *that*. I feel betrayed."

My eyes snapped wide. "Annie."

"What? I'm being supportive."

Luc's brow nudged upward—not because he heard her full sentence, but because Annie looked like she was trying not to squeal and failing miserably.

I nudged her forward. "Annie, this is Luc. Luc, Annie."

Luc's expression shifted to polite warmth, the kind he saved for people he wanted to make comfortable. "Welcome," he said in that smooth, sexy voice he didn't even try to soften.

He immediately braced a hand on the table as if to stand—because he was a gentleman—but I shot him a look so sharp it could've cut through the woodstove.

"Sit your *ass* back down," I warned under my breath, eyes flicking to his ankle.

He froze mid-lift, lips pressing together like he had a rebuttal ready.

I arched a brow.

He sat.

Annie blinked between us, confused, then opened her mouth to ask about the ankle—about everything—but I held up a hand.

"I'll explain," I said gently. "Just—come in, warm up first."

She started to nod, then her gaze snagged on my temple.

Stopped.

Tracked slowly down my cheek, my neck, the faint bruising along my arm where my sleeve had slid up during the hug.

Her whole expression changed.

"Emme..." she breathed, voice dropping into something raw. "What exactly happened out there?"

No yelling.

No theatrics.

Just sharp fear sharpening into protectiveness.

"Annie—"

She stepped closer, fingers hovering like she was scared to touch me and scared *not* to. "These are real bruises. You said you were okay. You said it wasn't that bad."

"It was the force of it. The truck got slammed around pretty hard."

"I know," she snapped—quick, emotional, too honest. "I'm not an idiot. But this—"

Her fingers trembled as she gestured to the side of my face.

"This looks like more than a bump, Emme."

Her jaw was tight now, eyes bright, scanning me like she needed to find every mark just to believe I was still standing.

"Annie," I murmured, catching her hands. "Hey. I'm okay."

"You were in an avalanche," she whispered, and the crack in her voice nearly undid me. "Inside a truck that could have flipped. Alone. Buried."

Each word dropped like she was hearing it for the first time.

"I wasn't alone," I said, voice gentler than I meant.

That made her glance at Luc—instantly, sharply.

Then back to me.

"Explain," she said quietly.

Not bossy.

Not dramatic.

Just... a sister looking at me like she couldn't inhale until she heard the rest.

I took a slow breath, grounding both of us.

"I will," I promised. "All of it."

Her shoulders softened just a fraction.

And then—barely audible—

"Good... because I didn't realize how frightened I was until I saw your face."

Chapter 31

Seismic Truths

EMME

B Y THE TIME WE were ready for dinner, the table looked like one of those spreads travel photographers stumble into by accident and brag about for the rest of their lives. I hadn't noticed it earlier—not really—because this was normal here. But when Annie lowered herself into her chair and finally stopped moving long enough to take it in, her breath hitched.

"Emme."

She wasn't whispering, but she wasn't exactly talking either. It was the tone she used when she found a designer handbag on sale and pretended not to be emotional about it. "Why didn't you tell me your dishes look like this?"

I followed her gaze over the table. Glacier-blue ceramic plates with stone-textured rims. A Mapuche-patterned wool runner—deep reds, blacks, earth tones. Simple linen napkins tied with braided leather. Carved wooden trivets shaped like condors.

"These aren't from a boutique," she said, fingertips brushing the edge of her plate. "Someone made these. Like... with actual hands."

Luc shifted in his chair, then stood with a soft exhale, using his cane for balance as he moved to the stove. He propped himself there, stretching his back before checking the simmering pot.

Annie's eyes cut to Luc, widening in a way that said, *Oh. Oh, that's what you've been doing out here.* She swiveled toward me like I'd been hiding a three-carat diamond.

"You just—live like this?"

I shrugged. "It's just dinner."

She gave me a look that translated to: you're a traitor to sisterhood.

Luc stirred the pot, shifting his weight off his bad ankle. His movements were unhurried but tense—the kind of restless motion he did when too much stillness started pressing on him.

I didn't call attention to it.

Didn't offer help.

Didn't remind him to sit.

I knew what this was. He needed a minute upright, a moment where pain wasn't the only thing he was aware of.

Annie watched him for two beats, eyes narrowing slightly—not with judgment, but with study. Wilder sisters were chronic observers. Unfairly perceptive. Built to read rooms and people and contract clauses.

"She's watching you," I murmured.

"I know," he said quietly, stirring.

He wasn't wrong.

When he sat again—slowly, carefully—Annie reached for her spoon with the poise of a woman bracing for something life-changing. His breath left him on a low exhale, quiet but impossible to hide.

"What is this exactly?" she asked.

"Carbonada criolla," Luc said. "Simple."

It wasn't simple.

The stew shimmered with color—orange cubes of pumpkin soft enough to break with a spoon, sweet corn, beef cooked until it fell apart, potatoes, carrots, raisins, paprika. A warm, fragrant bowl that tasted like winter comfort and sunlit kitchens.

Annie took a mouthful—then froze, eyes widening.

"Oh my God. Luc. This is indecent."

Luc frowned. "It is just pumpkin." But the faint tug at his mouth betrayed him—the kind of pride he never announced but couldn't quite hide.

"That's a lie," she said, taking another bite. "This tastes like Patagonia comfort and God."

He looked down, a faint, reluctant smile tugging at his mouth.

We ate quietly for a stretch—comfortable, warm silence. The woodstove crackled. The windows reflected soft lamplight. The smell of stew and bread curled through the room, nestling into the corners like something tender.

But Annie never stays quiet long.

"So," she said, wiping a bit of broth from her lip. "The avalanche."

Luc's hand stilled on his spoon. His jaw shifted once, a small grind of teeth, before he forced his face blank again.

My stomach pulled tight.

"I know the surface version," she continued softly. "I want the one you haven't told anyone."

The air shifted.

Not heavy—just waiting.

I set my spoon down and laced my fingers together under the table.

"It started with a jolt," I said. "The kind that feels like the whole world just... cracks."

Annie leaned in.

Luc didn't move.

"I hit the door hard. Bit my lip. The taste of copper was everywhere. Martín—Martín was out cold. The dog lost it. And then the snow..." I exhaled slowly. "It sounded like a roar. Not wind. Just... power. All at once."

Luc's jaw flexed. The muscle there jumped once, twice. He held himself perfectly still, the kind of stillness that meant he was listening with everything he had.

"The windshield started to cave," I said. "It all went dark. And then everything stopped. Completely still. Like the mountain was holding its breath around us."

Annie's fingers curled around her napkin.

"I don't know how long we stayed like that," I said. "It felt like hours. It could've been minutes."

A moment of silence wrapped around us.

Luc pushed his bowl an inch away, fingers curling lightly on the table edge.

"You didn't see the outside," he said quietly.

I looked at him.

Careful.

Soft.

Waiting.

He breathed once—deep enough that his chest shifted noticeably—then spoke. The breath wasn't steady. It wavered, like he had to anchor himself to the table before the words could come out.

"The Brigada de Rescate found the truck," he said. "A local saw the debris and called it in. I went with them."

I'd heard bits of this before. Never the whole thing. Never from him.

"They had to use a winch," he said. "The truck was nose-down, buried almost vertical in the drift. No one knew if anyone was alive inside."

He paused, eyes fixed somewhere near my wrist.

"They pulled it up. Snow everywhere. Metal bent. Windows cracked."

He swallowed.

"And I... went in."

Went in.

A polite phrasing.

I'd already learned the truth from Rafa—how Luc pushed two rescuers out of the way, crawled into the barely-open passenger side, and refused to come out until someone physically tugged him.

He would never admit it.

"You weren't moving when they winched it up," he said. "I thought—"

He stopped.

His fingers curled against his knee, the only sign he hadn't managed to swallow the rest of the sentence. The unfinished sentence landed like a blade between us.

Annie didn't speak. Didn't blink. She just watched him the way only a sister can—seeing too much.

Luc sat back slowly, breath measured, as if anything more might unravel him.

The room held its breath.

Then he reached for the wine.

He didn't pour dramatically or ceremoniously—just filled each glass with a steady hand. The steadiness was a lie; his knuckles stayed pale around the bottle.

Annie eyed hers carefully.

"Fair warning," Annie murmured. "I'm a notorious lightweight with anything red and fermented."

Luc huffed a quiet laugh. "Try this one."

She lifted the glass, swirled it like she'd seen Juliette do, sniffed—

—and made a sound I can only describe as a sensual shockwave.

"Holy shit."

She took a long sip. "This is—oh my God. This is like velvet had a baby with a sunset."

Luc blinked. "It's just Malbec."

"No. No it is not 'just Malbec,'" she said, eyes narrowing in delighted betrayal. "If Emme isn't already in love with you, then I'm about to be."

My throat closed around air.

Luc froze mid-reach. Not shock. More like a flicker of thought stopping him, then disappearing beneath his usual calm.

Silence cracked like thin ice.

Annie, utterly unbothered, took another sip and moaned again.

She swallowed, pointed her glass at Luc, and said, "Also—sorry, I've been distracted by trauma—but does your accent always sound like that?"

Luc blinked hard. "My accent?"

"Yes." Annie gestured aggressively. "The thing you do with your vowels? Honestly *illegal*."

I kicked her under the table.

She ignored me.

Luc looked at me like he needed a translator.

I shook my head. "Don't ask."

He didn't.

A moment later, Annie sat up straighter—serious now.

"Okay," she said quietly. "Real talk time."

Luc stilled.

I did too.

"Summer is drowning."

My pulse stumbled.

"She's covering your new Patagonia vendors," Annie said. "Plus your Miami clients. Plus the Portugal retreat updates. She's... not sleeping."

My chest tightened.

Luc watched me carefully. A small softness passed through his eyes—barely there, but it landed.

"What happens if she keeps this up?" he asked quietly.

No judgment.

Just a man who understood pressure cracks when he saw one.

I exhaled, sharp enough to sting on the way out.

"She breaks. And if she breaks, the business breaks."

Luc threw me the quickest look, like he was checking if I was breathing or bullshitting.

Honestly? Either was possible.

The truth sat heavy in my lap—warmer than the wine and twice as unsteady.

"And Daisy—bless her heart—tried to help."

Annie let out a slow breath, something darker threading underneath it.

"And that's... not even the worst of it."

My stomach dipped.

"Summit's moving in on Patagonia," she said. "Hard. They were sniffing around one of the glacierside investments."

Luc's shoulders went rigid. He didn't speak, but the stillness around him changed—denser, sharper, like someone had just walked a blade across a fault line.

"They found out Wilder Horizons already locked down your contract with him," she continued, nodding toward Luc. "Now they're pissed. They're accelerating their own vendor deals. Throwing stupid money around."

A cold prickle slid down my spine.

"If you don't get back soon," Annie said softly, "they'll swallow Patagonia whole and call it synergy."

She leaned back, eyes gentler now. "Florida doesn't just need you... Patagonia needs you too. Not to run—"

Her gaze softened even more. "—but to lead."

A pause.

A very pointed pause.

Luc watched me.

Watched the guilt climbing up my spine.

I looked down at my hands. The weight of responsibility pressed against my ribs.

Luc leaned forward, just enough that his voice landed softer.

"Emme," he said. "Your sister can handle clients. She can handle chaos. She cannot..."

He hesitated, choosing. "...handle losing you." His voice held steady, but his hand trembled once on the tabletop before he pulled it back into his lap.

The words hit like they were meant specifically for the small, shaky part of me I kept hidden.

Annie swallowed, eyes darting between us like she was witnessing a confession neither of us had spoken aloud.

I breathed out slow, steady, and still not steady enough.

Something shifted.

Annie took a slow sip of wine, eyes flicking between us.

"Right. Noted."

Luc blinked. "Noted?"

"You know." She waved a hand between us. "The vibe. The breathing. The near-death devotion. All that."

I groaned. "Annie."

"What?" she said. "I'm observant, not blind."

Luc's mouth twitched—barely—but it was there, a tiny crack in the armor.

Annie stabbed another bite of stew, deliberately casual. "Anyway. This is culinary manipulation by the way..." she mumbled around it.

I pressed my lips together to hide a laugh. Annie could defuse a bomb with nothing but an eating utensil and some attitude.

We drifted into softer conversation after that—small things, lighter topics.

The wine loosened Annie's shoulders.

The stew settled warmth into my bones.

Luc shifted his leg carefully, the pain returning in small pulses he tried not to show.

I saw it anyway.

Eventually, the plates sat empty.

The wine low.

The candles softened to small, molten curls of flame.

We didn't move.

Didn't need to.

Just three people breathing in the same little pocket of warmth with more truth on the table than food.

Annie nudged me under the table. "You good?"

I nodded, even though my pulse disagreed.

Luc's gaze held mine—steady as a held breath, calm in that infuriating, unblinking way of his. There was something raw beneath it, a quiet plea he never said aloud, the kind you only recognize when you're already half undone.

No pressure.

No expectation.

Just truth sitting between us like a fourth person at the table.

My heartbeat flickered.

Too fast.

Too aware of him.

I looked away first.

Coward.

And God help me...

The jolt of that—of *him*—scared me more than anything the mountain threw at me.

Chapter 32

Too Close, Too Warm, Too Late

EMME

ANNIE SLIPPED UPSTAIRS NOT long after dinner—claiming she needed to "wind down," which, for her, meant cleansing balm, ten minutes with her journal, and falling into bed at a forty-five-degree angle. Her footsteps faded above us, soft thuds and the occasional zip-zip-zip of a woman settling in.

Luc and I moved to the great room, where it had settled into a low, breathing quiet. Firelight licking the stone hearth. Shadows stretching long across the rug. The kind of silence that doesn't ask anything of you.

He sat down next to me and immediately guided me into him, one effortless tug that set my back against his chest. His warmth wrapped around me before I could decide whether to resist or melt.

Jesus. One tug and my ribs unlocked.

Neither of us spoke.

But neither of us needed to.

I let my gaze drift over the dying fire, the orange glow flickering against the windows. Tonight felt... steadier. My shoulders finally lowered a fraction, like the room had exhaled with me.

Annie's words replayed in loops.

If you don't get back soon, they'll swallow Patagonia whole and call it synergy.

Florida doesn't just need you... Patagonia needs you too.
Not to run—but to lead.

For the first time, the pull toward home didn't feel like retreat. Didn't feel like abandoning Luc. Didn't feel like crawling back to safety because the air was too thin here.

It felt like... stewardship. Like showing up for the thing I built instead of hoping someone else would patch the cracks. Like choosing the life I wanted instead of reacting to whatever storm was next.

Luc didn't fill the silence. Didn't try to sway me or soothe me or make it easier.

He stayed behind me, solid and warm, his arms a steady wrap around my ribs—a quiet constant I let myself rest in.

"Your sister," he finally said, voice low, "she's sharp."

I huffed a breath. "Weaponized, some might say."

"Good," he murmured.

I turned. "Good?"

His eyes flicked to mine—slow, deliberate. "Someone needs to look out for you when you're busy looking out for everyone else."

Heat fluttered low in my ribs, my breath hitching before I could hide it. Not romantic heat. Something steadier. Older. The kind of heat that says *I see you. All of you.*

The fire popped softly.

I looked back at it, pulse settling into something even.

"Going home doesn't feel like running anymore," I said quietly. "It feels like picking up a thread I dropped when the world went white."

His inhale was slow. Deep. As if he tucked that sentence somewhere private.

"I'm not asking you to stay," he said.

"I know."

"I'm also not asking you to leave."

I smiled at the flames. "I know that too."

Silence, warm and full.

Somewhere above us, Annie opened a drawer too aggressively and muttered a curse.

Luc's lips twitched.

I nudged his good leg with my knee. "She's staying with me tonight."

"I assumed."

"You're not nervous she's up there compiling files on you?"

"I survived dinner," he said. "The background check is inevitable."

God, his deadpan. It disarmed me every time.

I leaned back into the couch, letting the quiet settle again, heavier now, but comfortable.

Eventually, I stood.

He rose with me—slowly—balancing on his good foot.

The ache pulled at his expression, but he didn't complain.

I reached for his elbow.

He let me.

We climbed the stairs side by side, our hands never fully intertwining, just brushing once—enough to make the air feel charged.

At the landing, he paused.

"Come back," he murmured, chin tipping toward his room.

My stomach dipped.

"I will," I said—too quickly, too honest.

Then I slipped into my room, feeling him linger behind me even after the door clicked shut.

Annie had already made herself at home—shoes off, hair piled up, her journal resting open beside her—perched on the edge of the bed like a cat with a fresh piece of gossip.

"You two were quiet down there," she said, one brow lifted. "Comfortable quiet or sexually-charged quiet?"

I dropped my sweater on the chair. "Annie."

"What? I'm gathering context."

"Context for what?"

"How worried I need to be about your heart and whether I should prep an 'Are his intentions pure?' questionnaire."

I laughed into my hands. "You've known him for three hours."

"And yet," she said, finger raised, "I've seen *enough*."

I shook my head but sat beside her anyway.

She softened—just a shade—like her internal gears downshifted.

"Emme," she said quietly, "you know I like him. I do. He's steady. He listens. He cooks like a Patagonia kitchen deity."

I snorted.

"But..." she continued, and the word landed gently, not as a warning but as an invitation, "are you choosing him... or choosing yourself right now?"

The question slid under my ribs.

I breathed in.

The truth rose without permission.

"Both," I said. "I need both."

There it is. The truth. Loud as a siren.

Annie's face broke into something small and proud and devastatingly tender.

She squeezed my hand. "Then it's the right next step."

I swallowed.

She let go first, like she knew if she didn't, I'd fall apart a little.

"We'll talk more tomorrow," she said. "I'm spending the day going over the Refugio numbers with Luc—annual projections, capital flow, partnership margins."

I blinked. "Does he know that?"

"Not yet," she said brightly.

"You're going to terrify him."

I stood and paused, fingers grazing the doorframe like my body wasn't sure where to go next.

Annie looked up, eyes gentler now. "Emme... go to him."

My throat tightened. "You good for the night?"

"Please," she said, already burrowing under the blankets, "I'm going to sleep like a sedated llama."

I choked. "That's not—"

But she was already waving at me, dismissing me with a contented grunt.

I turned off the lamp.

The hallway felt cooler, dimmer, quieter.

Luc's door waited at the far end, and my body followed the pull long before my feet realized they'd started moving.

His room glowed with a single warm lamp, soft light pooling over the wooden floors. He sat propped against the headboard, cast elevated, hair mussed like he'd run a hand through it too many times.

My heart stuttered once. *That look should be outlawed. And probably regulated.*

When he saw me, something in his face loosened. Not relief exactly—more like confirmation.

"You came," he said softly.

I closed the door behind me.

"Of course I did."

He watched every step I took, gaze steady and dark—something tightening in the space between us.

When I reached the bed, his hand slid along my hip—slow, asking nothing, promising everything.

"Emme," he murmured, voice rougher now, "Reste avec moi ce soir." *Stay with me tonight.*

Heat pooled low, slow and inevitable.

I leaned in, fingers brushing the line of his jaw.

"Yeah," I whispered. "I'm not going anywhere tonight."

He pulled me into him, the awkward bulk of his cast knocking against my leg, but none of it mattered once his mouth found mine. There was nothing clumsy about the way he kissed me—just heat and intent and a kind of focus that stilled the space around us.

His hands came up, framing my face like he needed to feel every inch of me to breathe. His thumbs brushed along my cheekbones, slow and sure, and then his mouth deepened the kiss—hungry, certain, undoing me one heartbeat at a time.

When he finally dragged in air, his nose brushed mine, our breaths tangling in the small, warm space between us.

"Je te veux, Emme. Tout de suite." *I want you. Now.*

A shiver ran straight down my spine, sharp and electric.

"Then take me," I whispered, voice low and wrecked, the words pulled from somewhere deeper than want.

My fingers were already on the buttons of his flannel, working them open one by one. He let me, his hands sliding under the hem of my sweater, searching for the warm skin along my back. His touch burned, even through the thin cotton.

He pushed the fabric higher and I lifted my arms without thinking, letting him pull it over my head and drop it somewhere on the floor. My bra was nothing special—just soft lace—but the sound he made when he saw it went straight through me.

Nope. Absolutely not. I am not surviving that look.

His knuckles skimmed the peaks tightening under the fabric, a light pass that sent heat shooting low and fast.

He shifted his weight and lowered himself to the floor in front of me, using the edge of the bed for balance. It wasn't graceful—his cast stuck out at an impossible angle—but the look in his eyes made it irrelevant.

Focused.

Intent.

Almost reverent.

His hands settled at my hips, thumbs sliding under the waistband of my pants and the thin stretch of my underwear. I braced my palms on his shoulders—solid, warm, familiar—and lifted just enough for him to work the fabric down.

He peeled them off slowly, dragging everything over my skin in one long, deliberate glide. His knuckles skimmed my thighs, light enough to make my breath catch. When the last scrap of fabric hit the floor, he blew out a quiet, rough breath.

I stood bare in front of him, the cool air brushing over heated skin. But the way he looked at me—hungry and sure—was hotter than anything in the room.

He didn't rush. He shifted closer, his cast angled awkwardly to the side, and pressed a slow, open-mouthed kiss to the inside of my thigh. His stubble scraped lightly across sensitive skin, and the breath punched out of me. My fingers slid into his dark, messy hair on instinct.

"Si beau." *So beautiful.*

Another kiss. Softer. Lower.

My knees wobbled, a tremor pulling through me as I widened my stance, giving him space.

Take me apart, then. Go on.

A quiet sound rumbled in his chest, approval and hunger tangled together.

He looked up at me then, eyes catching mine and holding, steady and dark and intent, as he leaned in—slow enough to unravel me before he even touched me.

The first sweep of his tongue was slow and sure, a warm, deliberate stroke that punched a sound out of me before I could stop it. I arched toward him, helpless against the way he tasted me—like he'd been thinking about this, needing this.

He hummed against me, low and rough, the vibration hitting straight through my center and stealing every coherent thought I had left.

Then he really started.

He wasn't careful. He wasn't polished. He was hungry in a way that felt real—raw devotion wrapped in heat and focus.

God. This.

His mouth traced every shape of me, learning me, claiming every reaction, before he found the tight, aching knot of my clit.

He circled it slowly at first, teasing, testing, then pressed in with more intent, more pressure, his whole focus zeroing in on the place that made my legs shake.

One hand slid from my hip, his fingers easing through my slickness—gathering it, spreading it. Like he needed to feel just how far gone I was.

"Look at me, Emme," he said—soft, but in a way that left no space for anything else.

Oh God.

I did.

My eyes lifted, heavy and unfocused with pleasure, and he caught them—held them—like he'd been waiting for that exact second.

Slowly, deliberately, he brought his slick fingers to his mouth. His lips closed around them, tongue curling as he sucked them clean, and the sight hit me so hard I felt my knees threaten to give.

A sound tore out of me—half moan, half disbelief.

His eyes darkened.

"Tu as le goût du paradis," he murmured, rough enough to vibrate through me. *Heaven.*

Then his mouth was on me again—no hesitation, no restraint—and the world dropped out from under my feet.

He devoured me.

His tongue found my clit with a rhythm so sure, so focused, it stole the air from my lungs. And when his fingers slid back into my slick, he didn't tease. He pressed one inside me, then two, stretching me, filling me, curling up in a way that detonated behind my eyes.

White heat. Stars. Nothing else.

"Luc... je..." The words tore out of me, broken and useless, my French collapsing under the weight of what he was doing to me—reducing me to nothing but sensation.

"Oui, viens pour moi," he breathed against me—*come for me*—his words melting straight into my skin. His mouth and fingers worked in a perfect, ruthless rhythm, pulling me higher with every stroke.

"Lâche prise... donne-moi tout," he urged, let go, *give me everything*, his voice low and coaxing as he drew me deeper into the heat of him.

Fuccck. This man is going to be the death of me.

The pleasure coiled tight and hot low in my belly, ready to snap. My cries slipped out in a jumble of English and broken French, my voice catching in places I didn't know could break.

"Maintenant, Emme," he growled—*now*—and my body obeyed before my mind caught up.

It was the command in his voice, the certainty of it, that broke me open. The orgasm hit hard, a white-hot rush that stole my breath and sent my knees buckling. A cry tore out of me—raw, shaking—as I clenched around his fingers, my body arching helplessly into the wave.

Luc held me through every second. His mouth softened, gentling, tasting me as the shudders kept coming. He didn't stop until the last ripple eased out of me and I sagged against him, boneless, my hands locked on his shoulders like they were the only solid thing left in the room.

He eased his fingers from me with a gentleness that made my throat tighten. Then he pressed one last, reverent kiss to the inside of my thigh, a soft seal over skin that was still trembling.

When he looked up, his face was slick with my release, his eyes dark—satisfaction, hunger, something deeper I wasn't ready to name all tangled together.

"Et ce n'est que le commencement," he said, voice rough with everything he was holding back. *And that's only the beginning.*

Chapter 33

Scaling Up, Holding On

LUC

T HE MORNING CREPT IN long before I was ready for it.

Not that I'd slept. Neither of us had, not really. We'd grabbed pockets of rest between the heat and the laughter and the kind of slow, breathless hours that felt stitched together from another lifetime.

By the time gray light pushed at the curtains, Emme was curled against me—warm, quiet, and tangled up like she belonged there. The woodstove downstairs had burned low overnight, leaving the quiet, smoky warmth that always settled into the rafters this time of year. My body ached in every place she'd touched, and my cast wasn't helping, but I wouldn't have traded a single second of the night.

Ça valait le coup. Chaque putain de seconde. Worth every damn second.

She pressed a soft kiss to my chest when she finally rolled out of bed. "Coffee," she mumbled, hair a mess, voice wrecked in a way that made something primal and stupid flare up in my chest.

If I could've walked without the cast, I might've followed her like a shadow.

Instead, I hauled myself upright slowly, breathing through the sting in my ankle. I'd barely made it to the top of the stairs when a small, decisive figure appeared in the hallway.

Annie.

Hands on her hips.

Reddish-brown hair with attitude.

Barefoot, trim, fit, wrapped in one of Emme's sweaters that hung off her petite frame like armor disguised as knitwear.

She took one look at me and didn't even pretend to be subtle.

"Oh," she said, eyebrows lifting. "So that's why neither of you slept."

I froze.

Pourquoi elle me regarde comme ça... like she's auditing my soul.

She did not.

"I mean, honestly," she continued, waving a hand at my face, "you look like you wrestled a puma and lost. And Emme—" she pointed toward the kitchen, "—looks like she won."

Heat crawled up my neck. "Annie—"

"Relax," she said, breezing past me with the confidence of someone who had already decided I wasn't a threat. "If I didn't approve, you'd know it. Loudly."

I blinked.

"And just so we're clear," she added over her shoulder, "I might be five-foot-four and built like a woodland nymph, but I can drop you in under thirty seconds if you ever hurt her."

Putain... un tigre dans une peau de chaton. A damn tiger in kitten skin. Figures.

I stared after her. "I believe you."

"Good," she chirped, disappearing down the stairs. "Keep that attitude."

By the time I made it to the kitchen, Emme was leaning against the counter with a mug, trying—and failing—to hide the flush at the tips of her ears.

Ce rouge-là, c'est à cause de moi. Bien. That blush? Mine. Good.

My fingers twitched on the countertop, stupidly ready to pull her back into my arms.

Annie took one look at her face and snorted. "Uh-huh."

Emme glared. "Not a word."

"Oh, love," Annie said sweetly, "I have *entire paragraphs*, but I'm choosing mercy."

Despite myself, I laughed. I didn't let it out fully—my ribs still felt tight from everything I wasn't ready to admit—but Annie caught it.

Her eyes softened just a fraction.

That seemed to be the thing about her—sharp edges, yes, but all of them pointed in the direction of love.

She claimed a chair like she was staking territory, crossed her legs, and slipped into what I could only describe as professional predator mode.

"So," she said, adjusting her braid, "we're going over your numbers today."

I blinked. "My what?"

"Refugio finances. Vendor agreements. Projections. All of it." She reached for her coffee like she was discussing the weather. "I figure we'll need a few hours."

I looked at Emme.

She mouthed, *I didn't know either.*

But she was smiling—small, proud, like this was exactly what her sister did. Fixed things. Protected people. Even people she'd met twelve hours ago.

A five-foot-four force of nature who could bulldoze her way through an empire with spreadsheets and charm.

Before I could respond, the coffeemaker sputtered.

Emme moved toward it automatically. "The beans are in the top cabinet," she offered, reaching up.

Her shirt rode just enough to distract me for a full second too long.

"Here," I said, stepping closer, trying not to think about the night we'd had. "Let me—"

"No, sit," Emme tugged me gently toward a stool. "Your ankle."

I lowered myself onto it, biting back a wince. Annie caught the micro-flinch and narrowed her eyes like she'd just diagnosed a structural flaw.

"Emme," she said lightly, "can you grab me a pen? I want to jot down a few things before we dive in."

Emme nodded and slipped out of the kitchen toward my office.

The second she was gone, Annie pivoted on me like a missile locking onto a target.

Her voice dropped.

Her expression sharpened.

She didn't bother pretending this wasn't intentional.

"Luc," she said quietly, "she hasn't told you she's thinking about leaving tomorrow, has she?"

A cold, clean drop landed in my stomach.

Putain... please don't let this be the part where everything turns.

"No," I said. Truth. "She hasn't."

Annie nodded once, like she'd expected that. "She only decided this morning. And she's still not sure."

My pulse thudded. "Because of me?"

"No," Annie said firmly. "She's trying to make the right call for the company. For herself... and for you."

I swallowed. Hard.

"I should've seen the weight she was carrying," I said, pulse hammering. "I'd never put that on her."

Annie studied me for a beat, like she was recalibrating whatever blueprint she'd sketched of me overnight.

"She's scared, yes," Annie continued, softer now. "But not of you. Of feeling more than she planned to. Of how fast this is. Of what it means outside a storm and a crisis."

My chest tightened, sharp and sudden.

She reached out and gave my arm a small, grounding squeeze, the first real softness she'd shown me.

"She's not running from you," Annie added. "She's trying not to run past you."

Those words hit like a blade—clean, precise, unavoidable. Sharp enough that I had to shift on the stool just to breathe.

I stared off for a second, like the room might give me an answer I didn't have yet. "I've already lost too much once," I said quietly. "I don't want to lose her."

A truth I rarely said aloud, because speaking it always felt like reopening a wound I'd stitched shut years ago.

Annie didn't flinch. "Then don't."

I met her eyes.

"In my gut," she said, unwavering, "I know she'll come back. That's not hope. That's who she is."

Footsteps returned down the hall.

Annie stepped back, sipping her coffee like she hadn't just reshaped the terrain beneath my feet.

Emme reentered with a pen tucked behind her ear, eyes softening when she saw me. Her hand brushed my shoulder—gentle, careful—and something warm cracked open inside me.

Tomorrow, she might leave.

But today...

Today I chose to believe she'd return.

Annie let the moment breathe exactly two seconds before she clapped her hands once, the sound crisp enough to cut through the fog in my head.

"Alright," she announced, sliding her tablet onto the table between us, "we're doing this properly." Outside, the wind pressed against the glass—steady, unhurried—like the mountain reminding us it was still here, still watching.

Emme blinked. "Annie—"

"No," Annie said, cool as an accountant about to audit a kingdom. "Luc deserves clarity. And Wilder needs alignment. And the sooner we build this bridge, the less chaos there'll be when the legal paperwork starts."

She angled the tablet toward me, tabs already open—expansion projections, service upgrades, insurance alignments, seasonal capacity planning.

I had to respect the efficiency.

Emme sank into the chair beside her. "Okay. How do you want to split this?"

"Easy," Annie said. "I handle finances. You handle vendors. Luc handles operations and on-the-ground logistics."

She pointed her pen at me first.

"Financial side," she said briskly. "Your last quarter tracked exactly where we expected—with waitlists six months out. But expansion means tightening a few things: insurance alignment, storm-season contingencies, and making sure guest capacity can scale without compromising what makes this place special."

I exhaled. "That's the part I care about. Growth without losing the soul of it."

She slid a page toward me with proposed expense buffers. "Refugio needs resilience built into the model—an emergency fund, two new seasonal hires, and a maintenance budget that isn't an afterthought."

"That's doable," I said immediately.

Both sisters looked at me—impressed, maybe. Or relieved.

"And staffing?" I added before Annie could continue. "Rafa does what three men do. It isn't sustainable."

Annie smiled, sharp and approving. "Exactly. You'll interview candidates remotely. I'll send a shortlist from the local job boards. We'll get someone before the next storm cycle."

"Good," I said. "Next."

She swiveled to her sister. "Vendor side."

Emme straightened, already in work mode. "Carmen's vineyard contract is drafted and ready for signature. Matías is reviewing the outfitter partnership terms. The artisan cooperative wants to scale slowly, but they're open to a winter-exclusive launch. And I've updated the logistics matrix—transport miles, delivery schedules, sustainability ratings."

Annie's brows lifted. "Damn. You've been busy."

"She has," I said quietly.

Emme's cheeks flushed, but she kept going. "I'll finish the vendor packet tonight. When I'm back in Maris Key, I'll handle approvals and legal formatting. If Wilder signs off, we'll have the Patagonia tier ready by New Year's."

"That timeline works for us," Annie said. "And for him?"

She looked at me.

"It works," I said. "It's fast, but it works."

"Good," Annie said. "Once Wilder's side is set, we start integration—Brynn on cross-marketing, Juliette on the legal framework, Rayann on bookings, and full insurance and liability alignment. None of this lands on your shoulders alone."

"Appreciate that," I said. "I just don't want Emme hitting the ground at a sprint the second she's home."

Both sisters froze for a beat.

Then Emme smiled—small, stunned, warm enough to flatten me.

Annie cleared her throat like she needed to reset the air.

She tapped the final tab open. "Last piece. Storm in-frastructure. The generator—"

"Replacing it," I said.

"Good," Annie said. "Not repairing—replacing. I'll send you three quotes."

"And I'm upgrading the emergency protocols," I added. "Trail closures, route markers, radio repeaters. Rafa and I talked about it before the avalanche. It wasn't enough. It will be now."

That got Annie's full attention. "You're already thinking ahead," she said, and this time her tone held zero teasing—just respect. "Exactly what we want in a partner."

Emme bumped my shoulder. "Told you he wasn't some cautionary tale."

"I did *not* call him that," Annie objected.

"You hinted," Emme said.

"I hinted that I didn't know him yet," Annie corrected.

Emme rolled her eyes. I tried not to smile. Annie pretended she hadn't been flustered.

She stood, stretching, her sweater sliding off one shoulder. "Alright. That's phase one. We'll finesse details later. But as of this morning, Refugio Cielo is officially on the road to full partnership with Wilder Horizons."

Something settled in my chest—not tightness. Not fear.

Purpose. A steady thing. A thing I hadn't felt since before the avalanche... maybe before my whole life tilted sideways.

"And Luc?" Annie added, pausing in the doorway.

I raised a brow.

Her voice softened. "When she comes back, you'll be ready. Not waiting—ready."

Prêt ? I'd level the ridge if it meant she walked back to me smiling.

Emme inhaled like the words hit her straight in the ribs.

Annie disappeared down the hall before either of us could speak.

The quiet that followed wasn't tense or fragile.

It was full.

Warm.

Alive with possibility.

Emme turned toward me, her knee brushing mine. "You sure you're up for all this?"

"Yes," I said. No hesitation. "I want this."

Her breath caught. A small, stunned thing.

She didn't kiss me. She didn't need to.

Her hand slid into mine—gentle, sure, hopeful. My thumb brushed her knuckles without thinking, like my body had already decided something my mind was still catching up to.

Ceci... ça, je ne le lâche pas. This I can hold onto.

Tomorrow, she might leave.

But tonight we had a plan.

And plans...

Plans meant she'd come back.

Chapter 34

Heat Shock

EMME

BY THE TIME THE plane wheels hit the runway, my pulse had been humming for three straight hours.

Florida humidity slapped me in the face the second I stepped off the jet bridge. Not metaphorically. Literally. The air felt thick enough to drink. A far cry from the thin, glacier-cold bite of Patagonia that still lived in the grooves of my bones.

Beside me, Annie adjusted her backpack straps and sighed. "God, I missed being able to breathe without my nostrils freezing together."

I didn't tell her that breathing here felt harder. Denser. Crowded.

A metal luggage cart slammed against another one up ahead, and the sharp clang shot down my spine so fast my vision pixelated for half a second.

It was nothing.

Just a noise.

Just Florida.

Just heat.

But my body didn't know the difference yet. My knees locked instinctively, stupid-fast.

Annie angled her head toward me, scanning the edges of my expression like only a sister could. She didn't ask. She didn't hover. She simply shifted slightly closer so our arms brushed each time we turned.

I pretended not to notice, shifting my bag higher on my shoulder—busy hands, busy posture. That was the mercy she offered: presence without commentary.

We made it through baggage claim and into the wall of sunlight outside. The brightness hit differently here—too white, too open—like something that hadn't learned to be gentle.

My phone buzzed as we crossed the curb.

LUC: Send me a picture when you land. Je veux voir tes yeux. *I want to see your eyes.*

I swallowed, thumb hovering over the screen.

ME: Landed. Sun's a little aggressive. You'd hate it.

Three dots appeared.

Then—

LUC: Ouais. You're where you need to be. I'll text when dawn hits the ridge.

A small, stupid warmth unfurled low in my ribs. Dawn on the ridge. He knew those words worked on me like a tether.

I tucked my phone away before I could cling too hard to it.

The drive across the causeway felt longer than usual. The Gulf was a sheet of blue glass stretching out forever, dotted with sailboats and jet skis and tourists who had absolutely no idea how lucky they were to exist in a world where mountains didn't fall on top of them.

A truck hit a pothole two cars ahead. The jolt cracked like a gunshot against concrete.

My fingers clenched around the seatbelt before my brain caught up.

Annie didn't look at me. Instead, she nudged the AC vent so the air hit my face directly. "Jet lag's hitting, huh?"

"Yeah," I said, grateful for the lie she offered me.

I wasn't ready for the truth.

Not yet.

Maybe soon.

The Wilder Horizons headquarters rose from the lush landscaping like it always did—coastal-modern, glass and whitewash and a ridiculous number of palm trees Juliette insisted were "branding." Inside, the staff sprang up like we'd returned from a month-long trek in the Andes.

I paused at the bookings board, eyes pulling straight to Patagonia. A dense cluster of red pins—surging, over-flowing, multiplying. The sight should've grounded me. Instead it felt like watching someone else's life take off without me.

"EMME!"

"Oh my god, you're BACK!"

"Tell us everything—wait, no, you look exhausted, don't tell us anything—should we get wine?"

I smiled. I even laughed. It wasn't fake. It just felt... misaligned. Like my emotions were half a beat behind the world. Like stepping off a moving walkway and mis-judging the floor.

When things quieted, I slipped into my office, in-haling the familiar scent of citrus cleaner and ocean air drifting through the vents. Normally soothing. Today it felt like my ribs cinched, like a belt had been yanked one notch too far.

Then a landscaper fired up a weed trimmer outside.

The high, buzzing whine—

God.

I dropped my coffee.

It splattered across the desk, dark and starbursting across a stack of vendor printouts.

Before I could move, Annie was already there, hand lightly braced on my elbow. No pity. No panic. Just stable gravity. Her presence alone leveled the tilt in the room.

"Sit," she murmured.

"I'm fine," I said. Reflexive. Useless.

She arched the Wilder-sister-bullshit-detection eyebrow. "You're many things. Fine isn't one of them."

I exhaled through my nose, steady but shaky underneath. The kind of breath you take when you're trying not to rewrite the past on a loop.

"It's loud," I said quietly. "Everything's loud here."

"That tracks," she said. Like I'd reported a weather update. "And you're allowed to feel that."

I rubbed my palms against my leggings. "I thought it would fade as soon as I left the mountain."

"Brains don't work on airport schedules," she replied gently. "You've been through something real. Your body's still talking."

I hated how those words cracked something open in me. My throat tightened like I'd swallowed ice.

Not weak. Just honest.

Annie crouched in front of me and took my hands—lightly, carefully, like I might bolt. "We'll get you someone to talk to. A professional. Someone who understands trauma responses."

"I don't..." A breath. "I don't want this to get in the way."

"It's not in the way," she said. "It's part of the path."

I stared at her. My steady baby sister, hands warm around mine. Patagonia's cold still lingering in my bones. Luc's voice somewhere between memory and heartbeat.

And for the first time since I'd landed, air moved easier through my lungs, as if someone had eased a window open in a stuffy room.

"Okay," I whispered. "Find me someone."

"I already have names," she said, standing. "I was waiting for you to catch up."

I let out a shaky laugh. "Of course you were."

Later, after a meeting with my sisters—an hour of cross-updates, vendor chatter, and Juliette's rapid-fire "we need to capitalize on Patagonia demand immediately"—I realized I'd answered half their questions on muscle memory alone. Their voices blurred; my responses came preloaded.

"Emme, do you want Daisy to move the Patagonia tier to the homepage?"

"Sure. Keep the language clean," I'd said, hearing the words before I actually decided them.

"Timeline for the artisan launch?"

"Monday. Margins intact."

My mouth did the talking, but my mind felt a half-step behind, like I was watching myself through glass while the room moved too fast, too bright, too loud. None of them seemed to notice—thank God—but Annie shot me one long, quiet look that told me she absolutely did.

After the meeting, after the unpacking and the slow, careful reconnection with a world that hadn't been buried in snow, I finally stepped onto my own balcony, the sliding door clicking shut behind me.

The sun was dropping fast—peach bleeding into the Gulf, the kind of watercolor haze tourists used for Christmas card photos. The air was warm and a little salty, brushing against my skin like Florida trying to welcome me back without asking too many questions.

My phone buzzed—a photo from Luc.

Dawn breaking over the ridge. Indigo turning gold.

LUC: Le matin te dit bonjour. *The morning says hello.*

I huffed out something between a laugh and a sigh. Right. Opposite seasons. Opposite schedules. Opposite hemispheres. Somehow still synced.

Florida behind me. Patagonia under his feet.

Two worlds. One life stretching between them like a tightrope I didn't mind walking.

I leaned on the railing, watching the pink-gold smear across the water.

The mountain wasn't gone from me.

Neither was he.

It wasn't perfect. But it was honest. And that felt like a good place to start.

The next morning, the Florida sun was already too bright by the time I walked into the small office suite Annie had somehow secured on zero notice. That was her magic trick: bending reality to her will with a phone call and a polite-but-terrifying tone.

The waiting room was quiet. Soft gray walls. A diffuser humming something lavender-adjacent. A framed print that said *You are safe here*, which I tried not to roll my eyes at.

A woman stepped into the doorway. Mid-forties. Steady posture. Kind eyes, but not the fragile kind that made you feel like you needed to apologize for taking up oxygen.

"Emme?" she said.

I nodded.

"I'm Dr. Taylor. Come on back."

Her office was simple: two chairs, a low table, a plant that was either very alive or very good at faking it. No inspirational posters. No clichés. A win.

I sat. She didn't rush. Didn't prod. Just settled into her own chair like we had all the time in the world.

"So," she said softly. "Your sister mentioned you've been through something intense recently."

Understatement of the decade.

"Yeah," I said. "Avalanche. Buried truck. Storm. Long story."

"And you're back home now," she said, reading between my lines without climbing inside them. "How has the transition been?"

I let my hands rest on my knees. Still. Too still.

"Loud," I said. "Everything here is loud. Doors slamming. Cars hitting potholes. Even the sunlight feels... sharp."

"Your body is still in survival mode," she said. "It hasn't been convinced it's safe yet."

Safe.

Right.

"What else are you noticing?" she asked.

I hesitated. Then—

"Sometimes it feels like I'm watching myself move through the day. Like I'm here, but not... fully in it."

She nodded once. "Dissociation. Very common after trauma. It's your mind giving you distance from things that feel overwhelming."

She said it like a weather report. Calm. Unloaded.

"And when something startles you? Loud noises? Sudden movement?"

"They hit harder than they should." I swallowed. "Sometimes I smell gasoline and I don't know why. Or I hear metal and it feels like—"

"The hook on the truck," she finished gently.

I looked up. "Yeah."

We sat there for a beat. Not in silence—just in something level.

"We're not going to force anything," she said. "Our goal is grounding. Getting your mind and body back into the same room. Slowly. Safely."

I nodded.

Grounding sounded doable.

Grounding didn't ask me to rewrite the whole storm in one sitting.

"We'll start simple," she said. "Breathing. Sensory resets. Reclaiming the moments that feel slippery."

Slippery. Yep. That was the word for it.

My hands rubbed over the fabric of my leggings; texture helped.

"And Emme?"

"Yeah?"

"You're not broken," she said. "You're responding exactly as someone would who survived what you did."

That landed. Not as comfort. But as truth.

I exhaled, long and steady. My shoulders dropped an inch, maybe two.

"Okay," I said. "Let's start."

Chapter 35

No Doubt

LUC

THE MORNINGS FELT COLDER without her. The empty pillow cooled faster without her weight.

Not just the air—*me*. The quiet had bite again. The kind that sank into bone if you didn't keep moving. So I did. Before sunrise, before the generator cycled, before Rafa yelled at me for touching anything heavy with an ankle that was "*not healed enough for your bullshit, jefe,*" I was already outside, checking routes, inspecting the perimeter, counting the pieces of my world like a prayer.

My phone buzzed in my pocket.

Emme.

I didn't even make it inside. I swiped the message open with fingers still stiff from the cold.

EMME:
First session done.
Her name's Dr. Taylor. She's... good.
Grounding techniques. Breathing. Sensory resets.
It helped.

I reread the last line twice.

Helped.

Something eased in my chest, a knot untangling from the inside out. My shoulders dropped a fraction, like the mountain had shifted an inch off me.

I typed with cold thumbs, slow but steady.

ME: Je suis fier de toi. *I'm proud of you.*

A few seconds passed. Then her voice note came through. I held the phone to my ear, breath fogging the screen.

Her voice—softer than usual, but steady.

"I told her about the noises. The sunlight. The... watching-myself-from-a-distance thing. She wasn't surprised. She said it's normal." A shaky little laugh. "Normal. Imagine that."

My throat tightened. The cold had nothing to do with it.

She kept talking—quiet, honest. The kind of honesty people only gave when they trusted you with places inside them that still hurt.

"And she said I'm not broken," Emme finished softly. "Just... responding."

I leaned my free hand on the railing, head bowing for a beat.

ME: *Oui*. Exactly that.

Her next text came fast.

EMME: How's Martín?

I huffed out something that might've been a laugh. Of course she asked.

I glanced toward the treeline, where Martín's cabin sat half-buried behind stacked firewood and a rusted old truck he refused to retire. He'd worked a night shift with the forestry service—too stubborn to slow down just because a mountain tried to kill him.

ME:
He's bien.
Still swearing at the snow like it owes him money.
Says the avalanche "le dejó los huesos enojados con él."
His bones are mad at him.

Three dots.
Then—

EMME: I want to check on him myself. Next time I'm there.

A low, stupid ache settled in under my ribs. Good ache. Human ache. Missing-her ache. I shifted my weight, like adjusting might make room for it.

I answered before I thought:

ME: Je signe. *With you.*

She sent no words back—just a small heart. Barely anything. But it hit harder than a paragraph.

I pocketed the phone before I started doing something pathetic like replaying the voice note.

Inside the lodge, papers were spread across the dining table—spreadsheets, staffing requests, insurance forms that Juliette sent with instructions that read like threats. I stared at the packet she'd emailed that morning.

From: JULIETTE

Luc, please confirm that you have reviewed clauses 17A through 17F.

If you skip them, I will know.

We always know.

I muttered, "Qu'est-ce qu'elle veut encore..." *What now?*

Rafa looked up from the stove. "Boss sister?"

"She wants me to confirm that I haven't been an idiot."

"Have you?" he asked.

"Probably."

He snorted.

Then my phone buzzed again.

A new message from Rayann this time. The Sales Director. The unflappable one. The one whose confidence could break men in half.

RAYANN: Hi Luc! Quick question—what exactly is your "digital sales funnel"?

I stared at the phone like it had insulted my mother.
"Digital... quoi?" I said out loud. *What?*
Rafa shook his head. "Don't answer that. It's a trap."
"It *feels* like a trap," I muttered.
Then another message.

RAYANN: *I can help set one up for Refugio Cielo! Shouldn't take more than a day or two.*

No. No no no.
Digital funnels meant emails, automation, graphics.
Things with colors and charts. No.
I typed slowly:

ME: Merci but no. We like simple here.

Her response came instantly.

RAYANN: Cute. Not an option.

Merde.

I put the phone face-down and prayed for a damn lightning strike. Anything. Just take me out of this conversation.

But nothing compared to the next ding.

Brynn. The one who terrified me. The one who smiled like she knew all your secrets and would use them for marketing.

BRYNN:

Luc. Need confirmation on brand colors for promo assets.

Sending you a palette.

A palette arrived. Neon coral. Electric teal. Something that looked radioactive.

I whispered, "No. Dieu non."

Rafa leaned over my shoulder and winced. "They want to turn Refugio Cielo into a Miami nightclub?"

"I think so," I said, horrified.

Emme's message appeared beneath it.

EMME: Ignore the colors. She's just testing you.

Of course she was. I exhaled.

By late afternoon, I'd answered thirty-seven emails, signed six preliminary staffing contracts, and walked the ridge twice—more times than my ankle doctor would approve of. The path still had a drop-off that made my stomach react before my brain did.

Avalanche memory hit like a flashbulb:

The shout over the radio.

The sprint through knee-deep snow.

The crushed truck half-buried and silent.

Her face—white, still, barely there.

My jaw locked. I dragged in a slow breath. Held it. Let it out.

Just like Dr. Taylor coached her through.

Just like I'd learned to do too.

It helped.

But not enough to sleep. The pillow still held her shape, and that didn't help either.

So I worked instead.

Rafa found me hunched over the expansion plans, rubbing the scar along my temple with absent fingers.

"You're going to pass out on that paper," he said.

"I'm fine."

"You're lying."

"Oui."

He sat next to me, arms crossed. "You miss her."

I didn't say anything. My silence answered for me.

He nudged my shoulder with his. "Good. Means you're human."

I huffed. "Barely."

We sat there for a long time, two men staring at a blueprint like it could solve loneliness.

Finally Rafa stood. "Sign the damn papers, jefe. She'll be back."

I picked up the pen.

Signed every page.

Sealed the envelope.

Walked outside into the kind of cold that bit clean and honest.

Held the envelope to my chest for a second—just long enough to feel the weight of the decision.

Then whispered into the empty air:

"Elle revient. I know she does."

And I mailed it.

The lodge felt too quiet when I stepped back inside. Not empty—just... missing its center of gravity. Even the fire crackled softer. Her energy changed rooms, warmed corners she'd never admit to touching.

I walked through the main room, where her scarf was still draped on the back of a chair. She'd tossed it there the night before she left—halfway on, halfway off, like she couldn't decide if she was cold or done with Patagonia trying to freeze her.

I reached for it.

Stopped.

Then quietly... I moved it back to the hook she always used without thinking.

Minimal.

Stupid, maybe.

But my chest eased a fraction the moment it rested there. Like the room exhaled. Like I did.

I sat heavily at the dining table, the paperwork spread like snowdrift around me. Expansion plans. Vendor contracts. Insurance forms that made me grateful Emme handled the business side because mon dieu... I would have set half of this on fire long ago.

My phone buzzed. Annie. A voice note.

I braced. Pressed play.

"Luc Moreau," she announced, in a tone that somehow combined CEO authority with younger-sister meddling. "If you think signing that contract means you're not joining the Wilder Horizons infrastructure, think again. We've already penciled you in for two quarterly check-ins and one annual retreat. No running."

A beat. The tiniest smirk in her voice.

"Oh, and I'm proud of you. Don't make it weird."

The message ended.

I blinked at the phone. "Trop tard," I muttered. *Too late.* It was already weird.

When the silence settled again, it wasn't gentle. It hit with that same low, metallic groan—the one the mountain was still making when I reached the ridge. Not the avalanche itself... the *after*. The twisted quiet. Snow still shifting. The truck half-buried, engine choking under the weight. And the knowledge—sharp and immediate—that she was inside... and that I'd almost been too late.

I inhaled slow—four seconds.

Held.

Exhaled.

The way Emme said Dr. Taylor taught her.

The pressure eased. Not all the way. But enough.

My phone rang next. A local number I knew well—Martín's sister.

I answered. "Hola, Rocío."

"Luc!" Rocío said, her voice warm and a little bossy in the way she used on everyone in the valley. "I'm calling to check on you. Martín said the lodge has been busy and that you've been pretending you're made of steel again. And I heard Emme flew back to Florida."

"I'm fine."

"Are you?" she asked, gentler now.

A beat. "No."

A laugh. "Good. Means you're honest today. And Emme? She's okay? Martín says she was quite shaken."

"She's working with a doctor," I said. "It's helping."

"Bueno." A pause. Softer. "Tell her we're thinking of her. And stop working too much."

Then she hung up before I could swear I wasn't.

I leaned back in the chair. Rubbed a hand over my jaw. The mountain wind rattled the windowpanes like it agreed with her.

Ding.

Emme this time.

I opened it instantly—before the screen even lit completely.

A photo.

Her notebook, open. Handwritten notes scrawled across the page in her angled print. A grounding list. Breath counts. Three sentences about noise, sunlight, fear.

Caption: **Doing the work.**

Something inside me dropped and rose at the same time. A strange gravity shift. I touched the edge of the phone like it might pick up warmth from my hand.

Another buzz.

A second message—this one a selfie. She sat in a café, hair pulled back, cheeks flushed, a paper cup in her hands. Her smile small but real.

Caption: **Told Dr. Taylor about you. About us. I'm sure.**

Heat spread low in my chest. I had to breathe around it.

My vision went soft at the edges. Not blurred—soft. I swallowed against it.

Elle revient. Et moi... j'attends. *She's coming back. And I'll be ready.*

The vow formed before I could stop it. Quiet. Absolute.

I stood and went upstairs because the silence in my chest needed something to do with its hands. The bedroom smelled faintly of cedar and the citrus soap she used. Her pillow still held the shape of the last night she slept beside me.

I stripped the bed—slow, deliberate. Pulled fresh sheets from the cabinet. Smoothed them corner to corner. Turned her side toward the window—the exact angle she liked to catch the first thin line of morning light.

I stepped back and dragged a hand over my jaw. The sheets were smooth, tight—made for her. For the way she moves when she sleeps, the way she curls closer without waking.

At the doorway, I stopped.

Turned.

Let myself feel it instead of fighting it—the hunger, the pull, the stupid, reckless devotion she didn't ask for but has anyway. My fingers tightened on the doorframe.

Elle revient. She's coming back.

And when she walks through that door—

I won't just be ready.

I'll be wanting her in every way a man can want a woman.

And she'll feel it the second she steps inside.

Chapter 36

Epilogue: Home

EMME

Maris Key always hit different in winter. The humidity let up, replaced by that windy, fifty-degree chill that Floridians swear is "arctic." Still salty, still sunlit, still too bright after Patagonia's granite-gray mornings—but familiar in a way that went straight to my bones.

I'd been back and forth for months now—moving in equal rhythm between the Refugio, Maris Key, and whatever corner of the world Wilder Horizons needed me in. My passport lived in my jacket. My suitcase never fully unpacked.

And on the weeks Luc managed to slip away from the lodge, he came to Florida. He met every one of my sisters—charms, threats, love, chaos and all—and still claimed he "liked them." He walked the beach with me at dusk, toes in warm sand instead of snow, and cooked in my Maris Key kitchen like it was the most natural thing in the world while I caught up at the office.

The Refugio's new high-speed Wi-Fi was supposedly for guests who "needed to Zen out without missing their spreadsheets," but it also meant I could work from the lodge without dropping a single ball. A laptop, a signal, and suddenly I could build contracts, negotiate partnerships, and run half the company from the edge of the world.

Somewhere in all of that, I'd started building a life there. Friends. Real ones. Sofi, the guide who dragged me on sunrise treks and taught me the difference between good wind and "go back inside" wind. Mateo, who insisted I learn proper crampon technique "for dignity."

As if I hadn't already lost that twelve times over.

Teresa, the helicopter pilot who brought empanadas unannounced and pretended it wasn't a love language.

My life—and my heart—were stretched across three latitudes: the mountain, the business, and the man I refused to lose.

God, when had that become the truth?

My pulse kicked, betraying me before my brain could scrape together an excuse. And somehow… it worked. At least for now.

Luc and I built routines around distance.

Morning messages. Nightly calls.

Maps opened side-by-side, pointing at new ridge lines and the future we were slowly charting.

I sent him videos of palm trees slapping the wind on Maris Key, then snapshots from Morocco—terracotta rooftops, spice markets, desert dunes that swallowed sound. Luc pretended he wasn't jealous. He absolutely was.

And I loved that about him more than I should probably admit.

Refugio Cielo was booked out eighteen months.

Eighteen. Months.

Rafa joked Luc would have to install a waiting list for the waiting list. I smiled at the message and felt that little tug in my chest—Rafa, with his unofficial big-brother role and quiet watchfulness, and Juliana, whose maternal fussing made everyone behave whether they meant to or not.

And in between the madness of peak season, Luc and I were sketching the first quiet drafts of something bigger—a second Refugio on the Chilean side of Patagonia.

Still early. Still secret. Just lines on a page for now, but lines drawn together.

So yes. Things were good.

Better than good.

Hard and busy. Beautiful in ways I never expected.

It was ours.

But coming back from Maris Key this time...

it felt different.

I'd just spent three days in full-family chaos: Brynn, heart-eyed and glowing; Summer grilling me about timelines; Annie "just checking in" on Luc over Face-Time every five hours; Juliette taking notes like my relationship required a quarterly review.

And then there was Brynn and Jerrick's celebration—a whole event in itself.

They all missed him over the weekend.

I missed him.

Missing him had become its own kind of gravity. Every message from him tugged my attention before the chime even finished.

And though everyone understood why he couldn't make it—peak season, weather audits, route planning, three last-minute guest emergencies—I still wished he'd been there. Wished they could've seen him in the sunshine, barefoot in the sand, stealing coconut shrimp off my plate and pretending it wasn't on purpose.

The moment my boots hit Patagonia's gravel again, the ache sharpened. The wind smelled like snow and cedar. The sky was turning gold over the ridge. Home, in every impossible way.

I dropped my bags at the lodge, fully aware Luc wouldn't be free the moment I walked through the door. Peak season turned him into a moving target—briefings, routes, weather calls, three different guests who "needed him specifically." Juliana was already bustling in the kitchen, and I assumed I'd catch only a glimpse of him before the dinner rush.

So I walked toward the overlook on my own.

Our overlook.

The place he brought me the first time he needed quiet more than oxygen.

The place where the mountain first felt like ours instead of his.

I reached the base of the last climb, breath fogging the air—

—and froze. Heat rushed up my throat so fast it felt like I'd swallowed light.

A lone figure stood at the top. Back to me. Shoulders rising like he'd run the whole ridge without stopping.

Luc.

My step faltered.

He wasn't supposed to be here.

What the hell was he doing?

He should've been at the lodge, wrangling twenty guests and five guides and whatever fresh disaster Patagonia had thrown at him today.

But he'd come anyway. Up the ridge.

To me.

He turned when he heard my steps. Hair wind-tossed. Jacket too thin for the altitude. Chest heaving like he'd sprinted the last stretch just to get here first.

"Luc?" My throat cracked around it.

His eyes—God—his eyes hit me like impact, knocking the breath right up into my throat.

I felt myself fall toward him without even moving.

"Je pouvais pas attendre." *I couldn't wait.*

He took one step toward me, breath catching.

"Pas pour ça." *Not for this.*

My throat tightened so fast it almost hurt, the word I meant to say caught behind it.

He closed the distance between us. Took my hand—not rushed, not frantic—just Luc, steady even when shaking.

He pressed something small into my palm.

Warm. Wooden. Hand-carved.

I opened my fingers.

The Refugio crest. The symbol of his home...

The place he built...

And the life we were building, stitch by stitch, across three latitudes.

When I looked up, his walls were gone. Every last one. His gaze didn't guard a single inch of itself.

His jaw had gone soft. "Emme."

My name broke out of him—soft, raw, and so sure it knocked the air from me.

"Marry me... soon, later, next year—whenever it's right for you. Je t'aime. Christ, I'm in love with you. Passionnément. Fiercely. More than I ever thought I could be with anyone."

Don't lose it, Emme. Not now.

My vision blurred at the edges.

He lifted my closed hand to his chest, over his heartbeat—steady now, like choosing me steadied him. He pressed his forehead to mine.

"I'm not rushing us. I'm telling you what I want our life to look like. Je suis à toi—*I've been yours*, depuis longtemps déjà."

His thumb brushed the token.

"Je veux seulement le oui." *I just need the yes.*

Five months of flights. Five months of bruises fading and trust regrowing and choosing each other through distance, doubt, and everything that came before—

My lungs finally unlocked.

Of course it was yes. It had always been yes.

"Oui," I whispered. "Yes. I love you. And I want you. I want this life we're building—every latitude, every season, every damn beautiful mess of it."

His exhale broke against my cheek—warm, relieved, wrecked—in the way only Luc could be wrecked by love.

He wrapped both arms around me, slow and certain, pulling me into him with the kind of steadiness I'd once believed didn't exist.

And something deep, something old and aching, settled in my bones.

And the mountain in him—and the fire in me—found their place.

The Penguins Made Us Do This

Luc here.

I don't usually talk to readers. Emme says I should "engage more."

So. Consider this me, engaging.

If you finished our story—and didn't throw the book when I opened my mouth at the wrong time—do Emme a favor:

leave Kate Sweden a review.

She's the woman responsible for putting a Florida sunshine hurricane in my lodge during peak season.

She'll call it "plot."

I call it "author-inflicted chaos."

If you laughed, swooned, blushed, or considered flying to Patagonia to find your own French mistake—tell her.

Reviews keep stories like ours alive.

Drop your review here: https://www.amazon.co m/dp/B0FX5JDTNW

And because Kate's relentless…

Next up?

Annie Wilder in the Galápagos.

Sunshine. Sea lions. And a professor who could use a personality transplant.

Yeah.

Good luck to him.

Emme here.

He's pretending this was my idea. It wasn't.

But since he already started…

If our story gave you even one moment of heated distraction, emotional carnage, or "I need a Frenchman immediately" energy—**leave Kate a review.**

She's an indie author. Reviews matter more than Luc's silence quota.

You know what to do: https://www.amazon.com /dp/B0FX5JDTNW

And as for what's next?

Galápagos Islands.

Fake dating.

Sea lions that bite.

And a man named Dr. Theodore Hale who absolutely deserves what Annie's about to do to him.

Buckle up, babes.

It only gets wilder from here.

Afterglow, Extras, and Contacts

Come Kick Off Your Heels in the Lounge

Looking for sassy sneak peeks, steamy reader chaos, and wildly inappropriate group chat energy?
You belong in Kate Sweden's Reader Lounge.⬜
I've got spoilers. I've got smut. I've got memes that will spiritually wound you (in the best way).
Basically, it's book club—but with less wine and more fictional orgasms.
Come hang out: → https://shorturl.at/qW1Sj.

Wanna Stay in the Wilder Loop?

Spoiler alerts, spicy extras, behind-the-scenes chaos, and the kind of newsletter that'll make your inbox blush?

Sign up for my newsletter here and let the Wilder shenanigans begin" → https://kateswedenromance.com/mailing-list

Craving More Chaos, Spice & Sneak Peeks?

Explore exclusive bonus scenes, upcoming release goodies, and the kind of behind-the-scenes extras that should probably come with a warning label—

Right this way, babe: www.KateSwedenRomance.com.

Let's Get Social (Yo Know You Wanna)

Come for the chaos. Stay for the thirst traps, TikToks, unhinged reader theories, and late-night overshares.

Follow me here:

Tik Tok – @kateswedenromance

Instagram – @katesweden_author.

Goodreads – Kate_Sweden

Link Tree – https://linktr.ee/kateswedenromance

Your Review = Our Happy Ending

Your reviews? *They have superpowers.*
They help new readers find their next favorite spicy escape—and keep authors like me doing the happy ugly cry in public.
If Emme and Luc left you wanting more, I'd be wildly grateful if you'd drop a quick, honest review on **Amazon** or **Goodreads**.
You rock. You're hot. I adore you.

A   m   a   z   o   n   →
https://www.amazon.com/dp/B0FX5JDTNW

Goodreads   →
https://www.goodreads.com/book/show/243018011-hooked-by-you

Emme & Luc's Afterparty

Finished the book and still emotionally compromised? *Same.*
So I made you something fun.

Want to *see* the Patagonia vibes, Luc's lodge aesthetic, or that winter wonderland in full visual glory?

There's a whole Pinterest mood board waiting for your unhinged deep-dive:

Pinterest Mood Board→ https://pin.it/3FNKGiE w8

Acknowledgements

To my Wild Magnolias team—thank you for cheering this book into existence, the third in the Wilder Horizons series, with endless pep talks, late-night messages, and a magically refilling glass of good red wine during my evening writing hours. You believed in this story long before it managed to put on boots and trek into the snow.

To my son, who sat across from me during home-school hours, solving physics problems about velocity and force while I was over here attempting to apply those same principles to certain... *ahem* bedroom dynamics between two fictional adults—thank you for being blissfully unaware of the scientifically questionable chaos glowing on my laptop screen. May your formulas stay clean, your experiments stay PG, and your mother's work remain a mystery for many, many years.

To my incredible beta readers—you were the steady hands and brilliant minds that helped shape this book into what it is. Your sharp eyes, big hearts, thoughtful notes, and unwavering encouragement made this story stronger, deeper, and so much more fun to write. I loved every moment of working with you.

Dana Appling, Jessica Aranda, Kimberly Boartfield, Erin Brower, Naomi Davis, Tina Fisher, Inês Galrinho, Rhonda Hunt, Dawn Krevokuch, Aimee Lavigne, Hilary Litzinger, Judith Miguel, Kelly Montgomery, Taylor Nixon, Cassie Springer, Farrah Stewert, Cheryl Thigpen, and Molly Young—thank you for helping Emme and Luc come alive on the page.

To my ride-or-die street team: thank you for shouting about this book from the rooftops (and TikTok, and Instagram, and probably to random strangers in Barnes & Noble). Your passion, hustle, and hilarious messages kept me going. I couldn't have done this without you.

And to my family—thank you for loving me through every whirlwind. Your patience as I hunker down behind my keyboard, miss the occasional event during crunch time, and chase the self-imposed deadlines I keep creating for myself means more than I can ever put into words. You're my steady place to land, always.

About the author

Kate Sweden is a romance author with a flair for funny, a soft spot for slow burns, and a love of happily ever afters with heat. A former Air Force officer, educator, and lifelong book nerd, she traded briefing rooms and lesson plans for plot twists and first kisses. These days, she lives in Northeast Florida with her husband, their teenage son, and a very opinionated dog named Sailor—plus a pantry that's suspiciously short on chocolate.

Hooked by You: Book Club & Reader Guide

Refugio Cielo Signature Sips & Bites

Buckle up! Make your book club spicy *and* delicious:

- **Snowmelt Malbec** – Deep red, dark cherry, a hint of cedar smoke, and enough altitude attitude to make you confess something you shouldn't

- **Sunshine & Frostbite Fondue** – Melted cheese, crusty bread, and the kind of slow-burn heat that starts fights and finishes them in bed

- **Glacier Wind Spritz** – Bubbly, crisp, kissed with citrus and cold enough to remind you who's in charge of the mountain

- **Frenchman's Fire Empanadas** – Pepper, smoked beef, and a reckless amount of heat—best paired with a man who raises his eyebrow and ruins your self-control

Tropes Checklist

Check off your favorite romance tropes featured in *Hooked by You*:

Grumpy x Sunshine (French edition)

Forced Proximity in a Snowstorm

Opposites Attract

Arrogant Hot Guy (with an accent!)

Remote Lodge Vibes

Slow Burn Tension

Emotional Armor + Hidden Soft Spots

Comical Sidekicks

Found Family

Spice Scale: How Hot Are We Talking?

Total Heat Rating: out of 5
(Your Kindle might need a fire extinguisher.)▢

Scene Breakdown:

- **Chapter 16 – French Twist**
  Location: Luc's room, Refugio Cielo
  Vibe: Tension fractures open—heated, breath-stealing, dangerous in ways no emergency kit is prepared for

- **Chapter 21 – Pressure Systems**
  Location: The Great Room, Refugio Cielo
  Vibe: Hands in all the right places, extra large blanket, two people pretending it's not the fireplace throwing heat

- **Chapter 22 –** Worth Every Fracture
  Location: The bedroom, Refugio Cielo
  Vibe: Care-turned-carnal, reverent, vulnerable dom energy

- **Chapter 29 –** Elle Veut (She Wants)
  Location: The Great Room, Refugio Cielo
  Vibe: Emotional   confession   turned

molten—raw, reverent, and utterly consuming

- **Chapter 32 – Too Close, Too Warm, Too Late**
  Location: Emme's guest room, Refugio Cielo
  Vibe: A hunger-soaked surrender where he takes her apart like a prayer he intends to memorize

Book Club Discussion Questions

Pour the wine. Grab the brie. Let's talk.
Bonus points if you share in our Link Reader's Group: Kate Sweden's Reader Lounge (yes, please!)

1. The lodge—and the mountain itself—shape the rhythm of Emme and Luc's relationship. Did you feel that Patagonia functioned as a kind of *third main character*? How did the environment push or reveal them?

2. Luc fights vulnerability at every turn. What scene showed you the crack in his armor most clearly? Why?

3. Which of Emme's internal battles resonated the most

with you: perfectionism, imposter syndrome, emotional self-protection, or fear of being chosen last?

4. Luc has a fierce, protective tenderness in private that contrasts sharply with his public quiet. How did this duality shape the power dynamic between him and Emme?

5. Which scene made you realize that Emme wasn't just visiting Patagonia—she belonged to it in some deep way?

6. Emme's relationship with her sisters—particularly Summer and Brynn—plays a huge part in her identity. What did this book reveal about her place in the Wilder family dynamic?

7. What was your favorite moment of bilingual banter or French-Spanish-English blend? How did language deepen intimacy in the story?

8. There are three major sex scenes that each reveal something new emotionally. Which one hit the hardest for you—and what did it say about where they were in their relationship?

9. Luc and Emme communicate a lot through silence. Did you feel those quiet moments were more powerful than the big emotional confessions? Why or why not?

10. How did you feel about Emme's "stepping away to think" choice? Did it feel realistic, frustrating, brave, necessary—or all of the above?

11. Which secondary character stole every scene for you—Annie, Juliana, Rafa, the guests, or someone else—and why?

12. What was your favorite grounded, tactile Patagonia detail—food, weather, wildlife, the storm, the lodge, the terrain? Did it make you want to go?

13. Emme's final decision to return to Patagonia at the end of the book: did you see it coming, or did the journey shift your expectations?

14. Which quote, line, or moment did you underline or screenshot because it hit emotionally, humorously, or thirstily?

15. The epilogue gives us a glimpse of Emme and Luc's life after the storm. What do you imagine happens for them next—both at the lodge and in their relationship?

Author's Note from Kate Sweden

This story was born from late-night research rabbit holes, too many cups of red wine, and a long-held dream of one day standing in the real Patagonia—feeling the cold bite off the glacier wind, hearing the creak of snow under boots, and watching the mountains breathe. Until I get there (it's absolutely on my bucket list), I let imagination and heart take the lead.

Hooked By You grew from a single question: **What happens when a sunshine woman collides with a man who's built entire walls out of silence?**

Add in a remote lodge, a soul-deep storm, bilingual banter, a Frenchman who cooks like sin, and the wild idea that love can feel both terrifying and inevitable—and Emme and Luc refused to stay quiet.

They're fictional. But the longing to be chosen for exactly who you are—the soft parts, the brave parts, the broken parts—that's real.

Thank you for reading. Thank you for swooning. And if someone in your life makes you feel seen, safe, steady, and just a little undone in the best possible way...

hold on.

That's where the magic lives.

KATE SWEDEN

A Fake Relationship
Romantic Comedy

Swooned
by You

Wilder Horizons Series

Preview of Swooned By You (Wilder Horizons, Book 4) - Annie's Story

Chapter 1: Collision Course

ANNIE

The boat shuddered as it bumped the dock, a hollow thud echoing across the quiet morning water. I steadied myself with one hand wrapped around the railing and the other around my emotional-support Diet Dr. Pepper. The can hissed when I cracked it open, fizz curling against the warm air. Salt wind slid across my skin, carrying the calls of sea lions from somewhere up the volcanic shoreline.

San Cristóbal looked exactly how the photos promised—wild, raw, untamed beauty. Black rock, turquoise water, sunlight burning the horizon gold. It hit my chest with a kind of ache. The good kind. The this-might-be-home-one-day kind.

I stepped off the boat, Dr. Martens boots thudding on the dock, the boards soft from salt and time. My Wilder Horizons badge swung against my chest, the laminated edge sticking to my sweaty collarbone.

Deep breath.

I could do this. Crisis management was practically a love language in my family, and this particular meltdown—well, it wasn't the weirdest thing I'd ever been thrown into.

The true crown still went to the *Ferret Passport Emergency* of last year, when a client attempted to board an international flight with a ferret dressed in a baby onesie and toddler sunglasses. I managed to talk three customs officers and one bewildered pilot out of detaining the creature like it was Jason Bourne. Both client and ferret survived the ordeal. No casualties. I counted it as a win.

Compared to that, a small-ship vendor violating wildlife distance rules?

Cake.

I adjusted my backpack strap and lifted the incident dossier under my arm. The printout glared at me like it knew I didn't have all the answers yet. A blurry photo on page one: a line of tourists too close to a cluster of Galápagos sea lions, one man practically nose-to-snout with a massive male. In the background, the boat they'd disembarked from—the boat contracted through a Wilder Horizons itinerary.

Not our fault. Not our operation. But our name was now tagged under the photo, climbing into the algorithmic fire pits of the internet.

My sister Juliette—the CEO of Wilder Horizons, our luxury travel company for the rich, picky, and occasionally unhinged—said, "Keep things quiet, Annie. Just see if the Galápagos could work for our restricted-destination list."

Summer, our COO and resident crisis-whisperer, added, "Text if you need help. You won't."

Classic sister faith. Equal parts comforting and terrifying.

I moved down the dock, dodging crates and coolers and a man hauling a stack of oxygen tanks. My boots squeaked on the damp boards. A pelican eyed me like it knew all my secrets.

I lifted my Diet Dr. Pepper to my lips—

—and slammed straight into a wall of sunburnt muscle and attitude.

I choked on soda and stumbled back. The man I'd collided with stopped abruptly, the metal harness he carried clanging against his thigh. He turned slowly, and when his wickedly green eyes met mine, something sharp and electric crackled between us.

He was tall. And broad. And built in the way men got built from hauling gear and diving in rough water, not from gyms with eucalyptus-scented cleansing towels. His dark hair was sun-bleached at the tips, a little longer than professional, curls stiff from salt. His eyelashes? Long. Unfairly long. And his forearms...

Jesus.

Board shorts slung low on his well-sculpted hips.

A half-zipped sun shirt plastered to his chest.

A mouth set in a shape that said he hated everything, including me.

"Watch it," he snapped.

I blinked at him. "Well, good morning to you too."

His gaze dropped to my badge, and something in his expression tightened.

"Oh," he muttered, disdain thick in his voice. "You're with that tourist company that pissed off my sea lions."

Shockingly, I didn't swoon under the flattery. "Wilder Horizons," I corrected, stepping around him.

He didn't move.

I did a polite little sidestep dance. He didn't participate.

"My fault for assuming professional courtesy was a thing here," I said, sliding past him and catching the faint scent of salt, sun, and whatever arrogance smelled like.

As I started to walk away, I felt it—his stare, heavy between my shoulder blades. Annoyed, confused, maybe irritated that I hadn't crumbled the way he probably expected.

Buddy, I've got five sisters. Youngest in the pack. I was raised by irritation.

I paused.

"Permit office?" I asked, because of course the man I'd just collided with seemed like the type who knew where bureaucratic misery lived.

He exhaled through his nose. "Was heading there," he said, jerking a thumb over his shoulder. "Forgot something. But... fine. I'll show you."

Oh, goody. A field trip with Captain Sunshine.

The permit office sat near the waterfront: a squat concrete building radiating heat like it believed in suffering.

Inside, the fan spun slowly, doing absolutely nothing useful—typical government energy.

A line of people filled the small room, half tourists with wide eyes, half local operators clutching stacks of forms. The air smelled like sweat, sunscreen, and the sweet rot of fruit someone had forgotten in a bag.

I stepped inside and switched mentally into CFO mode. Calm. Methodical. Unshakable.

Fix the vendor crisis.

Protect the Wilder name.

Determine if this place could be part of our ultra-restricted access offerings.

Easy.

Captain Sunshine disappeared the second we walked inside.

When it was finally my turn, the man behind the desk—an older gentleman sporting an impressive mustache—looked up from a pile of paperwork.

I smiled. "Buenos días. Vengo para hablar con—" *Good morning. I'm here to speak with—*

Before I could finish, Captain Sunshine's voice boomed from a side office marked AUTORIZACIÓN DE COHABITACIÓN—*Cohabitation Authorization*—like a man arguing with destiny itself.

"Esto es ridículo," he snapped. *This is ridiculous.* "My housing authorization was approved weeks ago."

I turned toward the doorway, but he was still inside—just loud enough to shake the walls. I could see forms covered in red stamps through the open door, and his voice edged toward volcanic.

The officer sighed. "Señor Hale, solo hay unidades para parejas en esta época del año." *We only have couples units available this time of year.*

Captain Sunshine—apparently Señor Someone-Who-Shouldn't-Be-This-Hot-At-This-Decibel Hale—shot back, "No soy una pareja. Soy un investigador." *I'm not part of a couple. I'm not cohabitating. I'm a researcher.*

The officer responded gently, "Entonces necesita un permiso individual aprobado antes de la temporada alta." *Then you need an individual permit approved before peak season.*

"I submitted that six months ago."

"And it was denied."

A frustrated thump echoed—something being set down too hard. Papers, probably. Maybe his soul.

Peak-season housing here was brutal. I'd learned that in my research. But hearing Sunshine lose his mind in real time?

I'd be lying if I said it wasn't entertaining.

"Si llega solo, no hay espacio." the officer added. *If you arrive solo, there's no space.*

Hale muttered, "Find space."

"Lo siento. No puedo." *I can't.*

Mr. Mustache shifted, glancing past me toward the side office. "Señor Hale... quizá ahora sí." *Maybe now we can.*

A pause. Footsteps. Then Sunshine stepped out of the office, still radiating fury. His gaze swept the line, landed on me, and froze.

Great. Of course the universe wanted me involved in this.

Mr. Mustache shifted, clearly remembering that we'd arrived together. His gaze bounced between me and the furious researcher behind him, and something clicked.

The officer brightened. "Oh, perfecto. Su pareja ya está aquí." *Your partner is here.*

"Mi—qué?" I asked. *My—what?*

Sunshine blinked. "I'm sorry—what?"

The officer pointed between us with bureaucratic confidence. "Su pareja. Ya podemos asignarles una unidad." *Your partner. Now we can assign you a housing unit.*

I blinked.

He blinked.

"No," I said at the exact same moment Sunshine said, "Yes."

He didn't look at me when he said it.

His eyes were already on the officer, jaw locked like he'd just amputated something to stop the bleeding.

I snapped toward him. "Yes?!"

He muttered under his breath, "Just—don't argue."

"I'm not your partner," I hissed.

He leaned closer, voice low and intense. "You *could* be."

I stared.

He grimaced. "For the permit. Not—God." He scrubbed a hand down his face. "Just go with it for one minute. Please."

"One minute for what?!"

"Saving my research project."

Mr. Mustache was already stamping forms like a man possessed.

"Unidad C-12," he announced proudly. "Perfecta para parejas." *Perfect for couples.*

Sunshine pinched the bridge of his nose.

I considered faking my own death.

"Un momento," I tried. "Hay un error—there's a mistake—"

"No error," the officer said cheerfully. "Muy buena coincidencia." *Very good coincidence.*

I stared at Sunshine.

He stared right back, green eyes earnest in a way I hated.

He mouthed, *Please.*

Fucking shoot me now.

I signed the form.

The officer clapped his hands. "¡Felicidades! Que disfruten su estadía romántica." *Congratulations! Enjoy your romantic stay.*

Sunshine winced.

I considered stepping into the ocean.

We walked out of the office in tight silence. Sea breeze whipped through my hair, the air thick with the smell of salt and sun-warmed stone. Sea lions barked somewhere nearby, the guttural sound vibrating through the dock.

Finally, I stopped. "Explain."

Sunshine stopped too, turning toward me with that same glacial intensity. "My housing got revoked."

"Yes, I gathered that much."

"I reapplied. They denied solo access because of seasonal restrictions. They prioritize couples—don't look at me like that, I didn't make the rules. They don't have enough units for single occupants right now."

"So you volunteered me," I said slowly, "to be your... couple."

"Partner," he corrected. "Not couple."

"You said pareja."

"They said pareja. I just didn't correct them."

I stared at him. "Wow. Romantic."

"It wasn't intended to be," he snapped.

"I know."

"I'm not looking for—"

"Trust me," I cut in, "whatever you're about to say, I also do not want it."

He blinked like he didn't expect me to hit that hard.

Good. He deserved it.

We resumed walking, tension thick between us.

I asked, "So you really think we can just... keep up this charade until your permit clears?"

"It won't clear," he muttered. "It's peak season. This is the only way."

"And I'm just the sacrifice?"

"You walked into me today," he muttered. "Seems like fate."

Oh my God.

I stopped dead. "Excuse me?!"

He turned to face me, expression unreadable. "You walked into me."

"Because you stopped walking!"

"It's a narrow dock."

"You take up a lot of space!"

He blinked, slow. "I do."

Infuriating man.

I exhaled, long and heavy. "Fine. Temporary arrangement. But I swear, if you even breathe the wrong way—"

"Understood."

I narrowed my eyes. "Well, Captain Sunshine," I said, "if we're fake-cohabitating, I should probably know what to call you... other than that."

His jaw flexed—once, twice—like he had to shove the words through unwilling teeth. "Theodore," he said. "Dr. Theodore Hale. Theo is fine."

I let a slow smile curve. "Theodore," I echoed, tasting it. "Very formal." I tipped my head and winked. "So... *Teddy*, then."

His entire body went rigid.

I added sweetly, "Or *sweetheart*. Dealer's choice."

He choked—actually choked—on his own breath. "Do. Not."

Oooh, he hated it. Oh, I loved that he hated it.

"I'm Annie. Annie Wilder."

"Annabelle." He smirked.

Prick.

Cabin C-12 sat on a raised wooden walkway overlooking the beach. Weather-worn pale blue paint peeled along the frame. A single window hung open, the lace curtain fluttering like it was waving a tiny white flag of surrender.

A sea lion barked from somewhere under the deck, the guttural sound vibrating through the wood as if it disagreed with everything about our situation.

Theo unlocked the door.

The hinges protested.

The room was small but clean and bright—whitewashed walls, a tiny kitchenette, a ceiling fan spinning lazy circles overhead.

And there it was.

One.

Single.

Bed.

I closed my eyes. "No."

Theo rubbed his face. "We can request a cot."

A knock landed on the door.

A lodge worker leaned in. "Perdón, we forgot to give you your Wi-Fi code." He offered a tiny card, then added, almost apologetically, "Also, if you need extra bedding... no hay catres. *We're out.* A large group came in."

Then he left.

As if he hadn't just set off a local earthquake.

Silence.

I walked to the bed and poked the mattress. Firm. Narrow. Not forgiving in any sense of the word.

"This is a terrible idea," I said.

Theo exhaled. "It's temporary."

"Temporary as in... a day?"

"Temporary as in... we'll see."

My chest tightened at the uncertainty.

Nope.

Not going there.

Theo set down his equipment on the small table, the metal clanking softly. Up close, he looked exhausted. A man held together by coffee, sunburn, and sheer, unreasonable stubbornness.

Something in my chest nudged—a flicker of empathy.

Nope. Absolutely fucking not. No softness for this crabby researcher man.

I turned toward the window for air—and froze.

Down on the beach, sunlight glinted off wet fur. At least forty sea lions sprawled across the black volcanic rock, barking, rolling, nudging each other. A taxi boat idled far too close, tourists leaning over the side with cameras out.

My stomach dropped.

This was the area.

The colony from the incident report.

The exact stretch of rock that Wilder Horizons would be questioned about.

Theo appeared beside me, following my gaze. His jaw tightened. Anger flashed, sharp and bright.

"Your vendor," he said quietly. "They were here too."

I swallowed hard as the boat crept closer, a ranger already striding across the rocks to intercept it.

The pit in my stomach widened.

"Oh no," I whispered.

This was *his* turf. *This* is what Dr. Theodore Hale was here to study.

Theo didn't look away from the water.

"Welcome to the Galápagos, Annabelle."

And just like that—the islands, the crisis, the man—all turned on me at once.

If this little disaster stroll with Captain Sunshine made you grin... just wait. Things get *much* messier in **Swooned By You**.

You'll want the rest of this, love. I promise.
https://www.amazon.com/dp/B0G4WX1TLT